**CIVIC CENTER**

# FLASHPOINT

**Don't Miss These Other Tales in the World of**

# FLASHPOINT

## CHRISTIE GOLDEN

Based on the video game
from Blizzard Entertainment

### G

**GALLERY BOOKS**

New York  London  Toronto  Sydney  New Delhi

G

Gallery Books
A Division of Simon & Schuster, Inc.
1230 Avenue of the Americas
New York, NY 10020

First Gallery Books hardcover edition November 2012

GALLERY BOOKS and colophon are registered trademarks of
Simon & Schuster, Inc.

For information about special discounts for bulk purchases,
please contact Simon & Schuster Special Sales at 1-866-506-1949 or
business@simonandschuster.com.

The Simon & Schuster Speakers Bureau can bring authors to
your live event. For more information or to book an event
contact the Simon & Schuster Speakers Bureau at 1-866-248-3049
or visit our website at www.simonspeakers.com.

Manufactured in the United States of America

10  9  8  7  6  5  4  3  2  1

Library of Congress Cataloging-in-Publication Data is available.

ISBN 978-1-4516-5962-7
ISBN 978-1-4165-6004-3 (ebook)

*This book is gratefully dedicated to those who have been so supportive of me during a very difficult time. You all are my Raiders.*

# CHAPTER ONE

**2504**

*"We all got our choices to make."*

Those were the last words Tychus Findlay—criminal, former marine, and traitor—would ever hear from his old friend James Raynor.

Tychus had made his choice first—to betray Jim's trust and friendship by attempting to murder Sarah Kerrigan, the former Queen of Blades, who now sprawled shivering and vulnerable in a red-black cavern inside the planet Char.

Jim had chosen not to let him.

*"I made a deal with the Devil, Jimmy."*

And for that deal, Sarah lay limp and trembling and alive, and Tychus Findlay lay stiffening in the armor that had turned out to be first a prison and then a metal coffin.

Jim lowered his pistol. Smoke still drifted upward from its muzzle, mingling with the steam that curled and coiled at his feet. The bullet meant for Arcturus Mengsk, the man he hated above all others, had instead ended the life of the man Jim had once called his best friend.

*What have I just done?*

Jim fought back the tidal wave of emotions that threatened to overwhelm him. This was no time for rejoicing that the artifact to restore Kerrigan had worked, for berating his own lack of judgment regarding Tychus, for mourning the giant of a man whose rumbling voice would never again utter either jokes or threats.

They needed to get out of this murky, hellish cavern, off this world, and fast.

With Sarah Kerrigan.

His men moved forward as their commander holstered his weapon, clearly intending to bring Tychus's body with them. Jim barked sharply, "Leave him!"

"Sir?" Cam Fraser asked, confused. "We don't leave no one behind."

"We're leaving *him*. I ain't gonna risk any of your lives for the sake of carrying the corpse of a traitor," Jim snarled. It was a valid argument. But even as he spoke the words, Jim knew it wasn't the only reason for his decision.

He *wanted* to leave Tychus behind. Findlay had cut a deal with Arcturus Mengsk. He would have traded Kerrigan's life for his freedom. Now Sarah Kerrigan lived, and Tychus would rot inside his suit. There was a brutal justice about it that Jim suspected would rack his soul if he thought about it too much. But, perhaps mercifully, there was no time for thinking.

They had come here, to the zerg base world of Char, to do what no doubt seemed like madness: to make the Queen of Blades human again. They had found her deep inside the volcanic, ashy planet. She seemed completely stripped of her zerg-given abilities and appearance. Gone were the bony wings, the scaly skin that had once covered her toned body. But her hair was still—

It looked like it had worked. And "looked like" was close enough for Raynor, for now.

"We need a dropship, Matt," Raynor said into his comm.

Matt Horner, captain of the battlecruiser *Hyperion*, sounded stunned. "It . . . it worked? That alien thing Valerian had us go find for him . . . it really worked?"

Raynor knelt and, as gently as possible in the giant metal suit, slid his arms beneath Sarah and lifted her. She whimpered, once, and his heart broke.

"Looks like," he said. He didn't voice his concern about her to Matt as his gaze was drawn again to what crowned her head.

The long red, silky tresses Raynor had once run his hands through were still only things of memory. This part of the Queen of Blades had not changed; instead of soft tendrils, what looked like a hideous cross between tentacles, sectioned insect legs, and quills adorned her skull. Maybe, like a tail that wasn't needed anymore, it was just a vestigial relic left behind after the artifact worked its voodoo.

Maybe it wasn't.

"I . . . really can't believe it, sir." Matt was still stuck in astonishment.

"I said we need a dropship, unless we've gone to all this trouble to free Sarah only to have her die along with the rest of us, Matt," Raynor said. He rose. Sarah's form, naked as any newborn's, shifted with the gesture, rolling closer to him.

If only he were really holding her in his arms, not just carrying her in his armor, he thought fleetingly. If only he could feel her against him, as he had once, a few years ago, a lifetime ago.

*Sarah . . . I'm gonna keep you safe.*

"Of course, sir," said Matt, snapping to attention again. "The zerg are going crazy without Kerri—without the Queen of Blades to direct them. Some of them are fleeing, but a whole mess of them are apparently just interested in suicide runs. It's going to be tough getting something down to you, but we'll do it."

"Attaboy," Raynor said. He headed back toward the entrance, carrying Sarah carefully. "Now listen up: We've got a little complication. Your dropship needs to wait for two groups, not just one. I had to split up my team. My group went to find out what the xel'naga artifact did to Kerrigan, and Lisle and Haynes stayed behind to protect it. Once you've figured out where you're going to land that dropship, they'll bring it with them and meet us there."

There was no way they were leaving the artifact behind. Jim could see it in his mind's eye: sleek and black, slightly longer than a man was tall, with blue luminescent lines that revealed where five separate pieces had come together to create a single astonishing device. Raynor knew that although they had only begun to understand what it was capable of, he would always remember it and be grateful for what it had done for Sarah.

"I'll start analyzing the terrain for the safest place to park one, sir," Matt said.

"You do that." Jim ended the conversation and switched to another channel. They stepped out of the cavern—

*—I killed my best friend and left him to rot in there—*

—into the red glow of what passed for sunlight on Char. It was an ugly and unpredictable world. The surface was rocky and black, or gray with ash, or simply just liquid fire. The atmosphere was survivable without hardskins . . . barely. It was Hell, pure and simple, and a fitting place for the zerg to call their home.

"Jim?" The voice was weak, but it was *hers*. Human. And she knew who he was.

"It's okay; I gotcha." And that was all he needed to say. He walked slowly, carefully, then, feeling her gaze, met her eyes. He did not give her a reassuring smile. His feelings ran too deep for that. He looked at her for a moment, then returned his attention to the ugly world around him. Words could come later. Right now, he needed to get her to safety.

"Hey, boys," he said into his comm, "it worked. You kept that xel'naga thing safe for me like I asked?"

"Yes, sir!" came Lisle's voice. "Had to fight back a bunch of 'em when it first started, but they've steered clear of it for a while. Was the damnedest thing—critters just started attacking each other."

"And I bet you ain't complaining."

"No, sir, not one damn bit!"

"I'll let you know the rendezvous point as soon as we know ourselves." Jim glanced up at the red sky. He could see that the battle was still raging above the planet; here and there were explosions, appearing as small puffs from this distance. He could even see the tiny shapes of mutalisks closer to the surface. "We—"

Kerrigan's body suddenly spasmed, and she began to cough. Jim swore. He should have thought of this. They still didn't know what, exactly, had happened to Kerrigan—it could be that the transition back to human had weakened her more than they thought.

"Medic!" he called as he placed Kerrigan on the ground, kneeling beside her. Lily Preston hurried up to him, striding swiftly in her medic's hardskin while pulling out a respiratory unit from her pack. She too knelt beside Kerrigan, fastening the unit over the gasping woman's mouth and nose. A thin blanket, featherlight but made of a material known as insulweave that would ensure that the patient's body heat stayed at a steady 37 degrees Celsius, was gently wrapped around Kerrigan. She whimpered softly as her limbs were lifted and tucked in like a doll's, but the coughing and spasming stopped.

Preston peered at Jim. "We don't know what she is anymore, Jim," she said. "I'm treating her like a human, but—"

"She *is* human, dammit!" Jim snapped, insisting on it even though he himself was gripped with a cold fear that Kerrigan really wasn't. "She has trouble breathing the air just like we do. Her body temperature—"

The ground on which the two knelt suddenly pitched like a wild animal, and there was a huge, reverberating sound that seemed to go on forever. Several other Raiders were knocked clean off their feet. Jim held Sarah close, trying to keep her stable. Out of the corner of his eye he glimpsed a huge red glow, and he whirled to see what had happened.

A gigantic chunk of what had once been a battlecruiser was now nothing more than blazing wreckage, burning sullenly in the crater it had made. Things out of nightmares were swarming all over it. They were zerglings, the smallest package in which zerg hell came. Hydralisks were a maglev trainwreck combination of insects with scythelike arms, snake bodies, teeth that never ended, and neosteel-penetrating spines they fired from their backs. Mutalisks were monsters that brought the ability to fly in atmosphere and in deep space, acidic blood, and parasitic glave wurms into the mix. What the zerglings lacked in size and unique attacks compared to their brothers, they made up for in numbers. Seemingly composed entirely of teeth and claws and carapaces, the zerglings threw themselves on the wreckage, attracted like insects to the brightness and the heat, and screamed horribly as their bodies were burned to a crisp. Jim glanced skyward and shouted, "Brace for impact!" as the rest of the battlecruiser, in fiery chunks as small as a helmet and as large as a house, followed, slamming into the surface of Char like an armored fist into an unprotected face.

Despite Jim's warning and the stability the hardskins provided, the ground trembled so violently that more than one of them fell. Jim hung on tightly to Sarah, swaying and fighting to remain steady out of sheer cussedness.

Many of the remaining zerglings were suddenly silenced, but others continued to scramble and shriek. Any second now the hideous things, utterly undirected, would no doubt turn and come for Jim and his team. Not because they were bearing away the zerg Queen of Blades, who had once controlled and directed them completely, but simply because the terrans were moving, and thus they were prey.

In his head, Jim suddenly saw the image that had haunted him for four years: the disturbed, broken fantasy of what Sarah's last moments as a human woman had been like.

He heard again her request for aid, heard Arcturus's despicable words: *"Belay that order. We're moving out."* Arcturus Mengsk—he who used people until he had used them up, then threw them away once they were of no more use or had become too dangerous. Jim heard himself screaming, *"What? You're not just gonna* leave *them?"* The disbelief—it had still been a question then. Jim had still somehow thought he had misunderstood, that Arcturus wasn't really doing what it looked like.

But that ice-hearted bastard had intended to do exactly that. Sarah's voice had come again, a slight tremor of worry in its normally cool tones: *"Uh, boys . . . ? How about that evac?"*

*"Damn you, Arcturus! Don't do this."*

*And you* are *damned. You are . . .*

*"Commander . . . ?"*

Pause.

*". . . Jim? What the hell's going on up there?"*

And then nothing. Jim had imagined her looking in all directions as they came, endless wave after wave of horror, chittering and shrieking in triumph. And after that? The Queen of Blades, part psionic human but more monstrous zerg, had been born.

He had tormented himself with wondering how she had faced what should have been her death: Firing till her ammunition ran out, then leaping on them? Standing quietly and letting them take her? Attempting to kill herself first?

*I thought they'd killed you. There were times—a lot of 'em—that I wished they had.*

*And now, even with all you've done, even with so many dead—I'm so glad you're alive.*

He heard the sounds of weapons being fired in the distance, and then the inevitable high-pitched chittering and screaming of the zerg. Jim rose and reached for his pistol, taking a huge step so that he stood protectively over Sarah. They would get her only over his dead body—literally. Except he would take the precious second to kill her before they got him. Sarah Kerrigan would never again be their creation.

And today was *not* a good day to die. Not when his life had a chance of restarting after hurtling to a heart-shattering stop four years ago.

Fraser glanced at him quickly, then away as he too took a defensive stance. "I kinda feel sorry for the zerg right now, tackling you, Jim."

"Me too."

Jim looked upward, relieved to see that, for now at least, the mutalisks were busying themselves attacking the Dominion vessels in the air, which were better prepared to fight them off. Of more immediate concern to him was the cloud of ashy gray dust stirred up from the enemy's approach. Jim could distinguish the shapes of multijawed, scythe-armed monstrosities slithering on their tail-torsos. He counted four hydralisks. Swallowed by the powdery dust were lumps that had to be several more zerglings racing forward like a pack of wild dogs, only infinitely more lethal and terrifying.

Jim took aim as the cloud drew closer and ordered, "On my mark—fire!"

His soldiers were good. Jim felt sweat trickling into his own eyes and blinked it back, ignoring the sting. He waited until that sweet second, when the attack would have the most effect but not be so late that they would be overrun. In some distant part of his mind, he lamented that he had become so familiar with how best to slaughter zerg that the timing was almost second nature.

Still they came, crying out for blood and death, crazed with the lack of guidance from their missing queen.

Jim waited.

"*Mark!*" he shouted. The clacking, gleeful screams of triumph and lust to kill changed abruptly into sharp keening sounds as the zerg were blasted to bloody chunks. Pieces of the insectoid horrors flew wildly into the air. A chunk of carapace thunked on Jim's helmet before sliding off. He didn't change his pace. He kept firing, moving the pistol with a steady sweeping motion back and forth, mowing them down as they came. He had never seen independent thought in their actions or movements, but he had often seen intelligence. Kerrigan's intelligence, directing and maneuvering them. Now, he saw only chaos and insanity glinting in their tiny, bright eyes, erratic choppiness in their movements.

He blew off the last one's head. It dropped six paces from him, spewing blood and ichor, twitched, and lay still.

At once Jim knelt beside Sarah. She was curled up in a ball, clutching the blanket about her. Oddly enough, the gesture reassured Jim. It was . . . very human.

"Matt, where is that dropship?" Raynor shouted into his comm.

"Sir, it just launched." Matt's voice was sharp with anxiety. Judging by what remained of the battlecruiser still smoldering nearby, Jim could make a good guess as to what he was dealing with up there. But there was no time for sympathy. They had to get Sarah aboard, and then they had to get the fekk away from this hellhole.

"Tell them I'll double their pay if they get here in five minutes."

"Sir, you haven't paid them in weeks."

"Well, if I'm dead by the time they get here, that ain't gonna change, now, is it?"

Matt's faint chuckle was heartening. "There's truth in that, sir. I'll let them know, but there's no guarantee when they'll get there. Rendezvous coordinates are bearing eight four seven mark eight."

"Good. We're not far from that plateau."

"Sir," said Fraser, "readings indicate that it's crawling with zerg."

"Of course it is," said Jim. "Whole damn *planet* is. We just got to get there and hold them off till the ship comes."

He gathered Kerrigan in his arms. Her eyes opened. They were now back to their normal shade of green, no longer glowing and terrifying. She gave him a small smile, the pale lips of her too-wide mouth curving slightly. Her hand lifted to touch his chest, then fell back limply as her head rolled and her eyes closed, her body exhausted by that simple effort.

Oh yes. He'd hold them off. He'd hold them off forever.


Jim had notified Lisle and Haynes where the dropship would be landing and had to simply hope that the two soldiers would be able to hold off the zerg on their own. The plateau where rescue would come loomed ahead, only a few kilometers and yet a world away. Even as they ran steadily, their hardskins carrying them gracefully and easily, Jim heard a distant, low sound. He was incongruously reminded of the hot summers he had experienced, growing up on Shiloh, of the descent of twilight accompanied by the droning music of insects.

This sound, though, snapped him to full attention. He could see the creatures now, heading toward him and his team. Uncontrolled, they were reacting like the beasts they were, scenting prey and closing in on it. Jim felt a flash of grim humor as he realized that Lisle and Haynes were probably safer than he was this time.

Without Kerrigan to control them, the zerg would likely be less interested in the two humans with the artifact than the four humans without it, simply because Jim's group would provide more food.

"Stand your ground!"

There was a clatter as the soldiers came to a halt, lifted their rifles, and stood ready to attack on his command. Jim could distinguish three separate packs. There was no order to them, no uniform numbers or types, no flanking on one side or the other, no strategy at all. There was only hunger.

*Wait . . .*

"Fire!"

The Raiders butchered the zerg relentlessly. Some of the things stopped dead in their tracks and whirled, turning on their fallen colleagues for sustenance with the same enthusiasm they would have turned on Raynor's Raiders. While Jim held Sarah, the others kept firing, dropping more and more of the wretches, and when at last no attacking zerg remained, only diners and dinners, he gestured to his soldiers to go around the feast. The Raiders ran past while zerglings cannibalized hydralisks. As he left the grotesque sight behind, he suddenly wondered if the zerg would find and devour the body of a man he had once regarded as "friend," cracking open the metal shell of Findlay's armor to get to what was inside. . . .

He recoiled from the image for an instant and then forced himself to harden his heart against it. Tychus was dead. He didn't have to be. He could have still been alive, have still been Jim's friend, if he had turned his back on his "deal with the Devil." If only he had not been about to murder the woman Jim loved. But Tychus had made his choice, and he had to have known going in what Jim would do. He knew Jim better than anybody.

*Tychus. Damn, there was a time when I'd have done anything for you. And when I thought you would've done anything for me. A time when you did give up everything for me.*

A zergling was charging up to him, slaver dripping from its jaws. Without a pack its run was suicidal, but it didn't know that. It just knew it was hungry. Jim cradled Kerrigan close and turned so his back was to the creature, protecting her with his own body. Fraser leveled his rifle and fired a spike right between the thing's gleaming eyes. It kept coming for a stride or two, as if its body required a few seconds to understand that its brain had just been impaled, then it collapsed. Fraser took a bead on a second one, but it was unnecessary. The other zergling came to a halt and began to tear chunks out of its pack mate.

"Behind you!" Jim shouted.

Fraser whirled and dropped two more. The other zerglings chattered excitedly at the banquet Jim and his Raiders had spread out before them. Jim didn't even bother to wrinkle his nose in disgust. He simply held Kerrigan and started, again, to run straight for the rendezvous point.

It would be hypocrisy to condemn the zerg for turning on their own. They, at least, had excuses. Once completely controlled by the Overmind and then by the Queen of Blades, now they were nothing but simpleminded beasts. What excuse did humans have for doing the same thing?

Mengsk had turned on Kerrigan without batting an eye, abandoning her to what he expected would be a horrifically brutal fate. Tychus, at least, seemed to have taken an instant to mourn what he saw as a necessity. *"Damn shame,"* he had muttered.

Before starting to squeeze the trigger.

Before choosing to murder a helpless, traumatized woman right in front the man who loved her.

*Damn him anyway.*

It was becoming brutally rote: Zerg, one or two or twenty, would come out of nowhere. Jim would shout the orders. His Raiders would fire, and the zerg would fall, sometimes quickly, sometimes not. And when enough were dead, as if there were some kind of tipping point unknown to the Raiders, the zerg would stop hunting humans and start eating their own kind.

He wondered if his people resented the fact that their leader, who had chosen to put all their lives in jeopardy, stood by, holding Sarah Kerrigan, the former Queen of Blades—the one responsible for the deaths of so very many—while they fought to protect them all. Jim realized with a sick sensation that no matter how well you thought you knew someone, you didn't. You couldn't. Only the protoss could know someone through and through, by linking their minds and essences in the great psychic meeting space they called the Khala. And even some of their own kind, the dark templar, had chosen not to reveal themselves so profoundly.

*I'm flying blind,* Jim thought as he kept running, trying to cover as much ground as he could while jostling Sarah as little as possible. *We all are. Every man, every woman. We're flying blind, and we never really know shit about any other heart or mind but our own.*


"Sir!" cried Fraser. "Look!"

Mortified, Jim realized he had been so lost in his thoughts that he hadn't seen the tiny speck in the sky that was growing larger and larger, its shape becoming clearer until he could see the familiar and welcome curves of the dropship *Fanfare.* It looked more beautiful to Jim than just about any other sight he had ever seen . . . except for the look Sarah had given him as he bore her away.

But as cheers and whoops of delight went up from the weary soldiers, the sound was joined by another—a buzzing, humming noise. Jim swore. The *Fanfare,* like all dropships, had no weapons, and it couldn't land to rescue them until Jim's team cleared the area first.

"Fire at will!" Jim ordered. "Ain't gonna let a few pesky zerg get in our way!"

The soldiers agreed, and they fired on the zerg with even more intensity than they had demonstrated before. Zerg blew apart into pieces, and this time the Raiders didn't spare those that stopped to eat. Jim and his soldiers kept going, winning the prize step by slogging step, spattered in zerg blood and ichor. And finally, blessedly, the *Fanfare* settled on the rocky but mostly flat ground.

The ramp extended and the pilot, Wil Merrick, beckoned furiously. "Hurry! There's a whole slew of them heading this way!"

"Any sign of the second team?"

"None," Merrick said, then his eyes fell on the blanket-wrapped form. "Damn, that her?"

"That's her," Jim said.

"She's in shock," said Preston. She reached to take Jim's precious burden away from him, lifting Sarah as easily as he did thanks to the medic's armor. Jim didn't want to let Sarah go, but she needed what the medics could do for her right now more than what he could do. He handed her over to Preston, feeling a lurch in his heart as he watched the medic carry her inside. Kerrigan was eased into a seat and hooked up to an IV drip and (what looked to Jim) about six thousand other tubes or portable monitors. The words forced themselves out of Jim's mouth, a quiet plea: "Be gentle."

The irony did not escape him; it was a hell of a request to show gentleness to the murderess of billions. But Preston understood, nodding wordlessly as she went about her job of trying to save Kerrigan's life. Sarah gave no sign that she was even peripherally aware of anything.

*Hang on, Sarah. You're tough; you can survive. Don't let it be too late. Not after all this. . . .*

"Damn, sir, we need to get going!" the pilot shouted. "We got another bunch of zerg incoming."

"What kind?"

"We had to evade a whole shitload of mutalisks just to get down here, sir," Merrick replied. "Once we hit atmosphere, they went after someone else, but sensors indicate there's a mess of zerglings and hydralisks that seem intent on finishing the job."

Jim glanced over at Sarah. He desperately wished she could be gone, out of danger, safely in the *Hyperion*'s sick bay, but he couldn't abandon the men who had risked everything to save her.

"We ain't leaving my men to be zerg fodder nor that artifact to be destroyed!" Jim snapped. "Keep her as stable as possible. Her survival is paramount. If I give the order for you to take off and get to safety and leave me behind, you do it, do you understand?"

"Perfectly, sir."

Jim looked again at Sarah, her skin painted an unnatural hue by the artificial lighting, then jumped out of the dropship. The doors closed behind him.

His Raiders joined him, one of them handing Jim a gauss rifle. While he had treasured every moment he had tasted with Sarah in his arms again, Jim was also glad to be hoisting a rifle and tackling an active role in the fight once more.

He could hear the zerg coming now, feel the earth tremble beneath their onslaught. Grinning a little, Raynor lifted his rifle, pointed it at the roiling cloud of gray dust, and began to fire.

# CHAPTER TWO

In the palatial bridge aboard the *Bucephalus,* Valerian Mengsk, Heir Apparent to the Terran Dominion, removed the stopper from a very rare vintage of tawny port, poured himself a small glass, and gazed out of the huge viewport window that occupied a full wall.

The ugly planet of Char, red and sullen-looking, was prominently featured. There, a battle was taking place. One whose outcome meant everything to Valerian. On that volcanic, inhospitable world, either Sarah Kerrigan was being reborn, or the Queen of Blades was slaughtering those who had come to save her lost humanity.

Out among the stars, too, a battle was still raging. The zerg were uncontrolled, which was both good and bad. Good, in that their attacks had no strategy; bad, in that they were so brutally random. His own vessels were involved, and he had seen at least eleven of the twenty-five battlecruisers he'd brought to the fight destroyed. Even the glorious *Bucephalus* was coming under attack.

There had been, and were still, so many *if*s. If Raynor could find Kerrigan. If his team could place the artifact close enough for it to work. If the artifact even *did* work. Valerian had had every confidence that it would, but, of course, as an old quote so sagely held, "The best-laid schemes of mice and men go oft awry." Fortunately, thus far, it seemed his gamble had paid off, at least if the out-of-control behavior of the zerg was any indication.

Even so, he kept his pleasure in check, mindful of the remaining *if*s. If, if, if . . . *if* Raynor survived long enough to get Kerrigan to safety . . . *if* he would agree to turn her over to Valerian.

Then the Heir Apparent would celebrate in truth.

In anticipation of the moment, Valerian had assembled a group of doctors and scientists. Granted, it was only an interim team until they could get Kerrigan to a more suitable facility, but a fine selection nonetheless. They stood by, almost as excited as he, ready to begin examining Kerrigan the second she arrived. Raynor was not a fool. The former outlaw had to know that these men and women were far superior to any so-called doctor or scientist he had on the *Hyperion*. Valerian was gambling that in the end, the man's concern for his beloved would win out, and Raynor would want the best treatment for Sarah.

Valerian swirled the amber liquid in his glass, his gray eyes thoughtful, and took a sip of the warming fluid. His tongue crept out to capture a stray drop.

The power that would soon be his . . . the power to finally prove to his father that he was as strong a man—and a better man—than Arcturus Mengsk. But even more important to Valerian was the knowledge that Kerrigan had stored inside her skull. At least, he hoped she still had knowledge. It could be that she would remember nothing of being turned into a monster, the glorious and terrifying Queen of Blades, the mistress of the zerg. It could even be that her mind had been completely destroyed by the transformation.

It would grieve him if such were the situation. More than power or wealth, Valerian was excited by and valued knowledge. Particularly ancient knowledge. And surely, Kerrigan had once been in possession of it.

The soaring music emanating from the vinyl disc playing on the antique phonograph swelled to a crescendo, then came to a halt. The room was filled with a faint scratching noise. Valerian extended a well-manicured hand, lifted the needle, and started to replay the album. Old instruments began once again to play, and a human female voice, its owner dead for centuries, began to sing.

One could use knowledge for personal gain, of course. But just like the opera to which Valerian was only half listening, it was beautiful, and precious, and held value simply for what it was. For simply being.

He took another sip of port and reflected on the power of something called "love." Valerian had loved his late mother, but other than that, he'd had little familiarity with the emotion. He'd known respect and affection for others, but never considered himself to have been in love. He hoped to, one day; as a man who craved understanding of all things, he wished to experience such a powerful force. More than once he had witnessed what it could do. Love had turned one R. M. Dahl, an extremely efficient and selfish killer, into a woman who would be willing to kill—and die—for not just the man she unexpectedly found herself in love with, but also the ideals he cherished.

And that man, Professor Jacob Jefferson Ramsey, not only had loved her in return, but also had learned to understand, admire, and, yes, love an entire alien species. Valerian freely admitted that he had not remained unmoved by the experience of getting to know these two people. It had made him regret even more what he had later done to Jake.

Now another man who loved with his whole heart had done Valerian perhaps the greatest service yet. The fair-haired prince well knew that Jim Raynor was the sole reason Sarah Kerrigan was alive now. Raynor loved her, despite what she had become, despite the atrocities she had performed. Loved her enough to risk his life and those of others, enough to walk right into the heart of the monster's lair without any idea of whether he would find his death or his beloved.

Remarkable, quite remarkable, all of it. Valerian swirled the remaining liquid in his glass and smiled slightly. He raised the glass, said in his rich, pleasant voice, "Well, then, to love," and drained the last drops.

The pair was on its way with the artifact, Lisle had told Jim what felt like about four centuries ago.

In those four centuries, which were probably more like four minutes, Jim and his team had piled up an impressive number of zerg bodies, although that pile had grown smaller when two hydralisks had come to attack the terrans. Jim's Raiders had blasted one of them into a chunky magenta salsa. The surviving hydralisk had impaled a zergling corpse on its scythelike arms and retreated.

The Raiders had whooped in delight, not wasting ammunition as the huge creature slithered away with its prize.

"The solution to the zerg at last," Fraser had said. "Cut off the head and feed the limbs to each other."

Jim had shot him a quick look, but there had been no malice in the comment. And it was true. The Queen of Blades was gone, although the human who had been her genesis was—he hoped—inside the dropship.

There was a click in Jim's ear. "We're a kilometer out," Lisle said. "Sorry, boss. This xel'naga toy is slowing us a bit. And we got us some ugly dogs to put down."

Jim couldn't help but smile as Lisle downplayed what Jim knew damn good and well was life and death. "Roger that," Jim said, keeping his own voice light. Keeping up their spirits. He pointed to two of his men. "Fraser, Rolfsen—you go ahead and meet them. Clear their path. We got plenty of distracting snacks for the next wave. Those boys ain't got nothing."

"Yes, sir," Fraser said. He and Rolfsen took off. "Sir," came the voice of the pilot in Jim's ear, "I'm getting reports that there's a cluster of mutalisks assembling between us and the main fleet up there."

The tone of the man's voice—carefully flat, too neutral— told Jim all he needed to know.

"Kerrigan is still out cold," Jim said. "There's no way she could be directing them."

"If you say so, sir, but they *are* gathering. They could be following us—can't quite be sure."

"They may decide they just like each other's company," Jim shot back. "Unless you can tell me that you know exactly how zerg function when they're not receiving orders, we're going to assume this is nothing but a coincidence." He realized he sounded angry and defensive, but he couldn't help it. He knew Sarah wasn't controlling the zerg. Knew it in a way he could never explain.

"Yes, sir."

Dust heralded something approaching on the ground. Jim couldn't tell how far away it was. He lifted his weapon, but felt a prickling at the back of his neck—the instinct of a man so used to fighting that the gut was sometimes wiser than the head.

He held his fire. Sure enough, three seconds later, he could plainly see that the powder of Char was not being stirred up by a cluster of ravenous monsters but rather by Lisle, Haynes, Fraser, and Rolfsen approaching, heading toward them at as brisk a pace as they could manage while bearing the protective case that housed the gleaming alien artifact.

A cheer went up, and the dropship's ramp lowered. Grinning, covered in gray dust, the four Raiders loaded the invaluable artifact onto the ship. Jim glanced past them into the ship's interior to see Sarah, still unconscious, still breathing, still looking almost less human with all the machinery attached to her than she had appeared when he had first found her in the cavern.

He looked over his shoulder and swore. Another dust cloud—and this time he could see ugly silhouettes in it. "More pets to the party," he said. "Looks like they did follow the dropship's path." He hoisted his rifle and took aim.

"Sir, we need to go!" shouted Rolfsen.

Jim didn't waste breath replying. They had to take off—but they would be more successful doing so without a bunch of zerg flinging their bodies onto the ship. He mowed them down as they came, experiencing neither remorse nor delight, then leaped into the ship and tumbled into the seat next to Kerrigan. Almost before the doors had closed, the passengers had fastened their harnesses, and the dropship was airborne.

Jim and the others opened their visors. Recirculated air had never smelled so sweet. As he inhaled gratefully, Jim was surprised to find himself thinking not of their escape—which was still in question—nor even of Sarah, but of Tychus.

*I get to stay locked up in this suit 'til I pay off all my debts.*

Tychus Findlay had carried his jail with him, had lived and died in it. If only there had been some other way.

Jim shook the thought away and turned his attention toward Kerrigan. Her body was secured by one of the harnesses that locked them all safely into place, her eyes closed. Her head lolled, the strange-looking hair, if it could even be called that, shifting not of its own accord but with the movement of the vessel. Preston had made sure the blanket was well tucked around

Kerrigan, preserving her modesty. Not that Sarah ever had been a shrinking, delicate flower when it came to such things.

"How is she?" Jim asked.

Preston, seated on Kerrigan's other side, looked up from a data log. "It's hard to say right now. I've got her stable, and she seems human enough from what I can determine. But she needs more care than anything we can provide here."

"What else?"

Lily hesitated. "I think she needs more care than anything we can provide on the *Hyperion,* either."

"The *Hyperion* was Mengsk's flagship," Jim said. "The facilities are excellent. What exactly are you saying?"

She gave him a level look. "I'm saying I'm not sure what we're dealing with here, Jim. We have top-notch supplies, but, hell—I'm not a top-notch doctor, and I'm certainly not an expert on the zerg."

"She's not zerg!"

Lily's answer was a shrug. "I can't look you in the eye and say that," she said quietly. "Not yet." She bent her dark head back over the data log.

Jim sat for a moment, thinking hard, then triggered the release on one of his gauntlets and removed it. He reached out and took Kerrigan's hand in his, careful not to disturb any of the myriad tubes attached to various parts of her body.

Warm human flesh to warm human flesh. His eyes burned suddenly, and he blinked hard. He had not expected the sensation to move him quite so much. He gazed at her hand as if he had never seen it before, noting anew the strength of it, the oddly long fingernails that had once been talons, and remembered the first time those capable fingers had curled around his.

She had told him once that she kept her nails short because it was practical. Just like why she kept her hair out of the way, always pulled back in a ponytail. Just like why she kept herself incredibly fit and had constructed around herself a wall a kilometer thick.

Practical. These were the sorts of things a warrior and an assassin would do.

Jim wanted to press the limp hand to his heart or to his lips, but did neither. He simply remembered.

There was an abrupt *thunk* and the ship bucked. If Kerrigan had not been securely strapped in, she would have gone flying. Jim knew, of course, what had happened. Quickly, he lowered his visor and jacked into the dropship's power bus. The vessel's surroundings began downloading to his heads-up display.

Mutalisks.

They had always been subject to bloodlust when attacking, and now, without their queen to direct them at all, Jim suspected they were more mindless than zerglings. Two of them had focused on the dropship to the exclusion of all else, including their own lives. The hideous things flapped their delicate-looking wings (useless in space, so Jim figured it was some kind of animal reflex) and spat their parasitic glave wurms, which could eat, slice, or dice through just about anything Jim could think of, in the direction of the dropship. One of the wurms had clearly struck the hull.

The ship dove so quickly that Jim's stomach flip-flopped in surprise. Kerrigan's head snapped forward; the rest of them had armor to protect against such whiplash, but nothing could be done for her right now. Jim knew they were in a fight for their lives, and the only things that could save them were piloting skill and a speedy rescue before the glave wurm ate its way through.

The ship swooped upward as abruptly as it had dived, then rolled and dove again. Through the display on his HUD, Jim saw the brilliance of the tactic. The mutalisks ended up facing—and inadvertently attacking—each other. They threw back their many-eyed heads, no doubt screaming in agony as their own acidic blood began to eat away at their carapaces. Jim almost wished he could hear it in the silence of space.

Two down, but who knew how many more were out there? Jim thought again of the chunks of battlecruiser that had rained down on Char like meteors.

"Mayday, mayday, this is the *Hyperion* dropship *Fanfare* seeking shelter immediately. We are under heavy mutalisk attack and are carrying both the commander and Kerrigan. Repeat, we need assistance immediately!"

"*Bucephalus* here. What is your bearing, *Fanfare*?"

"No," Jim said flatly, patching in for the pilot's ears only. "Not there. I'm not letting him have her."

The ship rocked again. "Sir," shouted Merrick, "I don't think we have a choice! That one muta got in a solid strike. We've got about seven more minutes before the wurm eats through the hull!"

Jim was torn. Valerian would not see Sarah as a person. He saw her as means to an end—a way to overshadow his daddy, to prove himself. She was a tool, nothing more, and Raynor was damned if he'd let that pretty boy get his hands on Kerrigan.

The words of the medic returned to him. What if the *Hyperion* wasn't equipped to give Sarah the help she truly needed? What if he was denying her the chance to recover completely?

"Sir, we're not going to survive another strike, and we're tracking four more of the sons of bitches on our sensors," the pilot warned.

"Shit," Jim swore. "This is Raynor to *Bucephalus*. Send your boys out to get these zerg off our tail. We're coming in."

"Acknowledged, Mr. Raynor. We will intercept as soon as possible."

Choices. Jim hoped he wouldn't regret this one.

He clicked off the comm and leaned back, thinking, to simply sit and be with Sarah until they reached the docking bay of the *Bucephalus*. And then, maybe take his rifle and make sure the welcoming committee was indeed such a creature. To his surprise, she was awake . . . at least somewhat.

"Sarah," he said gently, taking her hand again.

Preston said quietly, "She's fading in and out of consciousness. I'm not sure what she knows right now."

Jim nodded his understanding and returned his attention to the woman he loved.

"Hey, darlin'," he said, keeping his voice as soft as he could and unable to hide a tremor of emotion.

Her green eyes widened, but he couldn't tell whether she was seeing him or something that existed only in her mind. She moved as if swimming through mud, then she suddenly shrank back, uttering a feral cry.

Jim's heart felt as if a giant hand were squeezing it. Of course she was afraid. She was more vulnerable than she had ever been before in her entire adult life—naked and weak and helpless before a man who had once loved her but who had once also vowed to kill her. He wondered if she remembered that promise, and if she was glad or fearful that he had been the one to find her.

"Calm her down, Jim," Preston was saying. The other Raiders were watching intently. Jim could only guess what was going through their minds. "Her vitals are all over the place!"

"Sarah, honey," Jim said, still keeping his voice soft and calm, "I promise, no one's going to hurt you. Not me, not anyone, do you understand? I give you my word. I promise. I promise!"

Her struggles were feeble at best, but she quieted, gazing up at him, her face and eyes so familiar, so her, beneath that mass of strange quill-tentacles that formed her hair.

Sarah.

She nodded and closed her eyes, almost with the trust of a child, accepting that his word was good.

*Sarah. Sarah. Dammit . . . you're going to be all right. I'm going to make you be all right. Make you Sarah again. If it takes the last drop of blood in my veins, I'm going to keep you safe.*

"She's unconscious," the medic said.

"If you can do so without harming her, then keep her that way," Jim said. "Better if she doesn't see what might be about to happen."

# CHAPTER THREE

Valerian had instructed that all conversation from the various vessels entangled in battle—including that from those battle-cruisers and Wraiths not his own—be monitored if at all possible. He was finishing a small, perfect piece of dark chocolate, his eyes on the battling ships visible through the clear wall of his private suite, when a message from the bridge was patched through.

"Sir," said the *Bucephalus*'s captain, Everett Vaughn, "I think you should hear this. . . ."

Valerian turned and nodded, letting the confection dissolve in exquisite sweetness on his tongue. But even the chocolate was not as sweet as the sense of triumph that washed through him at the following words.

"Mayday, mayday, this is the *Hyperion* dropship *Fanfare* seeking shelter immediately. We are under heavy mutalisk attack and are carrying both the commander and Kerrigan. Repeat, we need assistance immediately!"

"Bring them in!" Valerian cried. He found he couldn't stop grinning. Just as Jake Ramsey had predicted, the xel'naga artifact had, in the archaeologist's words, "worked as intended." Or, at least, as Valerian had intended it to. And here were both Raynor and Kerrigan sailing right into his hands.

"*Bucephalus* here. What is your bearing, *Fanfare*?" Vaughn queried.

There was a long pause, and Valerian's smile faltered ever so slightly. He didn't wish to take Raynor's vessel by force, but . . .

"This is Raynor to *Bucephalus*. Send your boys out to get these zerg off our tail. We're coming in."

"Acknowledged, Mr. Raynor." Vaughn's voice was calm and cool. "We will intercept as soon as possible."

Valerian's smile returned, even broader. Today was a historic day for the Mengsk empire. For today was when history would record that the power began to shift from father to son.

"Captain Vaughn, I will meet them in the docking bay," he said, and moved so quickly that the red cape he wore fluttered energetically behind him.


Jim stood in his hardskin, gauss rifle in hand, side by side with four other men as the dropship moved slowly into the docking bay. He thought about the last time he had boarded the *Bucephalus*. How different things had been. Then, he'd had Tychus with him, and he had come aboard Mengsk's flagship with the intent of seeing justice done. They'd entered through the docking tubes, fighting their way through the ship until they encountered not Arcturus Mengsk, as they had expected, but that man's son, Valerian. Come to think of it, it wasn't so different this time.

He didn't care what would happen to him; he was planning on putting a metal slug through Valerian's patrician forehead if the man said or did one single thing Jim Raynor didn't like.

"He's here, sir," the pilot said. Jim glanced at the feed coming through his HUD and narrowed his eyes.

On-screen, Valerian appeared arrogant, aristocratic, certain of himself. But he didn't look as if he planned anything untoward. There were a few guards, but no more than were to be expected, and none of them appeared to be spoiling for a fight.

The seconds ticked past. Valerian looked at the dropship, seemingly directly at Jim, folded his arms, and lifted a golden brow.

"Mr. Raynor," he said, "I have given you absolutely no cause to mistrust me. I've been honest with you about my motives, and you may believe me now when I assure you that the care of Sarah Kerrigan is of utmost importance to me."

Oh, Jim believed that, certainly. But he also believed that Valerian was quite capable of killing him on sight and absconding with Kerrigan for his own purposes.

It was Sarah herself who settled the matter. He heard a soft whimper and winced. It was an old cliché—where there was life, there was hope, and Sarah was alive. But she might not be if Jim stood here much longer.

"Open the doors," he said, and lifted his visor.

The ramp lowered, and Valerian's gray eyes did widen slightly as he saw Jim and four other Raiders in full combat armor with their weapons pointed at him. Valerian's own men snapped to full attention. He lifted a graceful hand to defuse the situation.

"Lower your weapons, gentlemen," he said. "Mr. Raynor is not to be greeted in such a manner."

As Valerian's marines obeyed, Jim nodded to his own men and stepped forward. In his suit, he towered over Valerian, but to the younger man's credit, the Heir Apparent didn't seem in the least intimidated.

"Congratulations, Mr. Raynor. Where is the lady of the hour?"

She was coming down the ramp of the dropship on a stretcher at that moment. Rolfsen guided it while Preston lifted the IV drip clear. Sarah lay unconscious, her head lolling in a way that made Jim's gut clench hard.

"And there she is," breathed Valerian. He strode toward Kerrigan, his eyes fastened on the limp, shallowly breathing form. "Amazing, simply amazing," he said, shaking his head slightly. "She does look human . . . except for her hair—" Valerian reached to touch one of the strange extensions.

Jim's armor-clad hand shot out and clamped down hard— but not enough to cause pain—on the Heir Apparent's arm. There was a clattering sound as rifles were raised instantly on both sides.

"She ain't a trophy," Jim said bluntly.

"I didn't say she was." Valerian was admirably calm, but as his gray gaze flickered meaningfully to his trapped arm and then back to Jim, there was a storm gathering in its cool depths. "Let go, Mr. Raynor."

Jim did as he was told. "She's sick," he said. "My medic says she needs attention. Now."

"And she shall get it," Valerian said. There was a sharp tone in his voice. He nodded and several men in white lab coats stepped forward, taking the stretcher with a convincing display of gentleness. "We'll attend to her here as best we can, and then we shall take her to one of the Moebius Foundation's locations. We have an extensive laboratory there. As you know, our Dr. Emil Narud is an expert, perhaps *the* expert, in zerg physiology. We'll be able to do every kind of test—"

"She's not a goddamn lab specimen either!" shouted Jim.

"We don't *know* what she is, don't you understand that?" snapped Valerian, his patience clearly evaporating. "And until we do, we don't know how to help her! You've risked so much getting her back, and now you won't do what's best for her simply because you don't want to admit that perhaps she's not as human as you want her to be."

Fury out of all proportion to the comment surged hotly through Jim. "Listen, you arrogant little—"

Jim's sentence was abruptly cut off by the harsh blaring sound of a red alert. "Bridge to Prince Valerian!"

"Valerian here." Valerian, too, had instantly abandoned the argument. "What's . . ."

His question trailed off as he turned and peered out the massive viewports.

Dozens of vessels had warped in with no warning. Raynor found himself gaping at the other half of the Dominion fleet. Valerian also stared, his mouth slightly open.

Jim recovered first, whirling on Valerian. "You treacherous son of a bitch!" He pulled back his fist, ready to land the Heir Apparent to the Terran Dominion a good solid one on the jaw and damn the consequences.

To Jim's shock, Valerian darted back and behind him and cried, "Hold your fire!" Raynor turned around to see the prince standing with a small pistol he'd pulled from who knew where. It was pointed straight at Jim, but Valerian didn't shoot.

"Do you think I did this?" Valerian hissed. His finesse was gone, and Jim realized that, different as he was from his father, Valerian could be just as dangerous and deadly. All his grace was feral now—the grace of the jungle, not the drawing room. "Do you think I want to give you and Kerrigan to *him*?"

No. Of course he wouldn't. Valerian was going to make his name by using them, not turning them over to his father.

"Hello, Son, Jim," came a far-too-familiar voice. Jim didn't need to turn to the screen on the wall of the docking bay to know that Arcturus Mengsk was smirking in anticipation of triumph. Jim recalled that awful moment when, right before Tychus had taken aim at Sarah, they had all heard Mengsk's voice coming from the inside of Tychus's helmet: *"You have your orders, Mr. Findlay. Carry them out."*

*"Tychus . . . what have you done?"*

*"I made a deal with the Devil, Jimmy. She dies . . . I go free."*

Now Jim abruptly realized how it had been that Mengsk had been able to talk to Tychus via comm.

The bastard had been waiting here the whole time.

Lurking just outside of orbit, calculatedly evading detection. Mengsk had let his son do all the work and take all the risks, using Tychus to dispose of Kerrigan, and was now swooping in to claim the credit and the prize.

*Like hell,* Jim thought, and to his surprise, he saw his thoughts reflected on Valerian Mengsk's face.

"You've got something I want, Son," drawled Arcturus.

Valerian composed himself, lowered the weapon, and turned toward the viewscreen. "To the victor go the spoils, Father," he said with a calm that astonished Raynor. "You taught me that."

"You're not the victor yet," said Arcturus. "I'd rather not fire on you. Give me whatever's left of Kerrigan, or kill the bitch yourself. Turn over the criminal, and we'll stand together to deliver the good news that the zerg threat is no more and the Dominion is safe, thanks to us. Everyone's happy."

Valerian shook his blond head. "I can't do that, Father."

The smirk turned into a sneer. "You're too soft, Valerian."

"It's not softness, Father; it's wisdom. We have a unique chance to study her. We may learn things about the zerg that would enable us to defeat them once and for all. Surely you don't think they'll remain undirected forever? When the Overmind was destroyed, they eventually replaced it with Kerrigan. And they'll replace *her* with someone else."

That ugly thought hadn't occurred to Raynor. He glanced over at Kerrigan's stretcher. When the red alert had sounded, the scientists had frozen in place, awaiting orders. Precious seconds were ticking by while Mengsk Junior and Senior argued. He caught Valerian's eye and jerked his head in Kerrigan's direction. Valerian nodded almost imperceptibly, and the scientists left at once.

Jim wanted to go with them, but even more, he needed to know if Valerian was going to continue to stand his ground.

"I knew all about your little plan, Son, and it's a waste of time. Kerrigan needs to be put down like the mad dog she is."

Jim couldn't help it. He retorted, "Just like anyone who disagrees with you, eh, Arcturus? It's so like you to send a hardened convict to put a spike through the brain of a naked, helpless woman."

Arcturus chuckled. "Oh, Raynor, you're just a fool in love. Sarah Kerrigan hasn't been helpless since the day she came out of her mother's womb, and you know it."

And then Valerian said something that took both his father and Jim aback.

"She's more than a ghost or a zerg—she is the fulfillment of a prophecy!"

Jim gaped at him. How had Valerian known that?

He himself wouldn't have known if his old friend, the dark templar prelate Zeratul, hadn't sought him out at great risk to himself to give Jim a crystal that shared that protoss's encounter with Kerrigan.

They were coming back. The xel'naga were coming back. What had Zeratul said? *You will hold her life in your hands. And though justice demands that she die for her crimes, only she can save us.*

If Zeratul believed that, Jim did too. And apparently, so did Valerian.

Arcturus Mengsk's bushy brows drew together over his eyes. "What the hell are you blathering on about?"

"I've not been idle, Father. Over the last few years, I have learned a great deal. The protoss are an ancient race, and they believe that their creators, the xel'naga—the same beings who made these artifacts I've been collecting, which appear to have turned Kerrigan human again—are coming back. And that Sarah Kerrigan might be our only hope when they do."

"And you believe this?" Arcturus Mengsk's voice was a combination of incredulity and contempt.

"Whether or not I believe it, the prophecy exists, and it's important. Too important for us to act rashly until we know more. We could be sealing our own fates if we kill Kerrigan now."

"The only fate I'm interested in is the one I make, boy. And that should be the only fate to interest you as well. In case you haven't noticed, we're humans—not protoss, not zerg—and anything those knobby-skinned mystics have told you is likely to be full of more stardust and fantasy than anything solid. Now be a good son. Kill that mistake of a woman who just happens to be your father's worst enemy, not to mention humanity's, or give her to me and let Daddy do the dirty work."

"Valerian, you can't let—"

Valerian lifted a hand, silencing Raynor. He looked away for a moment, then returned his gaze to his father.

"No, Father. I cannot, and I will not, obey a command I deem to be shortsighted and potentially devastating."

"What would be shortsighted and potentially devastating is saving a mass murderer! We're talking billions dead, Valerian! You choose the zerg bitch and that traitor Raynor over your own *father*?"

"What I choose," Valerian said, his voice growing stronger with each word, "is not to sacrifice this sector to rashness and my father's personal vendetta. And we both know that's what it is. I'm not excusing what she's done—I'm calling you on what *you've* done." He stepped forward, hands clenching. "You can still choose with me, Father. Take a step back from your revenge. See with the eyes of a true leader all that's really at stake here—all that you are placing in jeopardy for your own selfish reasons!" He forced his hands to unclench and extended one imploringly. "Let us study the prophecy together, and be ready if the xel'naga do indeed come as has been foretold!"

Even on a viewscreen the emperor's eyes seemed to grow cold and hard. "If you won't give her to me," Arcturus said, his voice low, "then you may rest assured that I will come and take her. I won't let anyone, not even you, stand in my way."

The image disappeared. Valerian stood where he was for a moment, then, slowly, lowered his hand.

"Valerian," Jim began.

The prince's golden head whipped around. "Go to sick bay," he said. "It's where you belong. Whatever Kerrigan's done . . . for the love of everything sacred and beautiful and true, keep her safe, Jim."

And at that moment, the *Bucephalus,* the flagship of the Dominion, carrying the Heir Apparent, came under attack by its emperor.

# CHAPTER FOUR

Matt Horner slouched in his chair, grimly thinking, *I knew it. I knew this day would come.*

The day when Arcturus Mengsk would actually find the "terrorist" group known as Raynor's Raiders and bring to bear the full wrath of the Dominion upon the vessel that had once been his flagship.

With the calm balance that was such an ingrained part of his nature, Matt immediately realized that only *half* of the Dominion fleet was bearing down on them. The other half—originally twenty-five and now a total of fourteen battlecruisers and their contingents of Wraiths, dropships, and so on—was under the control of another Mengsk and firing back at Daddy's ships. Valerian had patched in the *Hyperion* on the conversation between father and son, so Matt knew which Mengsk he should be attacking. His friend and commander James Raynor was still on the *Bucephalus* as well.

Regardless, it was not by any stretch of the imagination a

pleasant event, and Matt wasn't at all sure they'd be able to escape this time. The emperor seemed to be quite willing to let familial love go by the wayside when his desires were being thwarted, and he was now actively attacking the vessels under his son's command. Hard.

So far, that was the only advantage, if one could call it that. The viewscreen was filled with the ugly red-orange planet Char and the ugly red-orange blossoms of fire as ships were struck. It was a war of titans, a battle of battleships, and the carnage was certain to be vast. The great battlecruisers moved more slowly than the Wraiths as they fired and were fired upon, and the spectacle was horrifically awe-inspiring.

"And I thought the zerg were going to be our biggest worry," Matt muttered to himself. Then he said more loudly, "Lock in on the *Bucephalus*."

"Locked, sir," said the navigator, Marcus Cade.

The image on the screen shifted and the *Gorgon*-class battlecruiser appeared. It had already sustained damage but was dealing as good as it was getting. Matt knew that as the flagship of Mengsk's fleet, it had the most up-to-date weaponry and defenses and was the most massive ship humanity had ever seen. Even as Horner watched, the *Bucephalus* fired its Yamato cannon. The small, focused nuclear explosion hurtling from the cannon struck its target with devastating results. The older and less well equipped *Behemoth*-class battlecruiser on the receiving end didn't stand a chance. A roiling ball of fire appeared, and the attacked ship slowed drastically, starting to drift. It, and the six thousand souls upon it, no longer represented a threat.

But another two *Minotaur*-class ships were closing in. As the *Hyperion* pulled closer, Horner saw a green field go up around the *Bucephalus*. The battlecruiser was operating its defensive matrix, and with any luck, it would hold until the *Hyperion* got within firing range.

There was a sudden blur outside.

Zerg.

The mutalisks were undirected but just as vicious as ever, and Matt gave orders to fire. Every second they spent blasting the zerg that were descending in near-suicide attacks was a second when the ship that housed Jim and several other Raiders was in danger.

"Destroy the zerg, every one of them that comes within range," Matt said. "And on a separate screen keep tracking the *Bucephalus*. We'll—" He paused. "Belay that order."

"Sir?" asked Marcus Cade.

"Fire toward the zerg, but not *at* them. Get their attention focused solely on the *Hyperion*. Draw them away from the Dominion ships and get them coming after us instead."

Cade looked puzzled, but obeyed. "Two more ships from Valerian's fleet are moving to intercept. He's down to fourteen now from twenty-five, and several of them look pretty bad."

"I hear you," Matt said. "Let's keep moving toward them."

*With a whole bunch of really pissed-off zerg in tow,* he thought, and he permitted himself a small, wry smile.

The *Bucephalus* rocked slightly under the attacks from outside. Jim didn't waste a thought on worry. There was nothing he could do now for either Valerian's ship or his own. They would get out of this (or not) without his aid.

There was one person he could do something for. Maybe.

The sick bay aboard the *Bucephalus* was similar to that of the *Hyperion,* but more advanced to Jim's inexpert eye. It was large, almost cavernous, and appeared coldly efficient.

Sarah was finally on a proper hospital bed. She was hooked up to several IVs, and a display panel above her head ticked information off in gold electronic lettering. Jim could read the words but didn't understand most of them. The three doctors and one scientist, however, were glued to the readouts.

Jim, out of his armor now, was in a chair by her side. He took her hand in both of his and whispered quietly, "I know these boys are scary looking, but you're safe now. Everyone here's going to try to help you. And if they don't, I'll personally kick their asses out an airlock."

For a long moment, he thought she was still asleep. Then her eyes fluttered open and she blinked a few times. She looked around and then finally met his gaze.

". . . Jim?"

"Right here, darlin'," Jim said, smiling down at her.

She started to smile too, and then he could almost see the thoughts click into place. The smile froze, became a grimace, and she closed her eyes and turned away from him.

"Whatever you did," she murmured, "I wish you hadn't."

His breath caught for an instant, but he kept his voice calm. "You don't mean that," he said. "Let these boys do their job. Don't worry."

"Don't *worry*?" Her head jerked back and she stared at him, her lips curled and her voice rising on the last note. It seemed to startle the doctors out of their fascination with her statistics, and they glanced over to regard the patient instead of the numbers. "How can you say that to me? Jim, I know what I did. I remember. Billions dead . . . because of *me!*"

"That was not you," Jim said firmly. "That was the Queen of Blades. What they made you into. You're back to being Sarah again. And we're together now. So just hush, honey."

He had put off touching the strange tentacles that adorned her head in place of hair. Everything else was so human, so much the woman he remembered, but that. . . . Now he did so, keeping her fingers entwined with his as he reached with his other hand to gently stroke back the spiny protuberances. He steeled himself for the contact. To his surprise, they felt warm beneath his touch, like skin. Like Sarah's skin. And any hesitation he'd had about still loving her—hesitation he had pushed down so deep into his soul that he himself hadn't been aware of it until right now—vanished like a bad dream.

But the touch didn't comfort her. She turned her head, trying to pull away. Respecting her needs, Jim withdrew his hand.

"It doesn't matter. Sarah Kerrigan, Queen of Blades . . . you don't understand," she murmured. "Maybe you can never understand. I've always been a destroyer of things. Anything I touch, anything I care about . . . that's why they picked me, Jim. *Because* I'm a destroyer of things. . . ."

She closed her eyes and slipped into unconsciousness. Jim sat back, trying to sort out what she had said. How much of it was real, and how much was the pain talking?

And despite what he had told Sarah—despite what he kept telling himself—he couldn't help but wonder how much of the massacre of billions had been only the Queen of Blades . . . and how much had been Sarah Kerrigan.

It was the most beautiful thing in the world, the *whole world*, and she had caught one, and she was going to show it to Mama and Papa.

Sarah's short legs pumped as she ran through the field of yellow flowers, their faces turned up to the sun. She held the most beautiful thing in the whole world carefully in the cage of her hands. She could feel it fluttering; it was frightened, but she would let it go free once she had shown it to her parents.

"Sarah Louise Kerrigan!"

Sarah's footsteps slowed. Belatedly, as she gazed at her parents on the front porch, Papa checking his pocket watch and Mama frowning, she remembered that they were going into town today.

"I'm sorry. I forgot," she said. Her huge smile returned as she extended her still-clasped hands. "But look what I—"

"Look at your hair!" her mother snapped, exasperated. She began to pluck the flower petals from Sarah's red hair, attempting to smooth the wild mane into a ponytail. "What are we going to do with you? You've got dirt all over yourself, and we don't have time to wash you, do we?"

"Well," said Papa, consulting the watch, "you'll both have to hurry."

"Why couldn't we have a nice little girl who liked to look pretty, and not some messy little—"

The words hurt, but Sarah had heard them before. It was all right. Mama would be as astonished and full of wonder as Sarah herself, once she saw what her little girl had found. Her mother's tirade faded into an angry buzz as Sarah opened her hands, anticipating the moment happily.

It was dead. The most beautiful thing in the world was dead.

And Sarah had killed it.

"Oh, now look what you've done, Sarah! You've smashed the bug, too, and gotten it all over your hands—"

Sarah screamed.

She screamed in fury at her mother's words. She screamed in horror at the death literally on her small hands and out of guilt that she had whispered promises of safety to this fragile creature.

The red went everywhere.

It pattered, warm and wet, on Sarah's face, on the porch floorboards, on the rocking chair, gore moving too slowly to be real, too dreamily to be so horrific.

Dimly Sarah heard her father screaming incoherently, but it was like listening to something underwater—muffled and indistinct and far, far away. She was transfixed by the sight of her mother's head—well, where her mother's head used to be. Because now there wasn't anything left but part of a lower jaw and jagged bits of bone and blood and brain.

The body collapsed like a puppet whose strings had suddenly

been cut. And with merciless abruptness the strange dreaminess went away, and everything came into sharp, brutal focus. Sarah understood then what her father was screaming over and over again.

"Her head came apart . . . her head came apart . . . !"

"What the hell's happening to her?" cried Jim.

Sarah had gone rigid as a board. Her green eyes had snapped open, and they were staring at nothing Jim could see, but the horror in their depths tore him up. Dr. Frederick came over, pale with worry, and checked Sarah's stats.

"She should be fine. No reaction to the meds—" Frederick stopped short of saying, "I don't know," but the words didn't need to be uttered.

Sarah gasped sharply and then began to thrash. Jim hadn't liked the idea of the restraints but was now glad his protests had been overruled. Sarah was prevented from hurting not just someone else but also herself.

Valerian stood on the bridge. His fists were clenched and his gray eyes were as hard as neosteel as he watched the battle unfolding.

He supposed he should have expected this. He hadn't thought he was clouded with ideals about Arcturus's nature, but apparently the son hadn't really expected the father to go quite so far. Anywhere from four to six thousand people were aboard each battlecruiser. The lives of others truly meant nothing to his father.

Not even that of his child.

It wasn't going well. Four of Valerian's remaining fourteen battlecruisers—the *Aeneas,* the *Amphitrite,* the *Metis,* and the *Meleager*—hung dead in space. More of his vessels were se-

verely damaged. Debris as big as a city suburb turned and
floated, interfering with attacks. Now and then there was a
sudden, sharp blaze as a piece of wreckage went too near the
atmosphere and caught fire. The ten other battlecruisers kept
up the harrying, and one of Arcturus's ships was taken out of
play under a well-coordinated assault by the *Antigone* and the
*Eos*. Each closed in from a different side, and despite a valiant
effort, the enemy battlecruiser was destroyed. Valerian said a
silent thanks to the men and women aboard all his ships, who
could easily have fled to the safety of the other side. Few would
have blamed them—not even Valerian.

He had been a fool not to plan for this contingency. Arcturus had once told him, "*You still have much to learn.*" And the
bastard had been right.

"Sir, the *Hyperion* is closing in on us," said Captain Everett
Vaughn. Young but already going gray, he had done surpris-
ingly well with the sudden turn of events over the last few days
on this, his first command. "I've just gotten a message from
Captain Horner. He says . . ." Vaughn looked slightly confused.
"He says to watch out for the stray dogs."

"What?"

The *Hyperion* moved slowly into viewing range, and then
Valerian understood. A slow smile crossed his lips, and he recalled a quote from a playwright whose works were even older
than the opera he had been listening to earlier: "Cry 'Havoc,'
and let slip the dogs of war."

The *Hyperion* was swarming with zerg.

Some were directly attacking it; others flew earnestly in its
wake. They buzzed about it like bees, with even less mindful-
ness than those insects. And the *Hyperion* was on what appeared
to be a collision course with the *White Star*—the ship that carried
Arcturus Mengsk.

"They're—they're not going to try to ram it, are they?"
asked Vaughn.

Valerian shook his head, unable to answer. Raynor and his Raiders were completely unpredictable. The prince didn't think that the young man who was captaining the *Hyperion* was prepared to destroy all aboard for the sake of Raynor and Kerrigan— but he didn't know. And that chaotic element gave the Raiders an enormous advantage.

Because if Valerian didn't know what Horner would do, then Arcturus certainly didn't.

The two mighty ships, the *Hyperion* and the *White Star*, drew closer together. Valerian frowned. The *Hyperion* was jury-rigged and souped up within an inch of its mechanical life, and thus theoretically might be able to hold its own for a time against the newer *White Star*. Still, it was definitely the one that had the most to lose. He was glad that Raynor wasn't watching this; Valerian somehow didn't think that the man, outlaw and hater of Arcturus Mengsk though he was, would condone blowing up his own ship and all aboard on an attack that might not even work.

"Sir, they are most certainly on an intercept course," said Vaughn.

"I can see that, thank you, Captain," Valerian replied coolly, unable to tear his eyes from the impending disaster.

The *White Star* ripped into the *Hyperion*. Wraiths dove at it like a mass of angry hornets, strafing as they darted past. The *White Star* fired its Yamato cannon, and Valerian squinted at the brightness of the attack. Luck was with the *Hyperion*; it had been banking as the cannon fired, and the blow was a glancing one. Still, it was bad enough. Strangely, the *Hyperion* didn't return fire and just kept coming.

"Suicide," murmured Valerian. But . . . this made no sense. . . .

And then he laughed, a sharp, clear bark of admiring delight. Because while the *Hyperion* had indeed suffered the damage of a glancing hit, the attack had also served to anger the zerg. And

*all* of them—dozens by this point—began descending upon the
*White Star.*

"*Hyperion* to *Bucephalus*—get to clear space at coordinates
four one seven mark eight."

"Valerian here," he said, preempting the standard reply. "I'll
notify my fleet." He turned to Vaughn. "You heard the
gentleman," he said. "Get that message out, and make sure it's
run on encryption level three. I don't want to risk my father's
hearing about this."

"Aye, sir," said Vaughn.

Valerian turned his attention back to the battle that was
raging. The ships looked close enough to touch, and he felt the
*Bucephalus* rock as it was struck.

"Acknowledged, sir. The *Eos*, the *Patroclus*, the *Herakles*, and
the *Antigone* are all reporting various degrees of damage but will
make every effort to get there. The rest of the fleet have lost
their engines and are dead in space."

Valerian nodded. He was not surprised, judging by what
Arcturus was doing. But he would regret each life lost. This
wasn't supposed to happen. All had been going so well . . . but
that was a lesson he had learned early in life. Things could
change in a matter of seconds, and seldom for the better. This
was war now between father and son, and thousands would get
caught in the crossfire. That was the nature of the beast.

The zerg were still attacking the *White Star*, heedless of how
many of them died and buying Valerian and his soldiers precious
time. The *Bucephalus* and his other vessels slowly began to turn,
heading for the coordinates Horner had given them. Too
slowly . . . Valerian's jaw tightened as he saw a concentrated
volley nearly take out the *Eos*.

*Four.* Out of twenty-five. . . . Well, then, four it would be. He
knew the pilot was maneuvering the damaged *Bucephalus* at top
speed, but it felt like eons before Valerian started seeing stars
and empty space rather than Char, zerg, and explosions in the

viewports. Up ahead, bloody but unbowed, was the *Hyperion* waiting for them.

"*Bucephalus*, where are you?" Horner's voice demanded.

"We are en route. Four other battlecruisers have reported they will be jumping with us."

"They better get here soon. We don't have time to wait. Looks as if your absence has been noted."

"Rear view," snapped Valerian, fixing his gaze on the viewscreen. Sure enough, several of his father's ships were also starting to turn in lumbering pursuit. Valerian saw his own four vessels trying to follow him. Even as he watched, the emperor's fleet opened fire, and the *Eos*, already damaged, suddenly halted and began to drift.

*Three.*

"Come on," murmured Valerian. He felt sweat gather at his brow and reproached himself. He took pride in his constant, controlled demeanor, but he'd never been in this position before.

"Sir, incoming message from the *White Star*," said Vaughn.

That surprised Valerian. For a moment he debated ignoring his father. He didn't particularly feel like enduring more threats and angry comments. But what if Arcturus had changed his mind?

Doubtful. More honestly, impossible. But Valerian would never know unless he agreed to listen.

"Sir?"

"Put him through," Valerian said as he stepped to the console, pleased that his voice, at least, did not reflect his current agitated state.

The image of his father appeared in front of him. "Because you are my son and, at least until today, my heir, I am going to do something I have never done with anyone I've ever fought before. I'm going to swallow my pride."

Hope, painful in its joy and fear, pulsed sharply through Valerian like adrenaline. *Is it possible?*

"I will ask you one final time to reconsider. You have the enemy on your ship, boy. We can kill them together. I'll let you share the credit. I promise you that. Don't throw away your life and those of your crews on some wild protoss goose chase . . . if they even have geese."

*No.* Valerian had been right the first time.

He spoke, his heart heavy and melancholy with resignation. "You've already killed thousands, Father. I owe it to those who lost their lives defending me to stand up for what I believe in. And what I *don't* believe in . . . is you and your *promises.*"

He stabbed a finger down, and the image disappeared. A light began to flash almost immediately, indicating that Arcturus wanted to have the last word, but Valerian was done.

Behind him, the *White Star*, having shaken itself mostly free of the zerg, moved slowly around to fire on one of the ships trailing the *Bucephalus*. It landed a perfect hit on the *Patroclus*, and more red-orange death sprang up.

*Two battlecruisers, then.*

Two of the twenty-five that had accompanied Valerian would be able to make the jump with him. The captains of the ships that were crippled and of necessity left behind might or might not surrender to Arcturus; the emperor might or might not accept that surrender. Either way, it was out of Valerian's hands now. He had made his choice, and despite the losses that were mounting by the second, Valerian knew in his heart it was the right one. In his sick bay, he had Sarah Kerrigan—key to the prophecy about the return of the xel'naga. He could not—would not—jeopardize that.

"Sir, the *White Star* is moving within firing range," said Vaughn.

"Warp out," said Valerian.

# CHAPTER FIVE

They came, so many, so very many, all descending upon her. She felt hot breath, slaver on her face, and saw the flash of rows of teeth and the waving of sharp limbs. She had fought until her weapon clicked empty, only to realize that no evac was on its way, no help was going to arrive. She'd expected death, and instead—

Darkness . . . captivity, the inability to move toward freedom. But something was moving. Inside her body, her bones and muscles and sinew were twisting, contorting, reforming, and it was agony. Other minds touched her thoughts as she was being remade.

The power. So much strength, so many lives bound to hers, so much love—

*Love*—

She had known love before they had been bonded to her. Had tasted it as a simple human female lying quietly in the arms of a strong yet gentle man with a weatherworn, bearded face.

James Raynor. Marshal, outlaw, father, widower. Lover.

*Jim—*

The brief surcease of pain faded. Images of carnage took its place. Of uncountable zerg swarming across the faces of planets, infesting anything living they came across, including her, including—

She could feel her bony wings, each tip as sharp as a dagger, flexing, extending. Her head felt heavy, adorned not with light strands of hair but with something weightier, something that moved of its own accord. Her eyes could see farther than they ever had before; her mind had opened—

*—had been stretched—*

—to accommodate so much *more* than she had been able to process even as a ghost. To know, to feel, to wield power unimaginable.

To slaughter in numbers unimaginable.

How many?

Seas of faces. But one was etched in her brain. Kerrigan had never met her, but through the eyes of her zerg, Sarah had watched her die.

Watched a mother struggle to lift her sobbing daughter out of harm's way, when there was no path out of harm's way. . . .

Oh yes, Sarah had killed before. But each time, the taking of a life from another person had taken something from her as well. She recalled a dance of death she had performed, which the journalist Mike Liberty had unfortunately been forced to behold. Phasing in and out of invisibility, slashing here, snapping a neck there, firing a slugthrower, disappearing from one spot only to reappear in another. Faces gone, torsos ripped. She had left a trail of death like bread crumbs for Liberty to follow. And finally he had found her, sinking to her knees in exhaustion. . . .

"Waffles," she murmured.

"What's that, darlin'? Getting hungry on me?"

A voice from the past. One that had spoken soft words once,

had threatened to kill her another time. It had to be from the past, because he couldn't be here now—

Waffles. One of the techs she had killed during that *danse macabre* on Antiga Prime had died wishing he had eaten the waffles offered for breakfast that morning.

*I am a destroyer of things.*

And then suddenly the corpses rose up, their faces rotting or bloody or disfigured. Not just from that day but from every day she had dealt death as a human and as the Queen of Blades. Every man, woman, and child who had fallen since the moment she had become first a ghost and then the queen of the zerg— their *mother*—now lifted gore-covered hands to her, some pleading for her to return what she had ripped from them, some demanding vengeance for lives cut far, far too short.

They were a sea of ripped and bleeding flesh. She looked, dazed, as they flooded every corner of her vision and beyond. Dozens . . . hundreds . . . thousands . . . millions . . . billions . . .

. . . and two—mother and daughter. . . .

Their screams of agony and rage and fear filled her throat, and Sarah Kerrigan gave voice to them all.


The screaming made Jim's hair stand on end. Sarah's beautiful face was contorted in a grimace of pure terror and torment, her mouth gaping open, all the sounds of grief and fury pouring from it.

"Sarah!" he cried, grabbing her shoulders and shaking them first gently, then more firmly. "You're safe! It's all right!"

The screaming mutated into wails, then soft sobbing so lost and despairing that Jim felt himself start to weep.

"Talk to her," Frederick snapped. "Her brain waves indicate that she can hear us; she's just not letting any of this reach her."

Jim gazed at the woman on the bed and said a silent prayer to any deity, real or imagined, who might be listening.

"Sarah, honey, do you remember how much you hated my guts when we first met?"

More sobbing. There was no sign that she had understood him. Jim glanced at the doctor, who waved at him to continue.

"You sure were something else, honey. You looked mighty fine. And, oh, my thoughts betrayed me then, didn't they?"

## 2500

Antiga Prime. It was not the first world Sarah Kerrigan, former ghost and now second-in-command of the rebel group led by Arcturus Mengsk, had been assigned to, nor was it likely to be the last. As planets went, it was worse than some, better than others. Arid, dry, brown. It was known that the inhabitants were not all that fond of the Confederacy of Man. Mengsk believed that with a little bit of encouragement, they would rise up as they had once before, taking their world away from the clutches of the tyrannical Confederacy, reclaiming it for themselves. And, of course, for Arcturus Mengsk, their liberator.

So Sarah had been sent to make sure the situation for the overthrow was ripe. Her recon had borne fruit. Initial intel had revealed that the main problem was posed by a single Confederate detachment. Admittedly, it was Alpha Squad, but it was still only one detachment. It had not taken long for Kerrigan to discover that General Edmund Duke, commander of Alpha Squad and the battlecruiser *Norad II*, was nowhere to be found.

Mengsk had seemed pleased with the report and had told her to expect a dropship shortly with the "new boy," former marshal and now captain James Raynor, in command.

She had arrived at the rendezvous point and watched as the dropship disgorged its human contents, Mike Liberty still awkward in his powered armor, and they began to set up a perimeter. She chose to stay cloaked, wanting to take the measure of this Raynor for herself. Part of her training had been to size up the enemy, and these days everyone was a potential enemy—even those who claimed they were working for Mengsk.

Raynor was tall, well built but not overburdened with muscle, with deep-set wrinkles around dark eyes. He chatted amiably with the others, clapping one of them on the back. *Yes,* she thought. *He looks exactly like what he has been—a law-enforcement official on a backwater planet.* But there was something about him . . . something about the set of the jaw and the sharpness of his eyes. From a backwater world James Raynor might be, but he was no bumpkin.

Satisfied with her assessment and mindful that minutes mattered, Sarah stepped forward, removing her helmet to let her head cool and deactivating the cloak.

Liberty gave her a wry smile of recognition, but she didn't have time for pleasantries. She strode up to Raynor, saluting.

"Captain Raynor," she began. He turned around, lifting an eyebrow. "I've finished scouting out the area and—"

She was used to men finding her attractive, to giving them the telepathic equivalent of rolling her eyes and continuing with the conversation. But this man—the things he wanted to do to her. . . . Images of his hands on her, of their lips pressing together, of her legs wrapped around him—

"You *pig!*"

The pictures in his head were graphic, vivid, and . . . compelling. She was surprised by her own reaction to them, and she turned it into anger.

Jim's eyes widened. "What? I haven't even said anything to you yet!"

She gave him credit for not denying it but was too upset to acknowledge that. Besides, why should she? He *was* a pig!

"Yeah, but you were *thinking* it," she shot back. She wondered why she was so offended. It wasn't as if he was the first man to think such things. Sarah had thought there was an essence of goodness and decency about him upon first perusal. Clearly, she was wrong. He was just like all the rest underneath.

A pig.

"Oh yeah, you're a telepath," he said, infusing the word with . . . something. There were many emotions crowding his mind, and she didn't want to try to decipher them. He had the grace, at least, to appear embarrassed. "Look, let's just get on with this, okay?"

"Right." She bit the word off icily, again wondering why she was so angry. With the speed of practice, she recovered, still stinging a little, and filled in Liberty and Raynor on the situation. When Jim made a snide comment about her abilities, she rose to the bait for an instant before pushing her anger down. More important was the fact that she had observed something else on her reconnaissance . . . that the terrans were not alone on Antiga Prime.

"Crap," Jim said. "Confederates *and* zerg. They seem to go hand in hand. *Okay*, now let's roll out."


## 2504


Jim's mouth was dry from talking, from describing to the tormented young woman a time in their lives that now seemed so simple and almost sweet. He knew the *Bucephalus* had been in battle; even in the sick bay, deep inside the ship, they could feel it. He'd felt the ship take the hits. It had all gone on while he had been talking.

But Raynor was right where he knew he could do the most

good. As he spoke, Kerrigan's taut body relaxed slightly. Toward the end his heart lifted as something resembling her old smirk curved her full lips. Her breathing slowed, and the doctor came over to check her stats.

"She's asleep," Frederick said. "Not unconscious . . . just sleeping." Jim blew out a sigh of relief and sat back, still holding her hand. "Couldn't help but overhear," Frederick continued. "Just what the hell were you thinking when you saw her?"

"Way I was raised, son, a gentleman don't tell," Jim said, finding the energy to give the doctor a tired smirk. "But I bet you can make a good guess."

At that moment, there was a sharp whistling sound. "Mr. Raynor, this is Valerian. Please acknowledge."

Jim rose and went to the console, punching a button. "Raynor here. I'm guessing you and Matt got out all right, or else we wouldn't be having this conversation."

"You guess correctly. Although our escape from my father's fleet came at a great cost." The voice sounded genuinely regretful. "I'd like to meet with you and Mr. Horner aboard the *Hyperion*. We have much to discuss."

Click. It wasn't a request, of course, and Jim knew it. He was fine with that—it proved that he wasn't a prisoner, confined to sick bay along with Sarah. He didn't want to leave her, but she was clearly stable and in good hands. Jim gazed at her for a moment more, then glanced over at the doctor.

"Take care of her," he said. "Good care."

He'd given so much to find her. To save her. He'd turned on Tychus for her. He couldn't lose her now.


When Raynor and Valerian entered the bridge, Matt, huddled talking with the *Hyperion*'s chief engineer, Rory Swann, looked relieved. "Good to see you again, sir," he said. He nodded politely but coolly to Valerian and directed most of his attention to Raynor.

"Fill me in," Raynor said.

Matt did, describing the battle quickly and concisely. Jim watched Valerian sharply as he listened. Valerian still had that familiar poised, calm expression, but he seemed subdued by all that had transpired. There was a flicker of pain across the handsome face as Matt revealed to Raynor that only two other battlecruisers besides the *Bucephalus* had made it. Raynor said nothing, merely nodded sober acknowledgment. Mengsk was ruthless, but he wasn't stupid. If he needed the disabled ships and the crew aboard them, he'd spare them. If not—

"Well, Junior," he said to Valerian, opting for casual rather than sympathetic, "you found the artifacts, you put them together, and they worked. Sarah sure seems to be human again. Your next step was to take her to one of the Moebius Foundation installations and have your top-notch scientists take a look at her."

Valerian took a half second longer to respond than he should have, and Raynor saw just how rattled he really was. "Hm? Oh yes. Dr. Emil Narud will be of the utmost help to us at this juncture."

"We have a scientist here, you know," Horner put in. "And a rather good one. Egon Stetmann. We may not need Narud."

Valerian's golden brows drew together. "I've not met this Dr. Stetmann, but I assure you, there is no one in the galaxy who is more familiar with zerg physiology than Dr. Narud. We'd be foolish not to contact him as soon as possible."

"Let's see what Stetmann thinks before we make a decision," Jim said. He punched the control, and Egon's angular, eager face appeared. "Egon, how's the lab right now?"

"A bit of a mess, but nothing we can't either sweep up or fix up," Egon replied. "What's the plan?"

"Well, we're figuring that out right now," Jim said. "You heard that the xel'naga artifacts worked."

Stetmann's face brightened like a sun. "Oh yes, I did! That's fantastic! It's so exciting! Once we have the chance to study them further and, of course, talk with the Qu . . . uh, I mean Kerrigan, of course . . . science will have learned so much that—"

"That's what I want to talk to you about," Jim said. Left unchecked, Egon would prattle on for hours. "Our original plan was to take her to Valerian's Moebius Foundation. His father has made that considerably harder."

Egon frowned. "Oh, right . . . I can see how that could be an issue," he said. "That's bad."

"You don't think you can handle it? Kerrigan's human, but"—he grimaced, hating to admit it—"not quite all the way. She's going to need care and monitoring and examining so we know how best to take care of her."

The color drained visibly from his face. "Me?" His voice, always youthfully high, was a positive squeak. "Oh, sir—I don't think that's a very good idea. I mean, I know something about the zerg, but—"

"You know a hell of a lot, Egon."

"Well, while that's true, this—well, this is way beyond my pay grade. Obviously if we have no other choice, I'll do the best I can, but . . . sir, I'd hate to lose her, and not just because you'd come down on me like the zerg Swarm itself. I don't know that I'd be able to handle any, uh, emergencies that arose."

Considering Egon tended to slightly exaggerate his capabilities, Jim believed him now that the young scientist was clearly so uncertain. And uncomfortable.

And right. Jim *would* come down on him like the zerg Swarm if anything happened to Sarah.

"So. Guess we're seein' Narud again," he said. Not that long ago, the Raiders had saved Emil Narud and many of his team from the Queen of Blades. He hadn't liked the man much then and disliked him even more now.

"I know this is difficult for you, Mr. Raynor, but I assure you, Sarah will be in the best hands possible. We—"

"Captain Horner!" cried Cade. "We've got incoming vessels. The Dominion has found us!"

# CHAPTER
# SIX

Jim swore an oath that would have made Tychus Findlay do a double take. "How the hell did they track us?"

"No idea, sir," said Cade. He looked as flustered as the rest of them. "Captain Horner gave instructions for a calculated and encrypted coordinate jump. There's no way Mengsk could have broken the encryption so fast!"

Matt didn't waste a second to excuse himself. He moved back into his role as captain and began issuing orders. "Battle stations! Shields up!"

Jim whirled on Valerian, closing the distance between them and shoving his face to within a centimeter of the prince's. "Something you need to tell me?"

Valerian's eyes narrowed. He lifted a hand, placed it on Jim's chest, and firmly pushed Raynor back. "No," he said. "And I resent what you are implying."

"We're being followed. And the *Hyperion* sure as shit isn't leading them to us."

"And neither am I!" Valerian shot back. "I lost several battlecruisers full of human beings, Raynor, to ally with you, and—"

"Jim," broke in Swann's gruff voice. "He might be clean. Stupid, but clean."

"What do you mean?"

The viewscreens filled with fire and the *Hyperion* rocked. Valerian snapped, "I must return to my ship!"

"Not till I hear what Rory has to say," Jim said. He, too, burned to get back to the *Bucephalus*, to be beside Kerrigan, to figure out what was going on and put a stop to it. The more they were delayed by Papa Mengsk, the more time elapsed between Sarah and treatment.

Rory eyed Valerian but addressed his comment to Jim. "When you, uh, relieved Mengsk of the *Hyperion*, you will recall you had a whole mess of trackers and recording devices aboard it that had to be scoured off. From what you said, it took a bit of time to do it too. I'd bet that the *Bucephalus* is just as buggy, seeing as it also was once Mengsk's flagship. We got a head start this time, in that you recorded where things were rigged on the *Hyperion*. I'll wager that Arcturus simply ordered any bugs to be set up in the same pattern."

Jim frowned but nodded. "That's the likeliest explanation, all right."

"I'll take some of my crew over to the *Bucephalus* and start poking around." He eyed Valerian from under bushy brows. "We're a lot more used to being on the run and having to escape quick-like than you are, Prince Charming."

"Swann is a bit of a miracle worker when it comes to ships," Jim said, clapping his friend on the shoulder.

Valerian frowned slightly, no doubt disliking the idea of this gruff man poking about on his lovely vessel. "Very well," he said. As if he really had a choice. "Considering how well you've done eluding my father before now, I daresay you do know a thing or two." He smiled, and it looked—and felt—genuine. "Any help you can offer, I will gladly accept. But please, let's go. Men and women under my command are being attacked. I'd like to stand with them."

"I'll be there before you can blink," said Rory.

Annabelle Thatcher had been pulling double shifts, but then so had everyone else. She had found that being one of Raynor's Raiders consisted of hours of boredom spent either in helping her boss, Swann, repair the *Hyperion* or attending to its seemingly endless maintenance tasks; hours of slightly less boredom spent hanging out in the cantina with her friends, drinking some of bartender Cooper's magnificent mai tais; and minutes of stark terror.

Recently, those minutes had seemed even longer. Things had happened so fast that half the time the battle was raging, Annabelle and many others didn't know exactly who was fighting whom.

First, there had been the whole arriving-at-Char-and-dezergifying-Kerrigan part. That decision had caused some of the crew to feel uneasy, even to the point of openly speaking out against Raynor. To those such as Milo Kachinsky, the most vocal of the dissenters, it appeared that Raynor had been siding with the Dominion. Even Annabelle had wondered.

Tychus Findlay, who would, Annabelle thought, be scary even out of his hardskin and sound asleep, had fanned the flames. He'd taken jabs at Raynor's drinking—something that Annabelle herself had been more than a little concerned about—and bluntly stated that given the chance, Raynor would hightail it out of danger and leave his crew behind.

Annabelle didn't believe *that*. Raynor had walked in, flicked his cigar at Tychus, and an old-fashioned bar fight had broken out. Despite the apparent advantages of being in full armor, Tychus had been soundly—and publicly—trounced. Even Milo had said of Jim, "Now *that's* the commander I've been waiting on."

Once they had achieved orbit around Char, and the attempt to save Kerrigan had been made, things had happened so quickly and so violently, Annabelle was hardly sure what was what. Horner had made an announcement that the recovery of Kerrigan—in human form—had been successful, but then suddenly Arcturus Mengsk had appeared out of nowhere. No one knew what was going on, only that they were again in danger, and everyone focused on obeying orders and firing where they were told.

Again on orders, they'd jumped and were now . . . well, Annabelle sure as hell didn't know where. They had had what felt like six nanoseconds to catch their breaths before, somehow, Mengsk had found them, and they'd come under fire from the emperor a second time.

"No rest for the wicked," muttered her friend Earl. He, like Annabelle and the rest in engineering, was dirty and weary-looking.

"You should know," Annabelle shot back. The ship rocked, the curious gentleness of the motion belying the fury of the battle raging outside.

"Shut up, you two, and come with me," Rory said, stomping into engineering. Normally Swann was a bluff, genial sort of fellow, but he had a temper, and his team knew to not poke at the bear when such moods were upon him. Earl and Annabelle exchanged glances and shrugs, but obeyed, slinging tool kits over their shoulders and hurrying to keep up with their boss as they strode down the wide, carpeted corridors of what had once been Arcturus Mengsk's flagship.

"Sir," Annabelle ventured, "where are we going?"

"To the *Bucephalus*," Swann replied curtly. He broke into a trot, and the other two emulated him. "You probably couldn't tell, but in that last battle and in this one, too, Senior was fighting against Junior as well as us."

Annabelle's eyes widened. "Nope, down in engineering we just concentrated on keeping the *Hyperion* in one piece while zerg and Dominion battlecruisers swarmed all over us."

"Junior and a couple of his ships came with us. But once we jumped, Mengsk found us inside of fifteen minutes. So now we're going to go over to the golden boy's ship to check for transmitters and other technology that Senior might have planted on it."

"Because if we don't, Mengsk is going to be able to follow us anywhere we go," Annabelle finished. "Boy, does *that* sound familiar." She'd been aboard when Raynor had first acquired the *Hyperion*, and well remembered scouring the vessel for bugs. She was not looking forward to doing it again, but it was much preferable to being chased and attacked by the emperor. They hurried through the docking tubes and stepped out into the interior of the *Bucephalus*.

"First," said Rory, "engineering."

Valerian stood on the bridge. He had not felt this angry and helpless since he and his mother had been forced into hiding, hunted by Confederate kill teams. Though he knew he did an admirable job of concealing it, he was reeling at his father's betrayal. He still couldn't wrap his mind around Arcturus's decision. It was shortsighted and stupid—two things he had never believed of his father, but was forced to now.

He was also wrestling with another unusual emotion—guilt. He had ordered his soldiers to fire upon their emperor, then asked them to do what amounted to completely severing all ties in choosing Valerian over Arcturus. True, some of those who served aboard the battlecruisers were what were called "resocs"—marines who had had their memories altered in order to render them cheerful and utterly obedient. Even so, they were people, not machines like the adjutants, the humanoid-shaped computer interfaces. And there were many under his command whose minds were still completely their own—minds that had made a conscious choice to follow the Heir Apparent, not minds that simply followed orders.

Many of those men and women had died for choosing him. And now more were going to, because his father had been canny enough to plant trackers on the *Bucephalus*. He suddenly realized his hands had curled into fists and deliberately forced them to unclench.

As he watched, lips pressed together to form a thin, harsh line, he took a grim pleasure in noticing that if the number of his ships had been reduced, so had those of his father. It wasn't an even battle, but the odds were not as crushingly overwhelming as they could have been. Both he and his father had brought twenty-five ships to the battle, not counting the *White Star*, the *Bucephalus*, or the *Hyperion*. He did not dictate to his captain; Everett Vaughn knew his job well, and Valerian was wise enough to know the benefits of finding the best people possible for a position, and then standing back and letting them do their jobs.

His fists still clenched of their own accord each time one of his ships took a hit. One in particular, the *Antigone*, seemed to be the preferred target, other than the *Bucephalus* itself. The *Antigone* was the most damaged of the two ships that had been able to escape the previous battle. Mengsk obviously thought to cripple it permanently and remove it as a threat, while still firing at the *Bucephalus*.

Vaughn looked up at Valerian. "Sir, incoming transmission from the *White Star*."

"Ignore it. My father has nothing to say that could possibly interest me."

". . . Yes, sir."

There was, however, someone he did want to talk to. He strode to one of the bulkheads and punched an intercom. "Valerian to Swann. How are you progressing?"

"I'd be going faster without having to listen to your yapping," came the engineer's growl. "We're moving as fast as we can, Junior. Remember, it ain't just you and this pretty ship that's getting fired on."

"Of course."

"That said, we've found three bugs down here already. We should be up to check out the bridge shortly."

"I confess I hadn't expected to have three of Raynor's Raiders on the bridge of the *Bucephalus* in the middle of a battle," said Valerian. At that moment, orange filled the viewports and the *Bucephalus* rocked.

"Damage reports coming in from levels four and seven, six casualties," said Vaughn.

"Sooner we get up there and do our sweep, the sooner we can all jump again," Swann chimed in.

"Sir," said Vaughn, turning to Valerian, "I'm getting a message from the *Herakles* and the *Antigone*. They're taking severe damage and they both express uncertainty about the ability to make another jump without time to effect repairs."

Valerian grimaced. "Contact Raynor," he said. Raynor's face appeared on-screen.

"How you holding up, Valerian?"

"Your Swann appears to indeed be working miracles, but not quickly enough," said Valerian. "My two other ships might not be able to make the jump if we wait much longer."

"Well, no sense in doing it if we're just going to have to jump again right after."

Valerian's gray eyes were riveted to the sight of the battle, not on Raynor. The two ships were still fighting, but it was obvious that the *Antigone* was in bad shape, and the *Herakles* wasn't far behind.

"We're going to have to. It'll buy Swann and his team time to keep working."

"They're just going to find us—"

"I don't care!" snapped Valerian, whirling back to face Raynor's hologram. "We'll jump as many times as we have to in order to save my people, Raynor. And if you don't understand that sentiment, then I have misjudged you terribly."

Raynor frowned. Valerian didn't need to be a telepath to know what he was thinking. Raynor was no doubt wondering if this was simply noble posturing on Valerian's part, or if perhaps Junior was indeed a better man than Senior.

"I hear you," Raynor said at last. He turned his head. "Matt, get us some new jump coordinates. Even if it just buys us ten or fifteen minutes, it's worth it."

Valerian closed his eyes briefly in relief. "Thank you, Mr. Raynor." He clicked off the image. "This is Prince Valerian to the *Antigone* and the *Herakles*. Jump coordinates coming in from the *Hyperion* shortly. Wait for Captain Horner's mark, and then let's do it."

The next several minutes lasted forever. Valerian fought the urge to pace, instead practicing rhythmic breathing, an ancient art, to calm himself. The *White Star* was being attacked relentlessly, and it was taking damage. But not enough, nor fast enough.

*Come on, come on. . . .*

"Receiving incoming transmission from the *Hyperion*, sir— they're sending the jump coordinates and telling us to be ready to jump on his mark in less than two minutes."

For a brief, horrible second, Valerian wondered if their transmissions were being monitored as well. But almost instantly, he realized that they weren't. Because if they had been, then Mengsk and his fleet would have arrived a lot sooner than fifteen minutes later. It was a small consolation.

"Transmit to the *Herakles* and the *Antigone*," Valerian ordered.

"Both vessels to have an open channel to receive Captain Horner's mark. We'll—"

And he had to close his eyes at the sudden flash on the screen. When he opened them, it was to behold horror. The *Antigone* had been struck a definitive, deadly blow. Flames fed by the battlecruiser's own atmosphere still made him squint. There was a steady stream of debris and bodies pouring out from the gaping hole in the ship. As he stared, aghast, there was another strike, and the ship cracked in two.

The *Antigone*, and likely all the souls aboard it, was lost.

"Horner to fleet. Prepare to jump on my mark. Three . . . two . . . one . . . mark!"

The *Bucephalus* and a single other vessel of the "fleet" were all that accompanied the *Hyperion* as it fled to its next brief respite.

Anger burned, cold and seething, in Valerian's gut. He punched a button. "I'm sure you saw that, Raynor."

"I did, and I'm right sorry about it," came Raynor's voice. It was laced with genuine sympathy.

"We can't afford to lose any more ships or people."

"I agree, but I know that Swann and his team are working as fast as they possibly can. Judging by the last time, we've got about fifteen minutes or less before your dad finds us again, assuming that Swann hasn't gotten all the bugs yet. I understand he hasn't even tackled the bridge yet."

Valerian grimaced. "No, he hasn't."

"Well, come on over here then, while he does his thing there. Been talking a bit with Matt, and we might have a place to hide for a while once we get rid of your tracking devices."

# CHAPTER
# SEVEN

Jim looked up as Valerian emerged onto the bridge. The man knew how to make an entrance, Raynor had to admit. Compared with the rumpled, rather dirty appearance of his own crew, Valerian virtually sparkled. But the recent events had taken some of the shine off the boy. Jim noticed that, young as Valerian was, there were furrows along that high brow that hadn't been there before, and he didn't stand quite as proudly straight as he had earlier. Jim supposed he should feel satisfied, but instead, to his own confusion, he felt a little bit sad.

Horner was looking increasingly uncomfortable. Now he sighed and folded his arms as Valerian approached. He looked like he was about to volunteer to tickle a hydralisk. Valerian raised a golden eyebrow expectantly.

"First, Your Excellency," said Horner, "I want to say I'm sorry for the loss of the *Antigone*. I realize that had we jumped a minute sooner, it would have made it. I want you to know I went as fast as I could."

The coldness of Valerian's gray eyes thawed slightly. "Thank you," he said. "Any ideas you have to prevent further loss of life and get Sarah Kerrigan to proper care will be most welcome."

"Well, I . . . may have a solution," he said.

"Out with it, kid!" came Swann's voice. Jim was amused as Valerian looked startled. Then the Heir Apparent smiled self-deprecatingly as he realized that Swann was being looped into the conversation.

"I don't know that it's a *good* solution," Horner continued. "In fact, you know, the more I think about it—"

"Matt," Jim said, "spit it out. That's an order."

Matt nodded. "Yes, sir. I was thinking we might lie low in Deadman's Port for a while."

"Deadman's Port?" echoed Valerian, incredulous. "Mr. Horner, are you quite mad? That place is completely crawling with vermin! Pirates will be on us the second we warp in!"

But Jim was nodding. He thought he knew where Matt was going with this. "On the plus side, Valerian, your daddy won't be able to just bring in the big guns and force you to go to your room without any supper," he said. "The Dominion has absolutely no sway in that area. Arcturus would have to be prepared to launch a full-scale assault on the planet before he could even think about trying to find us, and I don't think he's prepared to do that. Maybe at some point, but not right now."

Valerian's shock had abated somewhat and he looked thoughtful. "That's true," he said. "He's lost the *Bucephalus* and the two— the other battlecruiser that jumped with me. And I have no idea what kind of shape the ones that *weren't* able to jump are in. But still—what's to stop the fine, upstanding citizens of the worst sewer in the galaxy from attacking us and taking the spoils?"

"That won't happen," said Jim, permitting himself a grin and clapping Horner on the shoulder. "We got ourselves an ace in the hole in that sewer. Don't we, *Matthew*?"

Horner actually blushed. "I, uh . . . do have a contact there, yes," he said. "Someone who would, I think, be willing to give us safe harbor for at least a while."

Swann burst out, "You're stark raving mad, Horner! Mira Han? That woman's a dirty merc!"

"Now, now, Swann," said Jim. "You better watch your manners. You're talking about the man's—"

"We don't need to get into that," Matt interrupted quickly. Valerian turned to Matt, eyebrows raised in inquiry. Horner didn't meet the Heir Apparent's gray gaze, waving his hand and saying, "It's . . . a long story."

"But, I imagine, one worth hearing at some point," said Valerian, clearly intrigued. He returned to the business at hand. "So this Mira Han would be willing to stave off the cutthroats and pirates that populate Deadman's Port and protect us from the Dominion, all for you?"

"It's a long shot, but I think I can talk her into it."

"Well, all I know is, she's got a real soft spot for *Matthew*," Raynor said. "Come on, Swann. You got a better idea?"

"With the Dominion sure to be on our ass every time we so much as try to blow our noses? Hell no, I ain't got a better idea. And you know it kills me to say it. How are you going to contact her, Horner?"

"I have a way."

Valerian stepped forward. "Mr. Horner, while I appreciate the fact that you are willing to do something you clearly don't enjoy to assist me—"

"With all due respect, I'm not doing it for you; I'm doing it for the Raiders." Matt's voice was icy.

"Point taken. However, considering the risk factor, I'd still like to know how you're going to be able to contact her."

Horner glanced at Raynor, who nodded. Jim was curious too. Matt slumped slightly, defeated. "She sends me information regularly about which channels are secure. Just in case I feel like talking to her. This would be the first time I've done so."

"Aww, poor Mira," said Jim. "Maybe I should get you some time off while we're there."

"Oh, please, sir," Matt said, quite earnestly, "I'd rather work double shifts."

"Well then, you better contact that . . . person," said Swann, clearly annoyed at the time-wasting banter. "And I better finish up here on the bridge. Let me know if you need me; otherwise, I'm over here doing my job. These little things ain't going to disable themselves, you know." There was a decisive click.

"As usual, Swann's right," Raynor said. "We're wasting time jawing. Valerian, you'd best get back to your bridge. We've got only a few more minutes until we can expect to see your father."

"A reunion most undesired," said Valerian.

"Actually," Horner said, "I've got an idea about that too."


Earl and Annabelle had been quietly listening in to the conversation their boss was having with Raynor, Horner, and Valerian. When the words *Deadman's Port* were mentioned, Annabelle grimaced and saw Earl make a similar expression. Swann's expression was even darker—a thundercloud in a normally sunny sky. Deadman's Port was a place to steer clear *of*, not to steer *to*. But as the old saying went, any port in a storm, and if Mira Han could keep the Dominion off their backs long enough for them to effect repairs, she supposed it was worth the risk.

Of course, they had to finish finding all the tracking devices before they could leap there. If Arcturus and the rest of the Dominion fleet materialized before the *Hyperion, Herakles,* and *Bucephalus* could escape, Annabelle knew that all the planning would be for nothing. Earl was an expert at nanotechnology. He knew where to plant things, and consequently, where others would be inclined to plant them. Between Earl, Annabelle (who remembered where many of the trackers had been on the *Hyper-*

*ion*), and Swann (with his overall knowledge and sharp instincts), it had gone fairly quickly—though not quickly enough. Generally, and rather unimaginatively, trackers or recording devices tended to be planted in the same areas: bridge, captain's and guest quarters, and engineering—rather than in some random place on the ship.

If the bridge on the *Hyperion* was luxurious, this was almost over the top. Open, airy, it felt more like someone's luxury yacht than the bridge of a battleship. While Raynor's Raiders had nothing resembling a uniform and often appeared rumpled and unshaven, the men and women here were all spit-and-polish. Their uniforms had nary a wrinkle; their voices bespoke wealth and education. Annabelle, who knew she'd taken a sonic shower and put on fresh clothes this morning, still felt like she smelled bad as she stood next to one of the navigators. The young man, dark-haired and dark-eyed and intimidatingly handsome, looked up at her inquiringly.

"I, uh, need to look under there," Annabelle said, giving a shy smile. "To look for bugs and stuff."

"Oh, of course." Immediately he rose from his chair, and she scooted underneath the console. Fingers that were nimble and sensitive, despite hard-earned calluses, felt about the cool metal and plastic. She smiled to herself as she touched a flat, oval object concealed in the shadows.

"Got one!" she called to Rory. Quickly, efficiently, she reached for a small tool with a glowing tip. Steady hands were required to detach the tracking device, as it was designed to break if it was removed inexpertly, continuing its devious mission with no way to stop it.

Suddenly klaxons began to blare. Annabelle started, but her hands stayed steady. She heard Rory, who swore under his breath. "Arcturus is right on time, the bastard."

"Shit," swore Annabelle. She wondered briefly if the handsome officer had overheard her, and if so, what his opinion of her rough language might be, then instantly dismissed the thought. She bit her lip, tasting the salt of her sweat, trying to decide if she should continue attempting to detach the bug or wait until the battle was over.

Without any warning, boots appeared three centimeters from her hip as she sat curled up beneath the console. The officer had made her decision for her—he was going to be at his station, and she was stuck. She shrugged and returned her attention to her job.

"Contact the *White Star,*" she heard Valerian say. Annabelle paused. Was he trying to stall, buy time—or was he going to surrender?

"Well, well, *now* you want to talk to me," came Arcturus Mengsk's voice. Annabelle shrank in on herself, just a little, at the sound of that voice, knowing the video image of the emperor was only a few centimeters away.

"Indeed I do," Valerian said. "Father, this is madness. You're throwing lives away chasing a woman who doesn't exist anymore."

"As long as she draws breath, she exists. She's a danger to me as the Queen of Blades or as Sarah Kerrigan. And if you weren't so dazzled by silly alien prophecies, you'd see that she's a danger to anyone around her, including you."

"No, Father. The best way to defeat an enemy is to make her your friend."

Arcturus guffawed at that. "That bitch is incapable of friendship. She was messed up long before I got my hands on her, and she always will be. You should have let Tychus complete his mission."

Annabelle started. Come to think of it, she hadn't heard about Tychus returning with the others—and Tychus was never one to stay silent. She had been too busy in engineering even for rumors to reach her. Had Tychus been hired to try to kill—

"Your puppet is dead, Father. You've failed. And you're always going to fail because you cannot see—"

"Enough of this! Your last chance, Valerian. Surrender, give me Kerrigan and Raynor, and we can put all this behind us."

"On this, I will defy you down to my last breath, Father."

"That can be arranged," came Arcturus's voice. "I've tried to be reasonable with—"

Another voice cut in abruptly. "Sir, this is Captain Roger Merriman of the *Herakles*. I regret to inform you that I am about to defy your orders."

"What?" Valerian didn't yelp, not quite, but his voice rose in pitch.

"Ha!" Arcturus sounded triumphant. "See there, Son? Your people are about to defect back over to the winning side."

"No, Emperor Arcturus. We pledged our service to Prince Valerian, sir, and our lives. We know you planted tracking devices on his ship, and that's how you've been able to follow our jumps. This ship is probably too badly damaged to make the jump—but we can buy the Heir Apparent time."

"No," cried Valerian, reasoning it out apparently at the same instant that Annabelle did. Her eyes widened in horror. "I forbid it. Fire on the *White Star*! If we cripple him, we can all—"

"No, sir," Merriman's voice continued. "This is the only way. Remember us to our families."

Annabelle clasped her knees tight to control her sudden shaking. Tears stung her eyes. Nearly six thousand people were about to give their lives for Valerian, for Raynor, for the hope that Kerrigan held out.

"Sir, the *Herakles* is approaching the *White Star* at full speed," someone said. "Time to impact . . . seven seconds."

Instinctively, heedless of how it might be interpreted, Annabelle reached out and brushed the leg of the navigator, desperate for human contact. She expected him to pull back, but instead, a hand reached down and grasped hers. She clung to it, wordlessly, squeezing, and he—she didn't even know his name—squeezed back.

Even from under the console, Annabelle could see the flashes of light that signaled the end of the suicide run.

There was a long, long pause. Then Valerian sighed. "It looks like it worked," he said. "The *White Star* is taking heavy damage."

"Damn, Valerian, you would have made a fine actor," came Jim Raynor's familiar drawl. "I think he bought it hook, line, and sinker."

"How are my crewmen doing over there?"

"It makes for interesting people watching, but so far no fights have broken out. Gonna be a bit crowded with nearly three thousand more mouths to feed, but we'll manage."

"What?" The word escaped Annabelle's mouth before she could stop it. The navigator scooted his chair back and peered down at her. A few seconds later, Valerian's own visage appeared, the small ponytail slipping over his shoulder as he bent over.

"Ah, Miss Annabelle," he said. "I'm afraid you were left out of the loop. My apologies."

She blinked, looking at Valerian and the navigator, both of whom regarded her kindly. "I—it was a trick?"

"One that worked," Valerian said. "We had just enough time to transfer the crew of the *Herakles*—which, sadly, had suffered great losses—to the *Hyperion* and the *Bucephalus*. We then had the captain speak from my personal suite about using the *Herakles* on a suicide run while the ship's adjutant piloted it right into the *White Star*. Arcturus won't be able to follow us for some time now, even if he eventually does discover where we are. The *Herakles* was in bad shape—but her crew is just fine."

"Oh," said Annabelle weakly. She wiped at her still-wet eyes and suddenly felt heat scorch her cheeks. "I feel so stupid," she muttered.

The navigator squeezed her hand, which he was still holding.

"Don't," he said. "The truth is, those men and women *would* have been willing to die for Valerian. They just didn't have to. And if you believed it, then sure as hell Arcturus did."

Valerian nodded, satisfied that Annabelle was all right. "Please continue, miss," he said. "I can't believe I'm saying this, but the sooner we get to Deadman's Port, the better."

She nodded and started to pull her hand back. The navigator held on to it for a second longer, then released it. Quietly, Annabelle asked, "Why did you do . . . that?" She gestured at his hand. "I mean—you knew it was a trick."

He smiled gently, his dark eyes kind. "*You* didn't," was all he said.

Sarah looked no better when Jim returned to the *Bucephalus*. He supposed he shouldn't have assumed she would, but somehow, knowing she was hooked up to all those tubes and such, he guessed he had. Frederick nodded as he entered.

"She's out, but she's stable."

"All right. Just going to sit with her awhile."

"Go right ahead."

Jim winced as his chair scraped the floor slightly, but Sarah didn't stir. She was indeed "out." He took her hand in his again, recalling that some people believed that even when in a coma, people were aware of such things. He hoped it was true.

Mentally, he went over the last few hours. He'd consistently kept putting his faith in Valerian, usually reluctantly, but thus far, the kid had been true to his word. It had been Matt who had suggested the initial plan for ramming the damaged *Herakles* into the *White Star*. Initially it looked like the only way to make it work was to leave a skeleton crew on the ship, but to both Jim's and Matt's surprise, Valerian flatly refused.

"I've lost too many loyal people today," he had said. "My father may go through his followers like tissue paper, but I don't. If we can't save the ship, we must save its crew, or I will not order it."

And so they had decided on mass evacuation—tricky to do subtly and quickly—and to program the adjutant to fly the empty ship to its doom and, one devoutly hoped, the doom of the *White Star* and Arcturus Mengsk.

But Jim had long ago lost that naïve hopefulness. Even if his ship didn't survive it, Mengsk would. He was like a cockroach— filthy but a survivor. He would come after them again, Jim was sure of it. The questions were when, where, and how.

It was almost impossible for Jim to believe that he had once been an ardent follower of the man. He'd slowly begun to become disillusioned with the terrorist and one-time ally who said what he wanted to hear, but even at his most angry, his most suspicious, he had never seen the betrayal coming.

Nor, bless her shattered soul, had Sarah. . . .


## 2500


After Antiga Prime had fallen to the zerg, Sarah still hadn't re-covered the color in her cheeks, nor had the blue-green circles under her eyes faded completely. She and Jim, after their first cups of coffee together, had gravitated to each other. Some-thing more than physical exhaustion seemed to be troubling her, but Jim didn't want to press. They had been aware that things were looming on the horizon, but after Sarah had been so drained from deploying the psi emitter, both of them were willing to shut their eyes to what lay ahead and simply enjoy the moment.

They had been summoned to Mengsk's office. It was the first time either had seen him since Antiga Prime. He looked relaxed and rested, and greeted them both enthusiastically as he pressed snifters of brandy into their hands. Kerrigan at first demurred, but, "I insist," said Arcturus, smiling kindly at her. And when Arcturus Mengsk insisted, one usually yielded.

He indicated two chairs, and they both sat. "Where's Mike?" asked Sarah. The reporter Michael Liberty had become a friend to both Kerrigan and Raynor, and seemed to be a special pet of Arcturus's. Even though, Jim mused as the thought formed, if Mike was a "pet," he was one of those dogs that occasionally growled at his "master."

"Normally I enjoy chatting with the three of you," Mengsk said, swirling the brandy in the snifter as he spoke. "But Liberty's devotion is somewhat . . . conditional. After what's happened recently, I wanted to take a few moments and speak to those who are more—let us say, in sync with my ideals. I wanted to thank you. Both of you. Things lie ahead and—well, no one knows the hour of his passing. It's more important than ever that we stay united. Work together for the freedom and betterment of mankind, as both of you have done."

He smiled, the neatly trimmed black-and-white beard parting to reveal white teeth. "I also wanted to say it does my heart good to see the two of you getting along so well."

Jim had thought he was a jaded cynic. But at Mengsk's words, he actually blushed. Not that Kerrigan would have any problem knowing what he was thinking without his telltale reddening.

Sarah, too, looked away for a moment, and then, evenly, regarded Jim. "I think we each misjudged the other," she said. "I'm glad Jim's with us."

"With you both cooperating, we can have what we are striving for. We truly can," said Mengsk, his compelling voice earnest. "We can have a better world without the Confederacy. Overthrowing that brutal, antiquated system—that's as pure a mission as any angel could follow. You two are my best soldiers—my angels."

Jim laughed out loud at that, scratching his neck. "Been called a lot of things before, Arcturus, but never an angel."

Mengsk chuckled, sipping the brandy. "Sometimes it takes others to see what lies inside a man's heart. I'm a good judge of character, Jim Raynor. It's let me get this far on my mission to, finally, rid this sector of the Confederacy and establish something that's just and lasting. You, my friend, do have an angel's ideals. And you, Sarah," and his voice grew warm with affection as he toasted her, "you are my avenging angel."

She lowered her eyes. Jim didn't have to be a telepath to sense her pain. But Sarah didn't protest. Because they all knew it to be true.

Jim was moved to speak. "You are right about one thing," he said, taking a gulp of the brandy. The liquid burned beautifully going down. "They've got to be stopped. Got to be. If there is an afterlife, those bastards are going to have to answer for a hell of a lot. Their policies are designed to line their pockets and nothing more, and they cost lives. Lives of good, decent people, just trying to make an honest living. People who trusted because, damn it, they *should* be able to trust. Trust that their government would feed them healthy, nourishing food, not poison. Trust that if they volunteered to go off and fight a war for the government, fight and maybe die, they'd be honored if they fell and taken care of if they came home. Trust that their leaders gave a rat's ass about them."

His voice shook, but he didn't care. Both Sarah and Mengsk were watching him, eyes wide, drinks forgotten in their hands.

"You see it too," he said to both of them. "Mengsk—they call you a terrorist. But you're a goddamned hero if you do what you say you're going to do. And history is going to look back at you and us and what we did and, dammit, why we did it, and it ain't going to be us that will be labeled terrorists anymore."

Mengsk extended his hand, and Raynor grasped it. Hard.

## 2504

*I trusted you, you son of a bitch,* Raynor thought. *Trusted Mengsk. Trusted Tychus.*

He glanced down at where his hand held Sarah's, and to his remorse realized he was almost crushing it. At once he loosened his grip. Sarah had trusted too.

Had.

For a long time now, Jim had kept a special bullet with the word *Justice* inscribed on it. He'd have to get another one now. The original had gone through Tychus Findlay's brain. And even as he swallowed hard at the memory, he realized something.

*Tychus—maybe this wasn't really your fault. I know what Mengsk can do to a person. I know how he can get under your skin and in your brain—make you think that you're doing the right thing. Maybe . . . maybe you really thought you were.*

*Like father, like son?* came another thought. *How far can I trust this pretty boy? So far he's been true to his word. So far. But Mengsk was at the beginning too. And so was Tychus. Mengsk took her from me once—and Tychus almost did it a second time. And I can't lose her again. I can't.*

*I won't.*

# CHAPTER EIGHT

"Matthew!"

The voice was purring, warm, and slightly accented, the voice of a sex kitten. The woman it belonged to had spun-candy-pink hair, but the rest of her was far from soft and pliable. One eye was sparkling in mischievous delight through a lock of the outrageously dyed hair, the other was red and glowing and cybernetic, encased by puckered flesh. The rest of her shape, though what was seen was appealing, was covered in protective gear. Mira Han was a curious bundle of contradictions.

"Matthew" smiled wanly at the image on the screen. "Hello again, Mira. Thank you for agreeing to help us."

"I am more than happy to help my dear, sweet husband," she said, her grin widening for a playful moment at Horner's obvious discomfort. Then, more seriously, she added, "For a while, anyway."

Matt frowned. "'A while'?"

"Of course. I cannot endanger my own people for too terribly long, now, can I? You would do the same."

Matt supposed he would. Sighing, he said, "Okay, how long is 'a while' in Mira time?"

"When I say so. I won't fight the Dominion for you, Matthew, so if they come, you and James and your new friend will be on your own. But, then again"—and she shrugged—"I know lots of hidey-holes here, and if I don't want something to be found—it isn't."

Raynor was so lost in his thoughts that it took a faint squeeze from Sarah's hand to draw his attention back to her. He looked at her at once, watching her eyelids fluttering open. "Hey, you," he said.

"Hey, yourself," she murmured, and there was the slightest hint of a smile. "This doctor can't keep his lab steady. Or is that just me?"

"Nah," Jim said. "It's not you, but it ain't the doctor either. We've been under attack, darlin'."

"Who from? Zerg, protoss, Dominion, Bob from down the hall?"

Jim tried and failed not to feel giddy at these admittedly feeble- and forced-sounding attempts at humor. At least there was some of Sarah's personality left. The giddiness abated when he realized that he probably would have to tell her about everything that had happened.

"Dominion," he said. The slight smile on her full mouth faded, and her lips pressed together.

"Arcturus," she said, the word a single sliver of ice.

"Yeah," Jim said. "He don't know when he's beat."

"He's not beat, Jim. He'll never be beat. He'll outlive us all, and have cocktail parties on our graves." She turned her head away and tried to disentangle her hand from his, but he wouldn't let her.

"Whoa, whoa now," he soothed, "you ain't got the whole picture."

"I don't need it."

"I think you do," Jim said. "We just gave old Arcturus a whipping he won't soon forget. He's sitting there on the bridge of his new flagship, licking his wounds and sulking."

"Your ally . . . he's the one who . . ." She lifted her other hand and gestured at her body.

"Yep," Jim said. "Mengsk's boy. Still don't trust him, but so far, he's kept to everything he said. Besides, his own father was trying to kill him. He starts to look okay in my book."

Her brow furrowed as she tried, through the haze of drugs coursing through her system, to comprehend what he had told her.

"Mengsk tried to kill his son?"

"Sure did. Came too close for comfort to killing us all. Valerian lost twenty-five battleships because of his decision to bring you back to me."

She froze and closed her eyes. Jim cursed inwardly. It was clear he had pushed too far.

"He didn't bring me back for you, Jim," Sarah said. Her voice was flat. "He brought me back to use me."

Jim caught movement out of the corner of his eye. The doctor was gesticulating and shaking his head, clearly wanting Jim to steer the conversation elsewhere. Jim frowned and shook his head. He'd never lied to Sarah before, and he wasn't going to start now. He thought about the conversation he'd had with Valerian about this same subject.

*"I want something more,"* Valerian had said. *"To prove that I will be a better emperor, and a better man."*

*"That shouldn't be hard,"* Jim recalled replying.

*"If I reform the worst mass murderer in history, make her human again, teamed with the famous outlaw Jim Raynor—that's all the proof I'll need."*

*"So I'm just a cog in your machine."*

*"If it gets you what you want . . . do you care?"*

*"Guess I don't."*

"You know, I thought that too," Jim said. "And it may still be true. No doubt helping you—and me too—is going to be a feather in Junior's cap. But that don't matter. You're back, Sarah, and he's got the ability to help you. We'll find out—"

"That I'm still a monster?" Sarah tore her hand from Jim's and grasped one of the long, snake-like tendrils that still served as hair. "*This* is human? I escape the certain death that Arcturus planned for me, only to become the queen of the zerg. Infested. Remade, cell by cell. And you've brought me back to hand me over to his *son*? Why didn't you just kill me when you could, Jim? Why didn't you? You promised you would. . . ."

And he had, long ago; he had promised he'd kill her rather than let her continue to rampage unchecked through the galaxy at the head of the Swarm. "Honey, I—"

She threw back her head and screamed. Not a cry of terror or pain but of rage and grief and despair. She arched, trying to pull free of the restraints, trying to launch herself at Jim. He clamped his hands down on her wrists, holding her long enough for the doctor to inject her with something. Three seconds later she went limp, and Jim caught her. Gently, he laid her back down on the bed, only then noticing the tears that had spilled from her now-closed eyes.

"I tried to tell you to stay quiet," muttered Frederick. "You should leave now."

Jim nodded, slowly. He touched Sarah's hand one more time, then rose and headed for the door.

"And you probably shouldn't come back," Frederick said. "I know you care about her, but you seem to be distressing her."

Jim froze, then slowly turned. "I'd like to see you try to keep me out," he said.

"I could make it a medical order," the doctor replied. "The care of my patient is paramount."

Jim took three long-legged strides and closed the distance between them. "You don't know *anything* about Sarah Kerrigan," he said. "I moved heaven and earth to bring her back, and I know that whatever harm my presence does her, it's doing good too. You thought so too."

"I did, until she—"

"It ain't me that's upsetting her," Jim said. "It's what I gotta be telling her about the world she's about to go back into. Your boss was the one who wanted to bring her back in the first place. Well, now she's back, and she's got a single goddamned anchor." He jutted a thumb at his chest. "Me. And I don't intend to abandon her. She's had to deal with betrayal once already. She'll deal with it again over my dead body."

Frederick didn't challenge him as he strode out of sick bay.

"We're going to do what?" Valerian couldn't hide the surprise in his voice.

"Hide in a junkyard," said the viewscreen's image of Matt Horner.

"That's what I thought you said, but then I realized that couldn't possibly be correct."

Matt smiled a little. "You've never actually been to Deadman's Port, have you?"

"Why no," said Valerian. "The part of my education involving traipsing about in an entire city full of murderers, thugs, and thieves appears to be sadly neglected."

"We'll bring you up to speed."

"How delightful."

"Anyway—if you've not physically been there, you don't

know what I mean when I say 'junkyard.' There are entire cities built on the junkyards of this planet. That's essentially what Deadman's Port *is*. Trust me . . . you could hide the whole Dominion fleet there if you had someone agreeing to look the other way. Two battlecruisers aren't going to be a problem."

Jim walked out from the *Hyperion*'s hangar bay into the gray, eye-stinging haze that was the "weather" in Deadman's Port. Blinking, he looked around and thought about his visit here, so many years ago, with Tychus Findlay. The place itself hadn't changed much—it was still an enormous trash heap that managed to be a city. Homes were made inside the wreckage of old ships; streets, if such they could be named, were merely pathways through the piles of debris. But people lived and died here, maybe even loved and dreamed.

Jim and Tychus had been on the run then from an assassin, forced to seek refuge and help from one Scutter O'Banon. O'Banon, who had run the planet at the time, had been bad news, even in the opinion of Raynor, who was an outlaw himself. Jim had thought then that Deadman's Rock, as the planet was known, was the single ugliest place he had ever seen, and O'Banon the ugliest soul he had had the misfortune to encounter.

O'Banon had indeed given them shelter and jobs. Jim tried not to think about walking through the "streets" of the city with Tychus, and the bigger man approvingly exclaiming, *"Can't swing a cat without hitting a whore."* He had thought he had known what world-weary was, had thought things were as bad as they could get.

He hadn't even scratched the surface.

*I miss you, Tychus. Not the betrayer you became . . . but the man you used to be. Dammit . . . I miss my friend.*

But Tychus was gone. So was O'Banon, who had been re-

placed by someone named Ethan Stewart, who was himself replaced by someone else whom Raynor didn't know. Presumably, whoever the new boss of this forsaken place was, Mira was
in good with him, or else she wouldn't have been able to offer
sanctuary. Raynor hoped that whoever it was, he had good security. The bosses of Deadman's Port didn't seem to be very
long-lived, and the last thing Jim needed was a transitional
power struggle when he was asking a favor.

"I . . . think I understand what Mr. Horner was trying to say
about this place," said Valerian as he emerged from the
*Bucephalus*, his voice dripping with distaste.

"Yep," Jim said, still looking, still remembering. A whiff of a
cigar from somewhere floated to him, and for a brief, wonderful
moment, he thought if he turned around fast enough, he would
see Tychus.

*Not in this life.* Jim turned to regard Horner and Valerian and
shook his head. The Heir Apparent to the Dominion had removed his bright military coat, but even in rolled-up shirtsleeves
and trousers, he screamed "mark" to anyone who caught a
glimpse of him. "We gotta do something about you, Valerian,"
he said, welcoming the distraction from too many old memories. "You stick out like a sore thumb."

Valerian glanced down at his crisply pressed shirt, knife-
edged trousers, and gleaming black boots.

"Well, well, here you all are, three cute boys for Mira," came
a voice behind them. They turned to see a tall, muscular woman
standing in front of them, hands on her hips and grinning.
"Well," she amended thoughtfully, eyes—both mechanical and
human—darting from one to the other, "two cute boys and one
scruffy one. James," she sighed, "do you never avail yourself of
the sonic showers on your lovely ship?"

The "lovely ship" she referred to, along with the *Bucephalus*,
was camouflaged so well that its own designer wouldn't have
recognized it. The crew Mira had sent ahead had done a spec-

tacular job of removing (carefully, under Swann's supervision) unnecessary pieces of the exterior, temporarily welding on other pieces, and painting it masterfully so that it looked like a burned-out hulk. To heighten the illusion, actual debris had been piled atop the *Hyperion*. The *Bucephalus* had received the same treatment. Jim could have sworn Swann teared up at least once.

"Yes, I do, and I enjoy it," Jim said. "But I guess I just keep attracting dirt."

Mira made a little moue of disappointment and pushed his broad chest playfully. "Some might think that was an insult," she said. "Good thing I know better."

She then turned her unsettling gaze on Valerian. "I've been told to call you Mr. V," she said, "and I will do so. You look taller than UNN portrays you."

"I hear that a lot," said Valerian. "Thank you for agreeing to shelter us. I won't forget your kindness."

"Let us hope your dear papa doesn't find out about it and also decide to not forget," Mira said. Jim knew Mira well enough to recognize a warning when he heard it. Coquettish she might be when she chose, but dangerous she was at all times. He knew better than to underestimate her. She smiled, softening the subtle threat. "And I am grateful to you as well—for giving me the opportunity to spend some time with my dear Matthew."

Now, at last, she strode over to Horner and slipped into his arms, planting a kiss on his cheek as she handed him a folded piece of paper. Matt stayed completely immobile, looking like a prisoner about to face execution—resigned, but clearly wishing the situation were otherwise.

Valerian was smiling a little. "So how did the two of you meet?"

"Oh, let's not get into all that," Matt said quickly.

Mira's grin widened. "He likes to tease me," she said, but it was obvious to anyone that it was Mira doing the teasing. "He doesn't write, he doesn't call . . . but we are here now, and we shall make up for lost time, yes?"

Matt nodded without enthusiasm. *This never gets old,* Jim thought. Mira was as far from a heartbroken maiden as you could get, and the two were most definitely "husband and wife" in name only. Even so, the affection she had for Matt was obviously real, if nothing more than playful.

"I hate to interrupt," Jim said, "but I believe Matt—er, Matthew told you that we have a very ill woman who needs medical attention and a quiet place to rest up and heal."

Mira turned to him, still leaning against Matt but all business now. "He did. He was also very cryptic about the nature of the illness and the identity of this . . . woman."

In the end, Mira Han was a mercenary. She was taking a terrible risk in hiding them at all. Matt, Raynor, and Valerian had all decided that she needed to know some things but not others. Valerian had agreed to reveal his own identity, in light of the fact that she should know at least one main reason the Dominion might choose to seek them out. But all of them felt that naming Sarah Kerrigan would be to seal her death warrant—if not from Mira herself, then from others who felt they had a score to settle. Marines, with their biologically wired loyalty, were one thing. The Raiders, with their devotion to Jim and his choices, were also completely trustworthy. But Jim wasn't about to trust Mira's people that far. As Queen of Blades, Kerrigan had been nigh unstoppable. Even as Sarah Kerrigan, ghost, she could have defended herself just fine, thank you very much. But the woman in sick bay was weak and vulnerable. Pinching an IV tube closed could kill her. It was difficult, almost impossible, to think of her this way, but Jim knew that for the first time, she was utterly dependent on him. And he would not let her down.

"We all got our secrets," Jim said.

"Ma'am," said Valerian, smiling charmingly, "we've dealt

with you in good faith. I've revealed my identity, and surely you know that places me utterly in your hands. You could easily send a message to the Dominion and tell my father that you have us. But Matthew assures us that we can trust you. Please— grant us the same courtesy."

She remained unmoved, gazing at Jim and Valerian with her unnerving cybernetic eye. Horner said, "Mira—we can't talk about her right now. Just trust me, okay?"

The hard face softened. "Matthew, you are a good man, and I see good men oh so very rarely. All right. For you, not only do I hide, I don't ask questions."

Relief washed over Jim. "Thank you, Mira."

"Mmmmm," she said noncommittally. "I can offer you a safe house where this . . . woman . . . can be tended to. I have contacted some doctors, but I cannot imagine they would be superior to those aboard your ship, Mr. V. Still, they are at your disposal. The place is isolated, quiet, and very safe."

"Sounds just about perfect."

"Good. I will send someone round for you in about an hour or so. In the meantime, Matthew and I have some catching up to do," said Mira, slipping a possessive arm through Matt's. Matt cast a longing look at Jim, who merely shrugged and mouthed, "You're on your own."

# CHAPTER NINE

An hour later, as Mira had promised, a small system runner appeared for Jim and Sarah. Jim was clad in grungy, nondescript clothing—which was to say, dressed as usual—and carried a blanket-swaddled Sarah. He took care that the blanket covered her strange-looking "hair." The exterior of the system runner looked like it had seen better days, but on the inside it looked fairly new, if a trifle ill-used. Jim gently eased Kerrigan inside, tucking the blanket around her and making sure it didn't slip off her head. She was awake but still groggy with drugs.

"Where exactly are we going?" he asked the pilot.

"Outside the city," he said. "The safe house is well protected. You and your lady friend shouldn't be disturbed."

Jim frowned. An idea fluttered into his mind, but he instantly dismissed it. It couldn't possibly be that place.

They lifted off and left the junkyard that was a city behind. Jim again marveled, as he had the last time he was here, that it only seemed as though the entire planet was a trash pit. Metallic hues gave way to green grass and brown earth and even the open stretch of blue that indicated a lake.

And then he saw it. His eyes widened. It was more rundown than it had been, but it was unmistakably—

"That's Scutter O'Banon's complex, ain't it?" he asked.

The pilot laughed. "Sure is. How'd you know?"

"We—I . . . was here before. A long time ago." They had been in trouble, of course—when were they not?—but somehow Jim knew the man he had been back then hadn't appreciated how he had been free of cares.

Including bearing the burden of murdering his best friend.

He was beginning to wish he hadn't come. There was only one ghost for him in Deadman's Rock, but it was one too many.

"Don't look so different from up here, but once you get down, you'll see that a lot's changed," the pilot said, adding, "Mira ain't O'Banon."

"And thank God for that," Jim said. He chuckled and shook his head ruefully. So—pink-haired Mira Han was the one who had taken over after Ethan Stewart—O'Banon's successor—had been turned into a zerg. Raynor had had no idea that her power base was so strong, and judging by what the pilot said, she liked it that way. He felt suddenly much better about their safety and the quality of care that would be provided to Sarah.

The security was still in place, but the swimming pools had been filled in, and the gardens and orchards had been permitted to go to seed. The mansion, for such it had to be called, looked the same from the air, although the beautifully manicured lawn was a thing of the past.

The landing field had been kept up, and Jim was surprised to see the same old-fashioned groundcar awaiting them. He was even more surprised that the driver had shocking pink hair.

As Jim helped Sarah in and then took a seat himself, Mira

turned and grinned at him. "You did not expect me!" she crowed.

"No, I sure didn't," Jim said. He checked on Sarah, pulling the blanket around her again. She was still compliant, but the sedative would be wearing off soon. "Not in any of this. You fooled us right good, Mira—or should I be calling you Boss Lady Ma'am?"

"Not if you value those rough good looks of yours, James," she said. Sitting beside her was Matt, who actually looked as if he might be having something resembling a good time. "Have you ever been in a groundcar, James?"

"Yep," he said. "Here, as a matter of fact."

"Oho! So you knew either the late Scutter or the late Ethan," she said. She drove the antiquated vehicle expertly, which surprised Jim, taking them on a smooth drive down a long, well-paved road. The trees Jim remembered looked about the same; a few years would not do much to change them.

"I did know O'Banon, though it was not a happy acquaintance," said Jim. "I am delighted you have stepped into his shoes."

"Because I am on your side?"

"That," Jim admitted, "and frankly, because you're a hell of a better person than he could ever be."

She met his eyes in the rearview mirror, and they were somber. "Thank you, James," she said quietly.

Attempting to lighten the mood, Jim asked, "Hey, did you keep Randall on?" Phillip Randall had been O'Banon's butler—elegant, poised, graying hair, sharp blue eyes. Nothing ever seemed to bother him, not Jim's and Tychus's scruffy appearances, nor Tychus's request for girls. Tychus, for once, had been joking . . . Randall took it quite seriously.

"I have heard stories about Phillip Randall," said Mira, "but he is also dead. Did you know he was an assassin?"

Jim and Matt exchanged glances. Suddenly the precision

with which Randall moved and the sharpness of those eyes took on an entirely different cast in Jim's mind. A phrase Scutter O'Banon had uttered when angry with them came back to him: *"Hell, boys, you're lucky it's Randall's day off, or you'd be bleeding on the floor right now."* Jim's eyes widened. He'd taken it as a joke. . . .

"Uh, no, I was not informed of that. I just thought he was a damned good butler."

"He was that too. You will find doctors here to help your . . . woman . . . but I am afraid you must cook and clean for yourselves."

She pulled the groundcar up in front of the mansion. Jim was surprised at how clearly he remembered the place. He carried Kerrigan, still drowsy, in his arms as they walked up to the huge entry door. Mira tapped in a code, and the massive old door swung open.

Here, at least, Jim's memory differed from the present reality. In Scutter's day, the old wood floors and beams had gleamed with careful, regular polishing, and the walls had been adorned with big-game trophies. Now, the room had fallen, if not into disrepair, at least into neglect. Dust lay thick on the heavy furniture. Most of the knickknacks that had cluttered the room—priceless antiques, but for Jim's taste too many and too garish—were gone. So were the animal heads, which was a significant improvement.

"I don't live here," Mira said. "This is just a place for people to come if they need to."

Jim shook his head at the thought of Scutter O'Banon's cherished estate becoming a safe house. It was wonderful.

The old wood creaked as they walked the uncarpeted floor to the curving staircase and ascended. Jim felt a jolt—the room in which he and Sarah would be staying had been the room assigned to Tychus.

He really did wish he hadn't come.

Mira fished in one of the pockets of her vest and came out with an old skeleton key. The room was as large as he remembered, but as with the entrance hall, most of the décor had long since been sold. The light slanting in from the window was as pleasing as ever, and the bed was the same—large and canopied and, Jim assumed, comfortable.

And just like that, it didn't matter at all to Jim that this room had belonged to Findlay. It was a safe haven for the woman he loved, where she could rest and, hopefully, recover. Jim noticed that the side tables beside the bed he remembered had been removed and replaced by portable medical tables.

Two men clad in white emerged from the sitting room, with the unmistakable superior expressions that some members of the medical profession often wore on their features. Jim adjusted Sarah in his arms and said, "I'm assuming I may rely on your doctor-patient confidentiality?"

They exchanged glances. "We work for Mira Han," one of them said. "But our first duty is to our patient."

"Is that a yes?" Jim pressed. He wanted to hear the words spoken. Sarah was too important.

"Yes," said the other. "Would you like it in writing?" he added sarcastically.

"Yeah, actually, that'd be great," said Jim, striding over and laying Sarah down gently on the bed.

Matt looked a little worried, as if Jim's brusqueness might offend Mira. Instead, she chortled. "Oh, James, you are so endearingly blunt. That is one reason I am so fond of you. I always know exactly where I stand with you."

"That's how I aim to keep it," Jim said, giving her a genuine smile. "I do appreciate what you're doing for us."

"I know," she said. "And I hope that Matthew and the charming Mr. V also appreciate it. And now, I will leave you and your little friend alone with the doctors. I hope they can help her. You can reach me through Matthew if you need anything." She turned to Matt. "Would you like to come on a long, *long* drive with me? There are some pretty and private places still left here, you know."

"Don't we have to get back to Mr. V?" Matt said, a little too quickly. "You promised to set him up with a secure channel."

"Oh, yes, so I did," Mira said. "Hm. I imagine he is chafing a bit, is he not? Yes, let's go and get him taken care of. *Then* we can have a nice drive."

She linked her arm with his and walked him out of the room. The doctors turned their attention to Sarah. One of them bent to pull back the blanket. Jim's hand shot out to grab the man's wrist.

"Your promise," he said. "Confidentiality."

"Of course," the doctor replied, rather testily. Jim released him, sat back, and watched the man's shock as he saw Sarah's snake-like "locks" fall free. The two doctors stared at him.

"Yeah, it's her," Jim said.

"You brought us the Queen of Blades?" one of them said, looking at Jim in shock.

"No. I brought you Sarah Kerrigan. And you're going to give her the best damn medical care you've ever given anyone in your life."

Not for the first time, Jim felt a terrible pang at seeing Sarah so weak. All his memories of her had been of a strong and powerful woman, whether she went by the name Sarah Kerrigan or the title Queen of Blades. To see her fight was to witness a ballet of weaponry and mind and muscle, a poem to the beauty of controlled, directed violence. She was trained to kill, but he knew what it took out of her to do so. If she could accomplish her goals without becoming an angel of death, she would do so. Jim understood. It was his choice as well. Something Mengsk could never quite understand.

And maybe that was why they had worked so well together—two superior killers who didn't like to kill.

## 2500

"Boy, there ain't nothing here to indicate anyone's home, is there?" Jim asked as they approached the single moon of the gas giant known only as G-2275.

Sarah threw him an amused glance. "That was the point of my briefing, Jim."

"Well, yeah, I know that, but it's kinda different when you see it for yourself."

She quirked a red brow, then looked at the viewscreen. It was a completely unremarkable moon, surrounding a completely unremarkable planet. There was no indication at all that beneath the surface was one of the great technological hubs of the Confederacy.

Sarah had briefed him, Mengsk, and Mike Liberty on the place earlier. After the victory on Antiga Prime, Mengsk was elated with his new toy, the psi emitter, that had enabled the rebels and much of the civilian population to escape with the Sons of Korhal, while the Confederacy's presence on the planet fell to first zerg and then the ruthless purge enacted by the protoss. But reports had started coming in that the goliaths, the twelve-foot-tall walkers that turned a man into a giant, had been adapted and improved.

Kerrigan freely admitted she was none too eager to repeat her psi-emitter performance, outrageously successful though it had been. She had convinced Mengsk that obtaining the plans of the upgraded goliaths would be more cost-effective, wide-reaching, and in the long run just as effective, and he had agreed. The tactical advantage the Confederacy had with the superior goliaths could prove to be a slow-growing but deadly one.

She even knew the likeliest place where such plans were being developed. "I've been there before, about a year ago," she said.

"Doing what?" Jim had asked before he could think, and winced inwardly at the sharp look she shot him that said, *What do you think?* "Oh."

She didn't elaborate on who or why, but simply continued. "They change the security codes religiously, of course. But there's a particular mathematical algorithm they use. It's complicated, but I know it. We can easily extrapolate it up to the hour."

"That seems foolish," said Mike, scratching his chin thoughtfully. "You learn the formula, you can walk through the door any time."

"Do not underestimate the arrogance of those who think they have a foolproof system, Mike," said Mengsk. "They are probably too busy patting themselves on the back for their cleverness to think about any danger."

"And don't underestimate the ingenuity of fools," quipped Jim. Sarah gave him a smirk, which he had hoped she would do.

"So, Sarah . . . you carried out a, uh, mission there once before. Think they'll have beefed up their security?"

"Doubtless," Kerrigan said. "But from the psychological profiles I've studied, they still won't have changed the algorithm. They will, however, probably have requested more than the dozen marines I had to contend with last time."

She'd been right, as she always was, on all counts. The smug bastards hadn't bothered to change the algorithm. It was child's play to obtain permission to dock, and once there, for an outlaw and a ghost to easily overpower the crew stationed in the docking bay and the two marines who had looked extremely bored before they had become extremely dead.

And after that, the true dance began.

The marines needed to be neutralized. If they were resocs, and they probably were, they would not stop fighting if left alive. Both Sarah and Jim realized that, and without a word to each other, went for the kill. This part of the dance was grim and joyless, but no less beautiful.

Their arrival had been approved, so no alarms were blaring. Sarah had memorized the layout of the station, and she went first, a beautiful red-haired woman shimmering into seeming nothingness, transforming into an unseen and unheard weapon. He watched her vanish, counted to five, then fired at the first marine stationed ahead. She went down, but her two companions started firing. One of them lifted a hand and opened his mouth to speak.

He died before he could utter a syllable, a single hole appearing in the chest of his combat armor as Sarah attacked from behind. Before the one remaining could even start to turn, he went flying across the corridor to slam into the bulkhead. He lay like a turtle on his back struggling to rise. Sarah materialized an instant later, ending the marine's struggle, her blue-and-white form taut and tense, a lock of hair hanging over her eyes. She was indeed a deadly weapon, capable of handling multiple foes at a time, silencing them all with acts of murder and grace.

Their eyes met. Something electric passed between them—a recognition, an acknowledgment of honed skills and strong nerves and a pool of deep regret that all of this, any of this, was necessary.

They'd found someone who knew where the plans were. Sarah had read his thoughts easily, and they'd left him and a team of fourteen bloody, unconscious, and alive. Mengsk had been pleased as punch, of course, and the rebellion's own goliaths had been upgraded. Once again, the odds had been changed.

Changed by Sarah Kerrigan, the ghost, the weapon who grieved.

★   ★   ★

## 2504

It was, Valerian mused as he leaned against the bar in the *Hyperion*'s cantina, a truly interesting path that had led him here. His father would not recognize the place—and that made him smile a little into his mai tai. The air was thick with smoke, and tinny music blasted from something he recalled was known as a "jukebox" suspended from the ceiling. It looked like it had been damaged and patched up, and his smile turned ironic as he listened to the singer caution about "suspicious minds."

"It had about twice as many songs before Tychus Findlay broke it," said Cooper, the bartender.

Valerian frowned slightly. Findlay. Valerian agreed with Jim's choice, but he knew it had been a difficult one for Raynor.

"Mai tai not to your liking?" Cooper asked, clearly worried at Valerian's expression.

"Oh, it's excellent," said Valerian, and meant it. "If the rest of your drinks are as delicious, then I must say your talents are squandered here."

Cooper, an amiable-looking fellow with dark hair and blue eyes, chuckled a little as he shook up yet another concoction for a customer. "Nah," he said. "I like it fine here. Been with the Raiders for a while. They fight hard and they risk everything. Least they deserve is a good drink at the end of the day."

"Or the start of one," said Valerian.

"You might not believe it, but we don't have a lot of drunks here," said Cooper, pouring the drink and handing it to a young woman. Valerian recognized her at once—and the gentleman who was keeping her company.

"Miss Annabelle," he said, and to the young man standing next to her, "Lieutenant Rawlins. Aren't you still on duty?"

"Sir, I'm a navigator, and right now, we're planet-bound," said Rawlins. "Captain Vaughn said I could buy this lady a drink. It's the least we could do to apologize for the trick we played on her."

Valerian smiled at the young woman. "I agree," he said. "And thank you. Your team did fine work under extreme pressure. I don't think the *Bucephalus* would be here if not for you."

Annabelle colored slightly. "Thanks," she said. "Just doing my job."

"I'm beginning to understand why Raynor's Raiders have given my father such difficulty," he said.

"We do our best to be thorns in the side," Annabelle replied. She turned back to her companion. "Thanks for the drink, Travis," she said. "Come with me. I know where the best table is."

"So tell me more about your idea for the dropships," said Travis. Although Valerian was aware that his navigator knew next to nothing about engineering, Travis sounded genuinely interested. Valerian smiled a little.

"And that," said Cooper, also watching the pair stroll off together, "is why I do what I do. Now a question for you, sir— why are you here and not on your ship?"

"I'm . . . not quite sure myself," Valerian said. "I imagine that since we have perforce joined together to stand against my father, I wanted to get to know more of the people I am working with."

"Sounds reasonable. Also, perhaps, to get some information?"

Valerian gave him a quick, sharp look, but Cooper merely smiled and began to rinse some glasses. "Come on; *everyone* talks to the bartender. You got questions, I got answers. But I got some questions of my own. Care to trade?"

"Sounds fair," said Valerian. "Although you must know there are some things I am not at liberty to share."

"Sure," said Cooper. "Matt and Jim are the same way. You go first."

"All right. What's your opinion of Mr. Raynor?"

"Wouldn't be here if I didn't respect him," said Cooper. "Lot of money to be had for someone who turns him in."

"So you never say a bad word against him?"

"I didn't say that," said Cooper. He began to dry the glasses. "There were moments I had my doubts. Like when he was so thick with that protoss Zeratul. And for a while there, I was worried that the liquor was getting the upper hand."

"What changed your mind?"

"Well, nothing's changed my mind about the protoss. You ever met them?"

"I have."

"Creepy, aren't they?" Cooper made a face. "No mouths, the way they move, and that whole reading-your-minds thing they do—no, sir, my apologies if you like them like Jim does, but I'd just as soon never have to look at one again. As for the drinking—well, Jim proved soon enough he's got the right stuff. He comes in now and then, and he drinks, and he has a good time, but I've stopped worrying about him. He's got his priorities straight."

"And those are?"

Cooper shot him a grin. "Ah-ah," he said, "that's more than one question I've answered. My turn."

Valerian toasted him with the half-full drink. "Fire away."

"Everyone knows that you've broken with your father over the whole Sarah Kerrigan business. But what now? We're not going to hide here forever."

Valerian eyed Cooper. "You don't beat around the bush," he said.

"No, I don't. I figure I listen to enough of that. I will level with you: the commander's decision to go to Char didn't sit well with the crew at first. Findlay tried to get people to not trust him."

"Hence the jukebox throwing."

"Indeed. And yet in the end, Tychus was on the floor and couldn't get up. And the commander told us, it was our choice to follow him or leave . . . just like it had always been. There wasn't a single Raider who left. But we want to know what it was all for, 'cause it sure didn't end with Kerrigan becoming human. If she even is. There's a lot of rumors running around."

Valerian was certain there were. He wondered what the safest course of action was, and decided that with this group, it was simply leveling. "She's obviously not completely well, or you would have seen her walking around."

Cooper's blue eyes held a trace of apprehension. "But . . . she's okay, mostly? She's not some . . . half-zerg thing being kept hidden from us?"

Valerian smiled. "Most certainly not." It was the truth. Kerrigan was okay. Mostly. "But the shock has been hard on her. She needs help, more help than I can give her on my ship. That's why we're here, by the good graces of one Mira Han, so that I can get her into the hands of people who can bring her the rest of the way back to herself."

"That Moebius Foundation, right?"

Valerian nodded his golden head. "Right. Any minute now—I hope—I'll be hearing from Mira that she's obtained a safe way for me to send a transmission. One can't be too careful."

Cooper grimaced. "I know. After Findlay—well, it wouldn't surprise me if your father had some spies on this planet too. You be careful when you go send that message." He gave Valerian a smile as he finished the glasses. "I hate to lose customers."

"You've lost too many," said Valerian. He put down a generous handful of credits. "You're going to be seeing a lot of my people here on the *Hyperion*. We had to divide the crew of the *Herakles* between the *Bucephalus* and your vessel. Treat them as well as you treat me."

Cooper gathered up the credits appreciatively. "You got it, Mr. V," he said, and glanced up at the entrance. "Well, look who's here," he said. "I'm surprised she let him out of her clutches—I mean, her arms."

The comment was a good-natured one, and Valerian turned

to see Matt Horner striding into the cantina. He went up to
Valerian and said, "We have a problem."

"I'll mix you another drink," said Cooper, turning to suit
action to word.

Valerian snapped to attention. "What's wrong? Was Mira
unable to get me a secure connection?"

"Oh, yes, that's been taken care of. The problem is, you need
to get to it."

The Heir Apparent frowned. "I don't understand."

"Let me put it to you this way," said Matt. He bent over, and
smeared his hand on the floor. It came up greasy with dripped
oil, smudged with dirt, and dotted with a few other things that
Valerian didn't want to think about. "See this?" asked Matt,
indicating his grimy hand.

Valerian made a face. "I do, though I wish I didn't."

Without warning, Matt reached over and smeared the filth
on Valerian's cheek. "That's a start," he said.

# CHAPTER
# TEN

Before Matt could observe it, let alone react, Valerian's hand had shot up, seized the captain's wrist, and twisted painfully. Matt's knees buckled, and Valerian heard the sounds of chairs being shoved back as the bar patrons prepared to come to their captain's defense. He let go at once but kept his gaze locked with Horner's.

"If you have a problem with me, say so," he snapped, his voice deepening with anger.

"I don't," said Matt, looking at him with a slightly stunned expression and rubbing his wrist. "You've got the problem. You look like . . . well . . . *you*. And if we're going to be taking a stroll through Deadman's Port, the less like *you* you look, the better."

Valerian had long ago learned to master his anger. Now and then it rose to the surface, as it had just done, to strike swiftly and surely like a venomous snake, but it always subsided quickly.

"I understand. You might simply have said so." He gestured to Matt's wrist. "Saved yourself a bit of pain."

"Don't worry about it," grunted Matt. "Gotta say I'm surprised you could even do that."

"Oh, you'll find I'm full of surprises," Valerian replied, taking a sip from the second mai tai Cooper had prepared for him. "But as to business. Why do we need to walk?"

"Mira says that even though the place is a total junkyard, most people walk if they need to get somewhere. The populace has swollen because of the recent zerg attacks. It used to be that mercs and criminals made up most of the population, but now it's composed mainly of refugees. Nobody's got money. Any kind of a vehicle or ship is going to attract attention."

While they spoke, Cooper had been wordlessly working on preparing another drink, and now gently pushed it toward Horner, who accepted it with a nod and a couple of credits.

"Very well," Valerian replied. He indicated the beverage. "I see you're a gin and tonic man."

"Tonic and synthlime, yes," said Matt. "I generally don't drink on duty. So we've got to get you looking as miserable, wretched, and impoverished as the rest of the population. And begging your pardon," he said as he took a sip, "that is going to be one hell of a challenge."

Valerian gave him a faint smile. "Perhaps less than you think," he said.

After about a half hour of asking around, Matt rounded up some clothing that was suitably worn. It came from one of Swann's people, who was, according to Matt, "someone who likes to get his hands dirty when he works."

Valerian eyed the clothing, trying not to look too offended by the, uh, fragrance wafting up from the oil-stained and patched trousers, shirt, jacket, and boots. "This should do nicely," he drawled.

"Too bad we can't wait a day or two for some stubble to grow out," Matt said, "but you'll have to do. A bit of dirt on your face and in your hair and you should look the part at least." Matt was trying to look all business, but it was obvious to Valerian that Horner was enjoying the thought of the Heir Apparent slouching through streets smelling like a refugee. The thought was equal parts amusing and annoying.

"'Look the part at least'?" he repeated. "Sounds like you don't think I can pull this off, Captain Horner."

"I admit, I'm worried. One wrong move and we're dead men. And the bunker is about five kilometers from here."

"You don't look terribly disreputable yourself," Valerian said. "Perhaps I should be worried about you. I take it the marines are to be left aboard the *Bucephalus*."

"Indeed, sir. The resocialized ones will be unable to deny their programming, and that makes them unsuitable for undercover work. And even your marines won't be able to shed their military bearing."

"Quite so."

"We could bring a couple of the less well-known Raiders to defend you. That is," added Matt, "assuming that you trust us."

The annoyance was starting to overwhelm the amusement. Valerian turned to Horner. "You don't like me," he said, "and you don't trust me. Yet here I am, putting myself in your hands. If we're going to work together, Captain Horner, then for pity's sake, let's work *together*, shall we? This posturing grows tiresome."

A faint flush of color rose in Matt's cheeks. Obviously Valerian's comment had hit home. "Of course."

"Besides," Valerian said, turning to regard the sour-smelling clothes once more, "this little task gets you away from Mira Han. I would think you'd be a bit more grateful."

The ice didn't break completely, but Matt struggled not to smile.

They stepped outside the makeshift shelter of the junk heap that was actually one of the most notorious battlecruisers in the galaxy, and again Valerian struggled not to cough at the thick miasma. Horner eyed him speculatively. He himself tended to err more on the "clean-cut" side of things than most of the Raiders, but Valerian had been a challenge. Other than the initial surprisingly fast—and painful—reaction, the prince had resigned himself to the charade. Looking at him now, Matt had to wonder if he might even get past his own father.

There was nothing they could do with the resources they had on hand about his patrician features, other than smear stuff on them. Which they had done. Valerian was chewing—something he had gotten from . . . someone—and bent over to spit out a quick stream of vile-colored liquid.

"I hope this comes off one's teeth," he muttered.

"I think it does, unless you chew regularly," Matt said.

The golden hair had come undone and Valerian had run fingers greasy with oil through it. They each sported pistols. The one Valerian had wanted to bring had been as spit-and-polish as the man himself. Horner had nixed it and substituted a more beat-up one from the *Hyperion*'s weapons locker. For a moment as he stood getting accustomed to what passed for air, Valerian was still ramrod straight, but even as Matt opened his mouth to comment on it, the prince shifted his weight to one hip, affecting a slouch.

"Good," Matt said.

Valerian's lips twitched, and he lifted a finger dangerously close to his nostril.

"Okay, you don't need to go that far," Matt grumbled, fighting back a laugh. "Let's go. We need to be careful. Even dressed like this, we still look better off than half the people who live here. Come on."

They clambered down from the "junk pile" and jumped the last meter down into the trough that served as a corridor. Matt observed that the layers of rubbish were almost like layers of sediment. Debris from newer ships was simply piled atop older heaps. He wondered what era his feet were treading on and what had happened to the men and women who had flown in what once had been part of a spacefaring vessel.

They headed north as best they could, following the directions that Mira had given Matt, breathily whispered into his ear and followed by a light kiss. He winced slightly at the memory and focused on the task at hand.

Valerian kept pace with him, putting a little swagger into his movements. The narrow corridor opened out onto a flatter area, and Matt shook his head. "This place is almost overrun," he said.

Valerian didn't answer. His sharp gray eyes were taking it in. There were dozens of people in this small area. Children, some of them barely clothed, were running about unsupervised, crawling into spaces and jumping about recklessly on the broken and twisted pieces of metal that had once been ships. There was color everywhere, from the pieces of clothing to the pieces of debris. Valerian's gaze seemed to be following one little boy who was intently scraping something off a large blue hunk of metal. "What's he doing?" Valerian asked quietly.

"Getting lunch," Matt replied. Even as he spoke, the boy lifted his filthy hands to his mouth and shoved something in it. Valerian looked away quickly. "Don't," Matt hissed. "You can't show any weakness. And don't get taken in by the kids either. Yeah, the poverty's real, but so are the child gangs that will lure you away so the bigger kids can take you for all you've got. Jim got suckered into that trap the first time he came here."

"I understand," said Valerian. His voice was resolute, but there was sorrow in it.

They shoved their way past the throngs of children who, once they saw the pair, immediately latched onto their legs and held out dirty, sticky, imploring hands, begging, "Please, mister, please, mister?"

"Get off," snarled Matt, with an anger and disgust he didn't feel, and pushed at them vigorously. He was firm, but not cruel. One of the children stumbled and fell. He didn't land hard, but one would never know it by how he filled his little lungs with air and let loose with a wail of pain. The boy was good, even came up with a few tears.

"What are you doing to by kid?" came an angry, deep voice. The words were slightly slurred, but no less ominous for that. Matt winced inwardly. Here it came. The man was taller than either he or Valerian, and if not quite as well built as Tychus Findlay, was still an imposing specimen. Another reminder of Findlay was the scar that ran down the side of his face, though part of this man's lip had been severed. He wasn't alone. Two friends, almost as nasty-looking as he, fell into place and advanced on Matt and Valerian.

"Teaching him manners," said Valerian before Matt could attempt to defuse the situation.

"You saying by boy ain't got banners?" The slurring was anything but comical, coming from that misshapen mouth.

"That's exactly what I'm saying. Keep him off us, and we'll be on our way."

Scarlip sneered, which presented a truly disturbing image. "I don't sink you're going anywhere." One dinner-plate-sized fist reached out, grabbed Valerian by his shirt, and lifted him up. Matt caught the glitter of knives out of the corner of his eye. He had just lifted his gun when . . . *everything* happened.

Valerian moved so fast he was quite literally a blur to Matt's eyes. Valerian's hands went instantly to the big one grasping his shirt, and a fraction of a second later Scarlip was on his knees shrieking. The big man's two pals both rushed Valerian, but suddenly the Heir Apparent simply was not there, but behind both of them instead. He leaped upward and kicked out, each booted foot landing on a broad back, and then—there was no other word for it—Valerian ran up the two men, pausing only long enough to knock their heads together before jumping off to land in a crouch, a knife that Matt had not known he possessed clutched in his hand.

The two men crumpled, not out cold, but definitely out of the fight. Scarlip bellowed and charged for him. Valerian waited, balancing on the balls of his feet, until the last possible second before darting out of the way. Scarlip's momentum propelled him forward, and he slammed with all the speed of his charge into a wall of debris. There was a solid thump as he struck, then a singing, stinging noise.

Valerian's knife pinned the other man's tattered shirtsleeve to what might or might not have been an old mattress.

Scarlip stared for a moment, then laughed. He tugged the knife free and turned, clutching it in his huge hand.

"You bissed," he snarled.

Valerian smiled beatifically. "No," he said gently, "I didn't. I have no desire to deprive a child of a parent—even of your sort." Both Scarlip and Matt noticed at the same moment that a second knife was in Valerian's hand. "Now," the prince continued, "do you want to let us pass, or must we follow this fight to its logical conclusion?"

The man's piggy eyes went from Valerian's calm face— damn, thought Matt, Valerian wasn't even *breathing* hard—to the knife, back to the face. He muttered something, tossed the knife down, and strode over to his son.

Valerian nodded, picked up the knife, and turned to Matt. Matt stared at him wordlessly for a second, then they continued on. They were not followed.

"I . . . had no idea you could do that," said Matt.

"Which part?"

"All of it. *Any* of it."

Valerian offered a small, tight smile. "You thought I was a bookish, effeminate weakling, didn't you?"

"I—" Matt didn't want to confirm it, but he didn't want to lie either. So he struggled to find a middle path. "Let's just say I certainly didn't expect you to handle yourself so well three to one."

"Three to two," said Valerian. "I saw that gun come out."

"You were moving too fast for me to get a clean shot."

". . . Sorry?"

Matt had to laugh. "Guess I owe you an apology."

"Not really. You know very little about me, Mr. Horner," Valerian continued as they trudged forward. "You've seen me cutting ribbons on UNN and heard me wax enthusiastic about ancient artifacts in person. You know I appreciate luxury and the arts, and I bear no obvious battle scars. What you don't know is that for most of my life, I was a secret. I've probably spent more hours in the company of military men than you have. Perhaps even than Mr. Raynor. I trained long and hard, with ancient weapons such as swords—"

"And knives."

"—and knives," Valerian agreed. "I know three different types of martial arts."

"Can you kill me with a spoon?"

"Only amateurs need spoons," said Valerian, so deadpan that for a second Matt wondered if he was serious. Their eyes met, and Matt saw mirth in the gray depths for a moment before Valerian looked away. "I never felt safe for a moment during my childhood. I've learned to be on my guard at all times, even when it's unnecessary. I picked the fight rather than backing down because word gets around in places like this. I don't expect we'll be troubled any further."

"You attracted attention," Matt said.

"I would rather be alive and have attracted attention, than dead and disregarded. As, I imagine, are most of those who die here."

"I did try to prepare you."

"You did, and I was. It's . . ." Valerian groped for words, then apparently could not find them. "A government is supposed to care for its people. But after the recent zerg attacks—they've been left here to rot, Matt. Men, women, children—the Dominion wouldn't lift a finger to help them."

"Well, the Dominion isn't exactly welcome here."

"And yet I saw there was food being shared, even though there were pockets being picked. Did you recognize the packs?"

"Uh," said Matt ineloquently.

"I notice everything," Valerian said. "I have to. I saw two packs that had the same insignia as Mira's jumpsuit. It's the sign of her so-called mercenary band. They're getting food to these people. Thugs and murderers and mercenaries seem to have bigger hearts than the people running my father's government."

Matt was silent. Mira had always struck him as an "out for herself" kind of gal. But he believed Valerian, and the revelation was forcing him to think of Mira in another light. Too, she had the damned Heir Apparent in her hands and had to know that Arcturus would reward her handsomely for turning Valerian in.

But she hadn't.

Not so far anyway. And Matt knew, though he wasn't quite sure how he knew, that she wouldn't.

"I wonder if we should tell her about Sarah," he said to Valerian.

"No," the prince said at once. "Tens of thousands of people here were displaced because of the actions of the Queen of Blades. Billions more died. If word gets out that Mira is harboring Kerrigan, all her charity won't buy Sarah a moment of life from those seeking revenge, and the streets are crammed with them."

His voice was both sad and bitter. "I won't return Mira's kindness by putting a mark on her head."

Matt didn't answer. He was ashamed the thought hadn't occurred to him first. "Hang on," he said, and came to a halt. He'd gotten so engrossed in the conversation he wondered if he might have missed the place. Quickly he checked the map Mira had sketched for him.

"This can't be right," Valerian said.

"I . . . think it is," Matt said. He showed Valerian the map, with some symbols sketched on it, then pointed to a piece of what had once been the chair of some long-destroyed ship. The same symbols were etched on it, probably with a knife. Valerian lifted a golden brow.

"Good thing neither of us is as big as Tychus was," said Matt, and slipped through the narrow aperture below the symbols.

# CHAPTER ELEVEN

Jim had been gone for only a little while. He hadn't wanted to leave Sarah alone with strangers at all, but he was a biological being, and his body had some needs that needed to be addressed. One of them was getting food. His stomach had rumbled so loudly that both of the doctors—Yeats and Becker—had looked at him askance.

Mira had been true to her word—no one was going to cook or clean for Jim. As he rummaged through the sprawling kitchen looking for something to heat up quickly, he found himself missing assassin-butler Randall. He was certain that man could have whipped up a culinary masterpiece from table scraps. He suddenly had a flashback to himself and Tychus in this kitchen once. The chefs had been annoyed but had not protested as Tychus helped himself out of pots of still-simmering food. More than once, they had stumbled into this kitchen at oh-dark-thirty, looking for something to stave off the inevitable hangover.

"Shit," Jim said. "Sooner I get out of here, the better."

He wasn't gone long, but apparently it was long enough. When he returned to Sarah a few minutes later with two plates of noodles and sauce from a stockpile of military rations, it was to find two dissimilar faces—one elderly and wrinkled and pale, the other dark as coffee and smooth-skinned—wearing similar expressions of concern.

Sarah lay on the bed, her breathing slow and regular, various tubes attached to her arms and chest. Her eyes were closed.

"How is she?" Jim asked, his own voice conveying his worry.

"Not good," the older doctor, Yeats, replied. "We had an incident earlier."

Jim's gut clenched. "What happened?"

"She tried to pull out one of her . . . well, we've begun referring to them as 'head quills,'" said Becker. "It tore slightly at the base, but it's a minor injury. We've repaired the damage."

Jim swallowed. "I see."

"Since then she's refused to respond to any questions and acts as if we're not present."

"She awake?" Jim asked, keeping his voice low as he gazed at the form lying under the sheet across the room.

"Yes," said Yeats, "but as Dr. Becker said, she's ignoring us."

"She won't ignore me."

Jim brushed past the doctors to take a seat in the chair beside Sarah. He scraped the legs loudly as he pulled the chair back, letting her know he was there. She was facing away from him and didn't move as he sat down. From this angle, he could see the wounded tendril; it had been carefully bandaged at the base.

"Hey, darlin'," Jim said.

"Quit staring at my head," she said without turning around.

"Reading my mind again?"

"No. I just know you. And I know the doctors told you what happened."

"Yeah, they did. You got pretty mad."

"You have no idea." Her voice managed to be both icy and full of heat. She was utterly furious and controlling herself by a sheer effort of will. He wanted to touch her but knew the gesture wouldn't be welcomed. So instead, he kept his voice light.

"You know, I reckon you're right about that. No one knows what's going on inside someone else."

"You do if you're a telepath."

Jim had to chuckle at that. "You got me there. Let's say that *I* don't know what's going on inside anyone else."

"We agree. Is this conversation over?"

"Do you want it to be?"

Silence. One hand moved up toward her head, as if to brush back the tendrils. But Jim knew it wasn't so innocent a gesture, and his hand shot out, gripping her wrist before she could do further harm.

"Ain't no cause to go hurting yourself," he said quietly. "Not going to bring anyone back. Besides—it wasn't you that did it. It was that damned infestation. They made you into their queen, Sarah. You didn't do it. Don't you ever forget that."

He was prepared for another outburst of rage and violence, but instead Sarah's hand went limp in his grasp. She let him guide it gently down beside her.

"I'm not so sure," she said softly. "About anything." Anyone else would have been fooled by the calm tone of voice. It didn't fool Jim for a minute. She was still full of rage, simmering inside, keeping a tight lid on it. And anyone knew that if you kept too tight a lid on something, it boiled over and made one hell of a mess.

He leaned over and whispered in her ear, "I love you, Sarah. You got that? No matter what."

★ ★ ★

## 2500

"We're going to get those people out, no matter what," Jim said firmly. "Our intel says that a lot of those scientists on Orna III ain't exactly happy with what they're being forced to do."

" 'Forced'?" said the young first officer of the *Cormorant*, the ship that was bearing Jim and Sarah to the science facility under discussion. The boy—what was his name, Jack Horner or something—was all dewy-eyed and wet behind the ears. Jim recognized the look. Not so long ago, he'd seen it when he looked in the mirror. Before the Guild Wars and betrayal had changed him.

"Forced," said Jim. "Not all of 'em, mind. Some of them probably enjoy what they're doing. In the name of science and all that. But a lot of them are as sick as we are at what's going on there. They're going to be rescued just as much as the, uh . . ." He turned to look at Sarah for the word.

"Experimental subjects," Sarah said coldly. Jim mentally shrugged. He'd been going for the word *patients* or something similar.

"With your permission, ma'am," said Horner, "we've heard a lot of rumors. They can't all be true." His assurance faltered under Sarah's unblinking stare.

"Rumors? You mean things like genetic splicing? Brain modification? Disease testing? Telepathic experimentation? And torture if there is noncompliance? Those kind of rumors?"

Horner looked uneasily at his captain, an elegant, dark-skinned woman named Sharyn Moore. She nodded that he could feel free to speak his mind.

"Yes, ma'am," said Horner, sounding a little less certain.

"Oh, they're true."

She didn't need to say anything more. The bridge crew looked at one another and shifted uneasily.

"The scientists in this facility are doing covert experimentations on their own citizens," Jim said. "Doing just what Sarah said they're doing. That's why we gotta stop 'em."

"How will you know who wants to leave?" Horner asked.

"I won't. Sarah will. Our job is to get these scientists with a conscience and the, uh, experimental subjects safely aboard the *Cormorant*. Your jobs are to be standing by ready to help us do that and then get us the hell out of here."

"We'll be rigging the place with explosives," Sarah said, "so time is of the essence."

Jim was startled, but he forced his expression to stay neutral. Sarah had said nothing about blowing up the facility in the briefing she'd given him, Mike, and Mengsk aboard the *Hyperion*. He decided he'd have a word with her in private. Right about now.

"We should be there in about three hours," he said. "All personnel—be ready. I understand you're our main contact, Jack."

"Um, it's *Matt* Horner, sir."

"Matt? I thought it was Jack."

Horner colored slightly. "Everyone does, sir," he said, resignedly. "And no, I don't sit in the corner eating pie. Also . . . I hate plums."

That was it—an old nursery rhyme about Little Jack Horner. Jim was a bit embarrassed. "Sorry," he said. Matt gave him a don't-worry-about-it grin.

Jim suddenly liked the guy very much. "You're our main contact, Matt," he repeated, more seriously. "You're our lifeline. Don't let me down."

Just that fast, Matt straightened and got that earnest look back in his eyes. "I won't, sir," he said. "You can count on that. With your permission, I'd like to go over the plan one more time."

"Fire away, Junior."

Matt cleared his throat. "Miss Kerrigan has forged documents admitting one wanted terrorist, James Raynor, to the facility for observation and study. The admission of said terrorist is very hush-hush. We have already received confirmation from the lead scientist to proceed with admissions. Mr. Raynor will be escorted by a ghost, so there will be little need for the sort of beefed-up security that might otherwise be required."

He glanced over at Kerrigan with a raised eyebrow. "So far, so good," she said, and Matt continued.

"The *Cormorant* has permission to stay in orbit until the ghost escort is satisfied that all requirements for Raynor's admission are met, and she has safely returned. Once you two dock, with Mr. Raynor apparently quite well secured, we start directing you where to go, thanks to the blueprints of the facility you provided, Miss Kerrigan. Then . . ."

A few moments later, their boots clanking on the metal floor of the old merchantman vessel, Jim said, "When were you planning to tell me about the explosives?"

She didn't look at him. "I planned to tell you about them precisely when I did, Jim," she said.

"Why did Mengsk order that?"

Now she looked up at him, her eyes intense. "He didn't order it. I did."

"What?"

"As the ranking member of this team here in the field, the decision is mine to make."

"That's a hell of a big decision not to at least run by the boss," Jim said.

"Arcturus doesn't own me!" she snapped. He blinked at her vehemence, and she calmed. "We can't let that scientific data reach anyone else," she said, her voice low and firm, but quivering slightly. "It wasn't even obtained for decent motives, like how to cure diseases or anything remotely humanitarian. It was obtained by *torture*, in order to perform *better* torture, in order to make innocent people who were too weak to stop it into monsters."

And suddenly Jim knew this wasn't about the mission. Or the information. This was about Sarah. He stopped, gently taking her arm to halt her as well. She jerked it away, but stopped, her jaw set.

"Sarah, adding an extra factor like setting explosives makes this mission more dangerous than it has to be—both for us and for the people we're trying to rescue," Jim said quietly. "I know you want—"

"This isn't about revenge," she said, reading his thoughts before he could speak them. "It's about justice. People who do what *they* do shouldn't be allowed to live. The knowledge they obtained by—by doing these things shouldn't be allowed to be known. Jim—I know about Johnny."

Jim went cold inside and took a step back. "What do you know? Who told you?"

"Mike . . . didn't exactly tell me. I read his thoughts."

"I see."

"No, I don't think you do. I . . . there's no one in this galaxy who understands how you feel more than I do. Your son suffered, Jimmy. I'm so sorry."

He nodded, swallowing. "I always wondered. Sarah . . . you can't tell me what they did to John. But . . . please . . . what did they do to you?"

Her eyes were wide and pleading. "Don't ask me that," she said, almost begging.

"I can't support this plan of yours unless I can understand why you want it so bad," he said.

Sarah looked away. "You'll hate me if I tell you. You're better off not knowing."

"I've always been a stubborn son of a gun," he said, and gave her a grin he didn't feel. "And I don't think I could ever hate you, Sarah."

She looked at him for a long moment, then began to speak in a calm, detached voice. "The Confederacy gave rise to the ghost program. There's so much *evil* that can be laid at their feet, Jim. And I don't use that word lightly. I can't, not having done the things I've done."

Jim thought about his son and his mother. One had been taken and subjected to horrors similar to those he was about to learn of; the other died from cancer caused by the government's utter and criminal lack of interest in providing safe food for the hungry. Oh yeah, he didn't have any qualms about using the word *evil* to describe the Confederacy.

"I was a child when they came for me—just like Johnny was. I had no control of my abilities. They wanted to know what I could do. They wanted me to display my abilities so they could analyze and classify me, figure out how best to use me. I was kept in isolation, except when they brought me out to try to test me. But one day they gave me a companion. A kitten. I had her for three weeks. A little black kitten with a white front and white paws. I named her Boots."

Jim suddenly didn't want to hear any more, but knew he had to.

"They implanted a tumor in Boots. It would kill her, slowly. Painfully. I was told I had the ability to end her life—and her suffering."

"What did you do?"

"Nothing." Her choice—to let an innocent creature continue to suffer rather than submit herself to the will of her tormentors— clearly distressed her, even to this day.

"Because you didn't want to let them know what you could do," he said.

"Because I had killed before with what I could do," she said, her voice thick with pain. "I knew what they wanted to turn me into. And I didn't want to do that to anyone, ever again."

"But you did," he said quietly. "And you still do."

It was a harsh statement, but one delivered with compassion, not cruelty.

"Yes," she replied. "I do what I have to do in order to stop this from ever happening again to anyone else. Inside that so-called science facility, they're doing things like what they did to me and worse on men, women, and children. I'm going to blow up this place, Jim. Because that's what needs to happen. You with me?"

Jim didn't even need to think twice. His mind filled with the images of a playful kitten slowly growing sicker and sicker, and a little girl whose heart broke more with each passing day. He gave her a sharp nod.

"I'm all in, darlin'," said Jim.

# CHAPTER TWELVE

## 2500

After what she had revealed to him, Jim was actually surprised that Sarah could content herself with blowing up the station and not tearing the mad scientists limb from limb. It was, he suspected, her real strength asserting itself. Anyone with a weapon—like a Colt Single Action Army revolver or a gauss rifle or telepathy—could be strong enough to kill. He knew that well enough. But Sarah's deep-rooted abhorrence of the act gave her the strength to choose not to kill. Now he understood at least a little bit of what drove her, and the knowledge only made him admire her all the more.

They had worked well together before, but this was different. The goal was more complicated. Finding and freeing the poor experimented-on sons of bitches was straightforward enough, granted. But they also had to find the decent men and women mixed in with the sickos and liberate them along with the victims. Oh, and rig explosives to blow the place up. And the only assistance the two of them would have in any of this was

Jack—dammit—Matt Horner's voice in their ears vectoring them in. Jim fought to keep his unease down, both for himself and to prevent a negative feedback loop with Sarah.

"I know," Sarah said, reading his thoughts again. "It's a tough one. And I'm making it tougher. But you know I'm right."

He nodded. "Yeah. You are. Let's do this thing." He held up his hands, and she snapped the cuffs around his hands and feet. To all appearances they were good, solid, Confederate metal cuffs and clanged quite satisfactorily, if completely ineffectively. She eyed him for a second.

"Sorry," she said.

"For what?" he asked.

The punch should have been expected but wasn't. For an instant, Jim saw stars. He could feel the swelling happening almost at once in his jaw and resisted the urge to wipe away the blood. He understood, of course, why she'd done it.

"Sarah, honey," he said, lisping a little around the swelling, "you hit like a girl."

She grinned, for the first time since their somber conversation. "I know."

He disembarked from the dropship first, and she followed closely behind him. A white-coated, older man with perfectly styled silver hair awaited them in the docking area. There were two armed guards with him, and they all looked excited.

"Dr. Orville Harris," he said, extending a hand to Sarah. Jim knew the name. This was the master of the house of pain, the chief scientist who oversaw every one of its horrors and knew all of its dark secrets. The one who gave all the orders. Sarah eyed the outstretched hand, then clasped her own deliberately behind her back.

"I don't shake hands," she said coldly.

"Ah," Harris said, forcing a smile. "Of course not." The doctor turned his attention to Raynor, eyeing him up and down like a prized beast brought for slaughter. Which Jim supposed he would be, if this scenario had been real.

"I'd like to inspect the facilities before releasing Convict 493 into your custody," Sarah continued.

"Of course," said Harris. "I must thank you for bringing me such a prize, Agent . . . ?"

"I'm a ghost," said Sarah. "You don't need to know my name. And these thugs," she continued, her too-wide mouth curling into a sneer, "dismiss them, please. Unless you think I can't handle a single bound prisoner?"

Jim fought not to grin. She was playing Harris masterfully. The man was practically deflating before Raynor's eyes.

"No, no! Of course I don't mean to imply that. As you were, gentlemen. This way, Agent . . . er, agent."

The door slid open, and the three—Kerrigan, Raynor, and Harris—walked into the corridor.

Two of them left it. Harris's body, Jim propped up in a corner, removing a small rectangular chip from the pocket of his spotless white jacket before tucking one of the small, blinking bombs—half the size of Jim's fist—into it. There would be many more of the bombs, and all would be activated at the same time. It was, Jim mused, so small to be so lethal. Something that caused so much destruction ought to be larger, more imposing.

"Got it," he said, showing Sarah the key.

She nodded briefly, not even glancing at the item. Sarah was like a predator on the hunt now, utterly focused on the task at hand. Her face held the expression Jim was starting to recognize meant *I'm listening to thoughts*: simultaneously laser-sharply focused and oddly distant.

"Okay, Matt," said Jim quietly, "Harris is down, we've got his key, and we're heading due south along one of the corridors." Sarah, of course, was familiar with the station's layout, but this way, she could concentrate fully on other tasks. If she didn't have to think about where to turn, she could listen to thoughts and be ready for any attacks.

"Keep going," came Matt's voice in his ear. Sarah had a similar device in her own ear and could hear Matt as well. "There's a door about ten meters ahead that leads into a more secure area. No guards, but Harris's key should let you in without a problem."

"I see it," Jim replied. He swiped the key, and sure enough, the door hummed and swung open. "We're in."

"Okay," said Matt. "Next up are three doors, two on the right, one on the left. The two on the right are a lab and an office; try not to attract attention. The one on the left takes you into the main, uh, holding area. The key will probably get you in there too, but there'll be a bunch of scientists and guards."

Jim and Sarah exchanged glances. "So we keep bluffing until we can make our move. I'll find the ones we can trust and give you a signal."

He nodded. "Sounds good."

Sarah refastened his fake manacles, and they repeated the bluff. The fabrication held. The guards were attentive but obedient to the orders of the scientists, and the scientists all appeared fascinated at the thought of, quite literally, picking the brain of the infamous James Raynor. But Raynor knew that for some of them, the macabre interest was as false as his bindings. Sarah's gaze flickered to Jim's for just an instant as she acknowledged the third scientist, then she gave the man a tight, faint smile. That, then, was the signal. She repeated it once more. Out of the eight or so scientists present, only two, apparently, had enough human compassion in them to secretly despise what they were doing. There was an Asian male and a blonde woman. And that was it. Jim hoped they would uncover more.

There was a question about the key; Sarah stared the man

down. She and Jim were accompanied by three other scientists through a heavily locked door and into another world.

Jim didn't bother to hide his shock at what he saw. It made the ruse more convincing, and besides, it was what he genuinely felt. Human beings, merely ordinary people according to the documentation they'd intercepted, sat, squatted, or lay in various positions. Some had had their brains affected, judging by the ugly scars on their shaven skulls. Others had pieces of who knew what grafted onto parts of their bodies. There was an odd, probably unnoticed compassion on display; the "subjects" were permitted clothing, which they almost universally used to hide their physical deformities. Jim barely kept his anger in check as a child, probably about ten years old, stood unmoving with his back to the newcomers. The scar on his bald skull was still new and ugly.

Their scientist guide, a heavyset, tall man with tanned skin and dark hair going stylishly gray at the temples, was saying something horrific about "adjusting and adapting on a genetic level" when Sarah's gaze met Jim's.

He roared, "shattering" the cuffs and diving for the other man. The guide stared up at Jim as he charged, all his smug, sick superiority gone as the outlaw James Raynor descended upon him. Jim didn't pull his punch, slamming it into the perfectly square jaw and dropping the bigger man to the floor. He fell at an angle that looked like it would be very uncomfortable. Jim wasn't sure if he was alive or dead, and he didn't really care. Not this time. He grabbed the key from the scientist's lab coat pocket and began to unlock the doors.

At the same instant, Sarah sprang for the other male, whose pale blue eyes widened with shock. With casual efficiency Sarah kicked his throat, crushing his windpipe.

Sarah whirled and grabbed the woman. The scientist inhaled breath to scream, but Sarah silenced her with a strong hand over her mouth. "We're here to get you out, if you want to go. Do you?"

Relief and something like joy filled the woman's eyes and she nodded vigorously. Sarah let her hand drop.

"Then help us. There are others who think like you. Dr. Phan, for one. Do you know of others?"

"I—I think so. We don't really talk about it. You understand why."

Sarah's face was beautiful and terrible in its anger, Jim thought as he glanced over, listening to the exchange as he released the inmates. "I do understand. Contact them. There will be dropships waiting starting in about ten minutes at landing area 4. Get these people out and take them to safety." She handed the woman a pistol. "Take this. You'll need it. And hurry. This whole place is going to blow soon."

The doctor gingerly took the gun, then moved beside Jim to assist him in opening doors. Some of the prisoners understood what was going on and were eager to escape; others looked frightened and cowered back.

"Okay, Matt, we're in, and we've got an ally, a doctor—?"

"Elizabeth Martin," the woman answered.

"Elizabeth Martin," Jim said. "She's going to take over this cell block and contact her allies."

"Roger that," Matt said. "Now, let's get you to the next section."

Jim turned to Sarah, finding her kneeling over the scientist Jim had coldcocked. She inserted the bomb into the coat pocket, then rose and turned to Jim. "Let's go."


There had been four holding areas in all. By the time Jim and Sarah made it to the final dropship and raced aboard, forty-four experimental subjects had reached freedom, along with thirteen scientists who had passed Sarah's inspection. Matt kept them on top of everything, alerting them when their cover had been blown and guiding them to hitherto unknown exits, twice just in the nick of time. Sarah planted a trail of bombs as they went, sometimes simply placing them on the floor. The more Jim saw, both of her and the station, of the scientists and the experiments, the more he understood. And the more he agreed with her decision. It had to end here, as much as it could end. There were other facilities, other scientists. But this particular branch of the horrendous tree of experimentation and torture would be cut off. Forever.

Sarah had held something in her hand as she placed down the final bomb. Jim didn't need to ask what it was. He knew. Instead, he asked, "How long?"

"Five minutes," she said.

"Man, you sure like to cut it close, darlin'."

"We'll make it."

And they had. Barely. The last dropship, bearing them, four scientists, and six inmates, was still climbing upward when the station exploded. The explosives went off in a little chain of destruction, from the first one placed on Dr. Harris's body to the last one plunked hastily down on a table, a series of nearly blinding flashes of billowing orange flames. Twenty seconds after the first one had detonated, all that was left was the black skeleton of the building and the hungrily licking flames.

Sarah was watching intently, her eyes fastened on the scene. Jim had expected to see righteous anger, or joy. Instead he saw something there he'd not seen from her before. Sarah Kerrigan wore an expression of tranquility. She had done what was necessary and had no regrets.

The words came completely unexpectedly. "Sarah? How about you come get a real drink with me once we get back?"

★　★　★

## 2504

Once Matt had edged through the entrance, turning himself sideways in order to do so, he emerged into a slightly more open area, dimly lit only by what light emerged from the entryway. In stark contrast to the random "construction" of the environment outside, this place had obviously been deliberately structured of plascrete. It looked like a small den. Valerian blocked the light for a moment, then stood beside Horner. This little antechamber appeared to be . . . it. But both men knew better.

"Start checking for a door," Matt said. Valerian began examining the walls. Horner squatted and patted the floor gently, his fingers searching for the slight groove that would indicate the presence of a door.

There was a clanking sound, and he jumped quickly to his feet as light outlined a square on the plascrete floor. The square slid back, and four men, all wearing Mira's merc symbol and pointing very large guns at them, popped out.

Valerian and Horner put their hands up at once. "Matt Horner and Mr. V," he said at once.

The weapons were lowered as they were recognized. "Damn, kid," one of the men said, "didn't Boss Lady give you the signal?"

Valerian looked archly at Matt, who shook his head. Damn the woman. She was the epitome of smart business sense and practicality, except around him, where she suddenly became all—how to put it—impish and playful. "No," he said heavily, "she didn't."

"Well, we've been expecting you, so come on down." As quickly as they had appeared, they were gone. Horner and Valerian followed them down a decidedly low-tech ladder and emerged in a high-tech world.

"I'm Gary Crane," said one of the men who had drawn on

them not two minutes earlier. He was tall, gangly, with lank black hair. His eyes were surrounded by crow's-feet, their color difficult to distinguish in the artificial light. "I'm supposed to show you around a little and take you to the private communication room."

Even an Heir Apparent on the run and Mira's "husband," it would seem, necessitated guards. Horner didn't object. It was most certainly SOP, and as long as Valerian got to do what he came here to do, he was fine with obeying protocol. "This is the nerve center of Mira's operation," Crane said, indicating the walls covered with blinking lights, buttons, switches, and visual displays.

"A bit risky, putting everything in one place," Valerian commented.

"Not as much as you'd think," Crane said. "Everything has a redundancy. If this place ever got hit or taken over, she could do everything she needed to do elsewhere. It's just convenient to have one spot for it all." He gave them a grin. "Besides, if you'd been bad guys and we hadn't succeeded in blowing you away right at first, you'd have been dispatched in seconds by all the security shit down here."

"I believe that," Matt said.

"Come on, follow me. We're all set up for you." He led them through the main area to one of six side doors. This room was completely devoid of anything resembling comforts. It was, in fact, completely devoid of anything save a lone console in the center of the room.

"Press this button here. It'll generate a random code. Enter that code here," he said, pointing to various places on the console. "It'll open a secure channel to anyone you want. You'll have six minutes to talk before the clear channel rescrambles itself. After that, you'll have to wait another forty-seven minutes for a second attempt."

"Understood," Valerian replied. "I'll be succinct." He looked pointedly at Crane, who looked back at him blankly for a moment, then said, "Oh, right. I'll be outside."

"Thank you." When the door had closed behind Crane, the grainy, jumpy viewscreen flickered wildly for a moment, then stabilized into the face of a distinguished-looking older man. He had the upright and commanding presence of a military officer from a bygone era, right down to the snowy hair, walrus mustache, and small tuft on the chin. His eyes, sharp even in the poor-quality hologram, fixed on Valerian for a moment. They narrowed, then suddenly the bushy eyebrows shot upward.

"Prince Valerian?" asked Dr. Emil Narud.

The Heir Apparent chuckled and executed a formal bow. "The same," he said. "Though a trifle rumpled, I fear."

"That's . . . putting it mildly. But you could look like the very Devil himself, as long as you are safe. I've gotten word of a battle that pitted Dominion ship against Dominion ship. It wasn't difficult to surmise what had happened. Your father . . . ?"

"I don't know," Valerian said, sobering. "He disapproved of my decision, as you can imagine. The *White Star* took a great deal of damage. We left before we knew what the final result of the battle was. I'm sure that if he's alive and well, he'll start hunting us again."

Narud's expression, already pleased and relieved, showed even more pleasure. "By 'we,' I assume . . ."

"Yes. We were successful. Sarah Kerrigan is alive and largely free from the infestation."

"'Largely'?"

"Well . . . you'll understand once you get here. Obviously I can't come to the major Moebius base now. Father will be observing it. You're going to have to come to us. There seem to be a few aspects of her, genetically speaking, that have not completely transformed. I am hopeful you will be able to assist us with that. And," Valerian added, "she's not doing very well. We need to get her to our backup base, and quickly, or I'm afraid we'll lose her."

The conviviality disappeared. Narud suddenly became all business. "That must not be allowed to happen. Of course, I shall come to you immediately. Where are you now?"

"At a scenic little spot called Deadman's Port."

Narud grimaced. "No wonder you are in disguise. You're assuming a terrible risk with her by taking her there."

"One and a half minutes," said Horner.

Valerian nodded acknowledgment. "I agree. Once you arrive, we're going to get out of here as fast as we can. I'm going to have to go shortly. The channel will rescramble, and I'm not sure we'll have another chance to speak."

"Don't worry about that," Narud said. "You worry about keeping the Queen of Blades as safe and stable as possible. And saving your own skin while you are doing it."

"We'll do our best. Make sure your facility is ready for us."

"We've been ready since you first contacted me, Valerian. Do be safe. Don't . . . you . . . moment of . . ."

The hologram sputtered, then froze, then blinked out of existence.

"He seemed to talk pretty familiarly to you," Horner commented. Valerian rubbed his eyes, then grunted as he remembered how dirty his fingers were. His eyes reddened and teared slightly from the grime as he spoke.

"Dr. Emil Narud is an absolute genius," he said. "I understand that when it comes to science, for all that I've studied and learned, I'm a mere child sitting at his feet. If anyone can help Sarah Kerrigan close the gap between what she is and what she was, it's him. And now," he said, "to take another scenic stroll through the trendy downtown of Deadman's Port."

★ ★ ★

"They there?"

"They are. Raynor's not, though."

"No, he's with Kerrigan, I'm sure of it. Are you and your men set up to move when I tell you to?"

"We are."

"His Excellency will be very grateful indeed. I'm certain that the little fief that Mira commands will pale in comparison to what you'll be given."

"It better. Whatever a 'fief' is."

A chuckle. "Whatever you do, do not act precipitously. All will be lost. Wait for my word. But once things happen—they'll happen very fast."

"That sounds just about right."

"Hey, Coop! What's going to happen fast?" Annabelle was grinning beneath her cap, her eyes bright and happy. Standing next to her was Travis Rawlins, from the *Bucephalus*.

Cooper smiled at them, ending the conversation at once. "Couple of people wanted their beers poured and ready for them when they got off shift," he said. "Told 'em I might not be able to do that, but it'd happen pretty fast once they got here. Now"—and he leaned forward, looking from one cheerful face to the other—"what can I get you two?"


Crane was waiting outside. He had one hand resting casually on the pistol at his hip, the other pressed to his ear. His lips were moving as Valerian and Matt came out, clearly finishing reporting in. He turned to them and nodded. "Checking in with the boss. Ready to head back?"

"More than ready," said Valerian. They followed Crane back through the main area. Matt glanced at some of the equipment as they passed and shook his head.

"You know . . . I knew she had connections, but I confess—I really didn't think that Mira was that big a fish here."

"Judging by what we've seen thus far, I would say she's the biggest fish," Valerian amended. "We are, all of us, accustomed to looking over our shoulders. I think probably she does it more often, and with more reason, than we do."

"Mira's a good leader," Crane said. "Treats her people fairly. Anyone tries to mess with her, they'll have to deal with all of us."

Matt nodded. He was glad to hear it. As they ascended the ladder to the surface, his mind was still on the contradictions and complexities that were Mira Han. And he hoped, sincerely, that her harboring of him, Raynor, Valerian, and Kerrigan would not turn out to be a generous gesture she would later regret.

# CHAPTER THIRTEEN

## 2500

The bar, Sam's Place, was middle-of-the-road. Not too tame, not too wild, not too dark or too bright. Jim wanted Sarah to feel comfortable, but he also wanted to show her something real, not some sanitized version of what a watering hole was like. He'd visited here before, and had a good relationship with Sam and the barkeepers. It wasn't Wicked Wayne's, the bar he and Tychus had patronized so much the place felt like home, but he'd moved way beyond that. Jim didn't need gyrating naked women and loud music any longer. He wanted decent conversation when he felt like talking and an icy cold beer to sip in peace when he didn't. Sam's Place offered both.

He tried not to keep checking his chrono and failed, tried not to keep looking back at the door and failed at that too. She was late. Maybe she'd decided not to come. Disappointment knifed through him at the thought, but he didn't suppose he could blame her. It was a completely new situation for her. The whole . . . relationship . . . thing . . . he didn't rightly know what to call it—that was new for her too. He was just reaching to put some creds on the counter and head out when he sensed her behind him. He turned, casually, so she wouldn't know how pleased he was she had decided to come, and prepared some smart-ass, cool comment with which to greet her.

What came out was a stunned, "You look . . . amazing."

Standing before him was indeed Sarah Kerrigan, but most definitely not the Kerrigan he knew. He knew the ghost, whose body was wrapped head to toe in a special formfitting suit that enabled her to appear and disappear at will. He knew the assassin who turned killing into a dance, even if she had many partners in that grim waltz. He knew the soldier who, even if she questioned orders, obeyed and gave her utmost.

He had never before met the woman.

Sarah had found a dress—God knew how—that fitted as if it had been designed for her. It wasn't a drop-dead gorgeous thing, nor was it skimpy and alluring. It was simple, a plain green sundress with a calf-length skirt and a halter top. It showed off the pale, sculpted shoulders, strong with muscle but still feminine and lightly dusted with freckles. For the first time since he'd met her, her long red hair was not in its customary ponytail but flowed loose around those sculpted shoulders in all its fiery glory. A small butterfly pin secured a lock of hair behind her ear. Her chest was covered, but there was a hint of cleavage. Surprisingly delicate feet were encased in light, strappy sandals, and she shifted her weight from one to the other nervously.

Sarah Kerrigan. Nervous.

"Thanks," she said, giving him a fleeting smile. "I . . . hope this was the right thing to wear. Someone loaned it to me."

"Perfect, darlin'," he said, rising and pulling out a chair for her like his father had taught him to do. He realized once again that she had an astoundingly flawless figure. Was there anything about her that wasn't perfect?

"Plenty of things," she said, then looked chagrined. "Damn. Sorry about that. Been trying not to—you know."

"Honey, as long as you don't call me a pig again, you can read whatever you want. I want to be an open book for you." The words just came, and he realized he meant them. She did too, and her posture relaxed, and her smile became more genuine. He realized that her mouth was just a little too wide for her face and wondered what it would be like to kiss it. To his astonishment, she blushed and looked down, her hair falling in her face. He reached out and covered her hand with his own.

"Now, what can I get you to drink?"

She gave a little shrug of those elegant, strong shoulders. "I have no idea. I don't drink except when Arcturus hands me something."

"Let's start you off with a nice cold beer on this hot day," Jim said. "And we'll go from there. Oh, and try these," he added, pointing to some snacks of fried—somethings. "They're delicious."

## 2504

"I have it on good authority that the food here is prepared by a better chef than on the *Hyperion*," Jim said, completely deadpan. He pointed to the noodles and sauce on the plate he set down before her. "Try this. It's delicious."

She eyed him. "You're a lot of things, Jim Raynor, but a chef isn't among them. And I recall you saying that about something before. I probably shouldn't trust your culinary judgment." She had hated the fried somethings.

He smiled, pleased that she remembered. Maybe she, too, was recalling the good moments of their past. There hadn't been many—they hadn't had time to make many good memories—but they were unspeakably precious to him. It seemed she, too, valued them.

"Well, maybe," he allowed, giving her an aw-shucks grin. "But you can't argue that it wasn't prepared with more care than even on the *Bucephalus*."

"Well, that's true." She peered cautiously at the food, and gave him a look equal parts bemusement and revulsion.

"Oh, come on now, they're rations, and I know you've had them before!" he protested, feigning insult. Then, relenting, he said, "Yeah, it's pretty terrible, but it's the best I could rustle up here. But wait until we get back on the *Bucephalus*. I figure if the food there is good enough for Valerian, it's probably pretty damn good, considering how snooty he is about what he drinks."

It was the wrong thing to say. Sarah's smile, faint to begin with, faded completely. Nonetheless, she struggled to sit. He was there to help her, his hands under her arms, easing her up. Once they had been strong with muscle. Now it seemed they were simply thin and soft, and he felt another by-now familiar twinge. She had to get help, real help, and soon.

"There you go," he said. Sarah made no effort to eat and simply stared at the food. She pushed the admittedly unappealing glop around listlessly. He watched her for about five minutes in silence, then said, "Darlin'? It ain't prime rib, but you got to eat."

She shrugged and then, like a sullen child, put a forkful of food in her mouth.

Jim wrestled with frustration and fear. He was able to choke it down for about another two minutes, then it burst out of him.

"Sarah, you're about as far from a stupid person as it's possible to get. But I gotta tell you, you're sitting here doing some mighty stupid things. You know you gotta eat. And yet you're just shoving this food around on your plate. You know you gotta talk to someone at some point about what happened, or else it's going to blow you wide open. You can't starve yourself and keep what happened to you all bottled up. Now, I get that you ain't the type to want to sit down with a head doctor, but I would have thought that after all we've been through together, you could feel that I was someone you could talk to. You did once."

She didn't respond at first, merely continued to sit with her eyes downcast. It unnerved him more than he cared to admit to see her like this, so listless and uncaring—she who had been all fire and passion, tamped down and controlled perhaps, but—

*—Sarah—*

She reached and squeezed his hand, tightly. He squeezed back. Almost at once, she let go, pushed her food away, then lay back down. She curled up into a tight ball, facing away from him.

"Sarah?"

"I'm not hungry, Jim. Just go. I'd like to be alone for a while."

Jim knew that couldn't be good. He knew what she would be thinking. And he felt a stab of guilt, knowing that by mentioning their date, he had led her to that place. He couldn't reach her, couldn't help her. It was like reaching out to someone who was about to fall. She had to hold on to his hand if he was going to be able to pull her back from that edge, and she just didn't seem to be able to.

Or maybe she didn't seem to be willing to.

He buried his face in his hands for a long moment, hoping against hope she'd turn around and say something. The only sounds were the gentle hum of the sick bay equipment and the soft, almost imperceptible drip of fluids from the IVs.

He said nothing as he rose and went out. He didn't know where he was going, and didn't really care. He simply let his feet carry him through the vast mansion that had once belonged to

Scutter O'Banon and now belonged to a pink-haired imp. He wandered its corridors, fists balled in his pockets, head down, seeing nothing of the once-beautiful home. He didn't even see Tychus.

He saw only Sarah, lying in his arms, her skin so pale it almost glowed in the dim light. . . .


## 2500


They had talked and had beers and laughed and eaten, and when the hour grew late, and Sarah finished the last of her beer and said, "What now?", Jim had not been afraid to simply extend his hand silently.

She had not gotten drunk. He couldn't imagine Sarah Kerrigan ever allowing herself to let go enough to be drunk. But she had permitted the alcohol to relax her, had imbibed enough so that both cheeks and eyes had a glow to them that Jim had never seen before, and she had given him the gift of her laughter—musical, throaty, more genuine than any other woman's laugh had ever been except for Liddy's.

*Liddy, I loved you. Always will. Stayed true to you till you breathed your last breath, and afterward too. But you're gone, my baby. And I know you'd understand and want me to be happy. And . . . I think I can be.*

He felt something inside him loosen as the thought formed, felt himself put down a burden he hadn't even realized he'd made himself carry. His heart was suddenly light, and he realized it was true. Jim Raynor was happy in this moment, with this woman, despite the horrors of war raging around them, despite the aliens who seemed to be always on their heels. He looked at Sarah, and he was happy.

So he reached out his hand. She gazed at it for a long

moment, some of the simple delight fading as she pondered taking a step that would turn a pleasant evening into something else—what, neither of them knew. An ending? A beginning?

And she slipped her strong hand into his.

He did not call for lights in the small cabin that was his room. There were always dim safety lights on, so that in case of an emergency Jim could quickly find the door. Now they bathed the simple room in a gentle blue radiance as he closed the door, leaned Sarah against it, and bent to kiss her.

It was gentle and soft and searching, this kiss that was their first. She was inexpert, shy, awkward—she, the epitome of precise movement and grace. He smiled against her mouth but kept kissing her, because quite simply, he didn't want to stop.

And she responded, hesitant at first, then with the growing passion he had known was there beneath the carefully controlled surface. Her arms slid about him and she arched up, no longer shy but hungry, yearning, as he was.

He didn't want it to be like this—rushed and wild. Not for their first time. And so he slowed her down, gently but firmly, making her understand that she could receive as well as give, teaching her that there was reward in patience.

It was she who interrupted the sweet silence afterward.

"You don't see it," she said, so softly that he hardly caught the words. It wasn't a question; it was a statement.

"Don't see what, darlin'?" he whispered back. Her head was on his broad chest, her ear pressed so she could hear his heart beat, her hair—so soft, like red silk—draped over them both. Her fingers trailed gently over his skin, tenderly, her passion spent for the moment, but still clearly wanting to feel connected to him. She didn't move to look at him.

She didn't reply at once, then said, in that same almost inaudible tone, "The darkness. The darkness that's . . . within me."

Her voice caught. He wanted to squeeze her tight, but refrained. She was like a wild animal, ready to bolt if he made the wrong move. She would shut down if he pushed too hard. He kept stroking her arm, sensing there was more, and after a moment she continued.

"It . . . scares me, sometimes. It's so strong. And so powerful."

"We all got light and darkness mixed up in us," Jim said quietly. "I've done a lot of things some folks would call pretty damn dark. And I know you have too. But, honey, you got free will now. You chose to accept that date tonight. You chose— you chose me. And I swear to you by all that's holy and a few things that ain't, all I see in you right now is a light so strong and pure I can't look away from it."

Sarah lifted her head. Her eyes glittered in the faint light as she searched his. She was more than likely reading his mind. He didn't care. He wanted her to. Maybe then she would see herself as he saw her. He smiled gently, lifting a hand to stroke that red silk and brought a tendril to his lips.

"I know that's what you see," she said. "And . . . don't think I discount it, but—you're not here." She tapped her head. "I am. This darkness . . . Jim, I need you to promise me something."

"What's that?"

She swallowed. He sensed that she had never been more vulnerable to anyone than she was in this moment, and the thought made his heart suddenly feel very, very full. "Promise me that if that darkness ever consumes me—you'll stop it. No matter what."

He opened his mouth, closed it again, and continued stroking her soft pale flesh. He didn't know what to say, what to do.

"Promise me!" Her voice was sharp, not with anger but with fear.

She wouldn't become consumed with darkness. Not after all she'd been through already. She had a tremendous power, and

unscrupulous people had made her do terrible things. But Sarah
Kerrigan was her own woman now. She would never be
anyone's toy. And so, she would never fall to that darkness.

It was with confidence and love both that he looked her in
the eyes and took her chin in his hand. "If it will make you rest
easier in my arms, darlin', then yes. I promise."


**2504**


*I promise.*

Sarah's eyelids fluttered open. While this room that passed
for a sick bay was never dark, with all the little lights of the
panels twinkling and soft illumination at night, it was still dim
enough so that she knew it was the small hours of the morning.

She thought back to her conversation with Jim earlier. He
couldn't know what she had been thinking. He couldn't know
that every time he urged her to talk about "what happened,"
she relived it: the "death" that was nothing so merciful, the
torment of her body twisting into its new shape, the sights and
sounds of so many people dying in agony, becoming either food
or raw genetic material for the zerg. *Her* zerg.

Her zerg that had descended upon a terrified but determined
woman, trying to lift her screaming daughter to safety.

*"Mama! Mama!" The girl didn't want to go, didn't want to be
handed off to the strong arms of a stranger who was trying to save her
life. She struggled.*

*In vain, all of it in vain. Mother and daughter and kind stranger
would all be dead within seconds—*

Jim wanted to think it was the Queen of Blades, that being
who was neither Sarah Kerrigan nor zerg proper, but a sick
mind's combination of both, who had done this. Maybe he was
right.

Sarah didn't think so.

She rolled over, slowly, and was both surprised and unsurprised to see a shape slumped over in the chair next to her. His head was tilted back, his mouth slightly open, a soft snore issuing forth. She closed her eyes.

*I promise.*

And yet, when the darkness was given full, hideous rein, he had not stopped it—no matter what.

Had he broken that promise? Or simply seen that, despite what she had thought and become and done, the darkness hadn't entirely consumed her?

Anger suddenly knifed through her, hot and keen. At who or what, she didn't know. There was a loud crash from somewhere, and her eyes snapped open as she heard a muffled curse from one of the night-shift medical personnel.

"What happened?" came a startled voice.

"Damned if I know," said another.

Sarah knew.

She'd done it. She'd felt her anger randomly select something in the room—even she didn't know what—and focus upon it until it . . . crashed? Exploded?

Jim awoke instantly, alert and ready, hand going to the pistol at his side.

"You all right?"

*Loaded question,* Sarah thought, but nodded. "Something broke." She didn't elaborate. She wasn't ready to think about the repercussions.

Jim looked over, saw that the damage was already being cleaned up, and nodded to himself. He turned back toward her.

"I know you asked me to go, but . . . I'd like to stay here. I won't bother you if you want to go back to sleep."

"It's all right," Sarah said. The telekinetic burst had alleviated some of the pressure. "I . . . was thinking about that night. What happened. What I said."

"Yeah," Jim said softly. "Me too." He was quiet for a moment, lost in thought. "You know, Arcturus didn't like the idea of you and me."

"Of course not," said Sarah, venom in her voice. "If we turned to each other, we wouldn't be dependent on him. He couldn't manipulate us anymore. He was afraid we'd be bad influences on each other."

"If by 'bad' you mean 'good,' as in thinking for ourselves— yep. Almost said as much to me after one of his little spies saw you leaving my quarters."

Sarah went very still, listening as if with her whole body. "What did he say?"

"Typical Mengsk bullshit," Jim said, with the bluntness and honesty she found so appealing. "He was trying to help me, he said. Warn me, so I wouldn't get hurt." Jim paused, obviously waiting for her to comment sarcastically, but she stayed silent. After a moment that almost became awkward, he continued. "Said that you weren't the sort of woman a guy like me should fall for. That you weren't some innocent little girl who needed rescuing but—" He stopped abruptly. Sarah didn't need to be a telepath to know what had happened. He had still been befuddled from sleep, and hadn't really thought through what he was saying.

"Go on," she said.

"It ain't important. Just, you know, like I said, typical stuff."

"Jim. What did he say?"

He sighed. "Said you were a weapon. A monster. Dangerous."

". . . I see."

"I . . . think that was when I first started to understand that I couldn't trust the bastard."

"He was right."

"You know, yeah, in a way. Not gonna argue that. You were *trained* to be a dangerous weapon, Sarah, and that's how he used you. And when you started to think for yourself and challenge his orders and start to open your eyes to just how bad he might be, you were a weapon that suddenly didn't shoot where he pointed it. You were a weapon that could turn back on him. That's why he tried to get rid of you. And that's when the monster was made." He leaned forward and took her hand. "But what one Mengsk made, another has given me the power to unmake. You're Sarah again, darlin', and I ain't gonna leave you again. *Ever.*"

# CHAPTER FOURTEEN

Jim, Matt, and Valerian sat in silence in the system runner as it swiftly bore them from the chaotic clutter of junk that was Deadman's Port to the barren, rocky dead space that was Paradise. "From one hellhole to another," Matt murmured at last as Jim looked about for a safe place to set down outside the town.

"Ah, but you must admit, there's such variety to the hellholes," said Valerian behind the two Raiders.

"True," said Jim. "This is a bit open for my taste. Why did Mira pick this spot, Matt?"

Matt gave him a quick annoyed glance. "You think I know? I don't understand anything that woman does or how she thinks."

"Well, it seems what she does and how she thinks have gotten her rather far here," Valerian said.

Jim's eyes narrowed as he sought out a place under a rock hanging not too far from the shabby-looking buildings that composed the town. "I don't know," he said. "Seems like a very odd place. But if Mira was gonna sell us out, she's had more than enough time to do so."

He guided the ship in for a landing and set it down gently. They all hopped out, their feet sinking a centimeter deep in soft, red dust. The sensation and the red hue reminded Jim of Char, and he felt a twinge. That was over. Sarah had been rescued, and Narud was, Valerian assured him, going to help her get well. He needed to focus on that, not the past, not shooting a friend who had once taken the fall for him, not any of that.

He felt Matt's eyes on him, but shook his head quickly: *I'm good.* Matt nodded.

"There's a bar in the town," Matt said.

"Vague that up for me, Matt," Jim said. "I'm sure there're more bars in this place than you can shake a stick at."

"This one's the first one we'll come to. Used to be a drug den, but Mira cleaned the place out. Still isn't going to serve port, I bet."

"I didn't come here to drink," Valerian said, not rising to the bait. Jim hadn't had time to ask Matt how their "expedition" into Deadman's Port proper had gone, but sensed that some of Matt's resentment toward the emperor's get had subsided. That was good. He didn't much care for the pretty boy either, but they all had a common goal right now, and as long as nobody whose first name started with Valerian and last name ended with Mengsk blew their cover, they should be all right.

The air was hot, with only a slight breeze, and Jim was glad of it; he really didn't want that fine dust scouring him when he was clad just in trousers, a shirt, boots, and a jacket. He had no fewer than three pistols on him, two in plain sight, and Matt and Valerian were similarly equipped. They strode without talking toward the outskirts of town.

Makeshift shelters were ringed nearly a dozen thick around the town of Paradise, along with shanties that were clearly older. The wind shifted, and Jim nearly gagged at the smell of stale urine, feces, and unwashed bodies. He saw whole families huddled together, eyeing them with suspicion, fear, or loathing as they approached.

"Whole lotta people got here suddenly, it looks like," Jim said quietly.

Matt opened his mouth to speak, but Valerian beat him to it. "Refugees," he said. "Apparently Mira is doing what she can to help."

"Ain't much," Jim said. It was in no way a criticism but merely a comment. There were simply so many.

"Okay," Matt said. "Mira said some of her people would be here in the crowds to keep an eye on us, but we probably wouldn't know who they are. She warned that some people here are simply angry and frustrated and looking for a target, so we should make sure our weapons are clearly visible."

Jim chuckled slightly. He had already done what Matt had asked before the *Hyperion* captain had spoken. Valerian, however, hastened to comply.

Jim felt eyes boring into him, some secretly, some openly. He coldly met the more brazen gazes and ignored the others. Valerian, fortunately, seemed to be affecting a walk that fit right in with Jim's and Matt's confident strides.

The buildings were similar to some of those that Jim had grown up with: prefab housing, but of a much lower quality than those on Shiloh. Many had already fallen apart and had been shored up with hunks of the native stone. There was an air of watchfulness and despair that hung thickly about the place.

"That building, second from the left," Matt said quietly, and they veered toward a dilapidated structure. There was no sign announcing the nature of the business conducted within, and Jim felt himself tense as he entered, pushing open the old, battered door.

A sweet, sickly smell lingered, announcing to those who knew the scent the previous nature of the place. Still, it was clear that recently, at least, the business had pedaled no vices other than the consumption of alcohol. There were a few tables and chairs scattered here and there. Patrons hunched over the tables, nursing their drinks. Matt walked up to the bar. The bartender, who had greasy muttonchop whiskers and a bald, tattooed head, eyed them for a moment.

"What'll it be?" he asked in a deep, almost challenging voice.

"Scotty Bolger's Old No. 8," Jim said.

"Same," said Valerian.

"Beer. Make it two; I'm thirsty," said Horner.

Exactly as they were supposed to.

The barkeep eyed Horner suspiciously, but the code of beverages, requested in precisely that order, wasn't really meant as an order or for his ears. Someone else was listening. They didn't turn around to see who it was who likely slipped off his or her chair.

The two glasses and two bottles were plopped unceremoniously on the bar. The whiskey slopped a bit, and the bartender made no effort to wipe it up. *Certainly ain't Cooper,* Jim thought as he picked up his glass. Even in the dim light, he could see thumbprints on it. He shrugged and knocked it back; the alcohol would kill anything unsanitary, and the hot trail down his throat was welcome. He ordered a second shot, then a third.

After a moment, they turned around and went to a vacant booth, of which there were many. "So far, so good," said Jim.

"Agreed," said Matt. "And by the way—Valerian, do a few of those fellows in the corner look familiar?"

Valerian made a slight face as if a twinge of pain had struck him and massaged his neck, turning slightly with the gesture. He turned back to the table.

"Crane, if I'm not mistaken. I see that Mira has indeed put some protectors in place."

Jim had just reached for one of Matt's beers—Horner was

only pretending to drink one anyway—when a figure slid into the booth beside Valerian. A hood concealed his features at first, but then he lifted his head and Jim could catch a glimpse of snow-white mustache and sideburns.

"Hello again, Doctor," Jim drawled to Emil Narud.

"I don't mind telling you, the sooner we get out of here, the better," the doctor said.

"Agreed, but we can't leave at once. Too noticeable," said Horner.

"Then, let me use the time to brief you as much as I can before we depart," Narud said. They all kept their voices low to avoid any listening ears. He turned to Jim. "I know you won't like this, but it's necessary that I run some tests on . . . the subject. She still has zerg mutagen in her genes, as is evidenced by the incomplete transformation of which Valerian here has told me. We'll need to determine if she is human enough to be trusted, or if we will be forced to contain her, for her own safety and that of—"

"*No.*"

Narud looked at Jim, nonplussed. "Surely you must understand—"

"*You* must understand *me,* and what I am saying is, you ain't gonna run no tests on her to determine if you'll treat her like a person or an animal. And don't cop a superior attitude with me. I'm sure you haven't forgotten how we saved your ass on Tyrador VIII."

Narud looked uncomfortable. "Er, no, of course not." If it had not been for the Raiders, the Queen of Blades might have obtained key information regarding the artifact that eventually returned her to her human form. And might have destroyed the scientists on the planet as a happy little side effect.

Valerian said quietly, "With the damage to our ships and the injuries to our crews, we're dangerously low on medical supplies already. Mira has been able to help us with some repairs, but anything more than the barest minimum would give the game away. We've got to get to a secret Moebius base for cover and get her the care she needs, if nothing else."

"They're right," said Matt. Jim looked at him angrily. Matt merely gave a shrug. "I can show you the list of our supplies and the holes in the ships if you want, sir. I don't like this any more than you do, but we can't stay here. Mira's done enough, and I don't want any harm to come to her because she helped us out."

Jim stared at his bottle, then plucked a cigarette from the pack he kept rolled up in his sleeve, struck a match, and lit it. He took a drag as he thought about Sarah lying on the bed in sick bay, all her fire dampened, her unwillingness to eat, the frightening frailty of a woman once so swift and lithe.

He didn't want Mira to be at risk either. Jim let the smoke trickle out his nostrils, his eyes narrowing speculatively as he regarded Narud.

"You don't do a damn thing to her—not even look at her—unless I'm there," Jim said. He spoke quietly but with an urgency that conveyed how deathly serious he was. "And if she isn't capable of refusing treatment, mine is the final word. You don't agree to that, we'll find some other way to get her help. Got it?"

Narud opened his mouth to reply.

Sarah Kerrigan's eyes flew open. Something was wrong. Jim—Jim was in danger. Or was it a dream? With the drugs and the nightmares and the holes she was finding in her memory, Sarah wasn't sure what was real anymore. She struggled for alertness through a drug-induced haze, opening her mouth and croaking, "Doctor . . ."

Yeats was by her side at once. "What is it, Sarah?"

"Jim . . . he's not here—he's not on the *H-Hyperion*, is he?"

"No, as a matter of fact, he isn't. He's with Captain Horner and Mr. V."

A glass half-filled with water went sailing across the room seemingly of its own volition. Sarah struggled to rise, throwing the covers off and placing her bare feet on the wooden floor.

"He's in danger—call him back, call him back now! *They want to capture him!*"


Swann didn't like being in command. He liked working with tools, getting his hands—both real and mechanical—dirty. He liked fixing things and working with a handful of people who thought exactly the way he did. Standing around on the bridge of the *Hyperion,* while they were safely ensconced beneath a pile of garbage no less, made him unhappy. Why did both Raynor and Horner need to go to see this Narud fellow anyway? Couldn't one go while the other commanded the *Hyperion,* so that Swann would not have to be up here and—

"Sir," said Marcus, "I—I think we're under attack!"

There had been no klaxons going off, no alerts, and Swann narrowed his eyes. "You 'think'?" he echoed gruffly. "What makes you think this when nothing else seems to report it?"

"Because someone's firing on the debris!"

Even then, it was so preposterous that Swann merely furrowed his bushy eyebrows farther.

"Sir—the debris that's—"

"—covering us," Swann finished. "Hell's bells. We've been found out. Get the *Bucephalus*'s captain, now!"

The image of Captain Everett Vaughn appeared on the console's viewscreen. "What is it, Mr. Swann?"

"'What is it?' We're under attack, you idiot!"

"I've detected activity on the surface, yes," Vaughn said.

Swann blinked. "Someone is firing on the debris that is hiding us, Vaughn," he said, making the words short and sharp. "What else can that possibly mean?"

"We have identified the ships as belonging to mercenaries,"

Vaughn continued. He was unflappable. "It's possible that this is a skirmish involving the individuals on the surface, and that we remain undetected."

"What?" Swann's voice climbed high into an angry yelp. "Are you nuts? We need to break cover and get out of here, fast—counterattack if we have to!"

Vaughn raised an eyebrow. "The *Hyperion* and the *Bucephalus* are battlecruisers, Mr. Swann. Formerly *flagships* of the Dominion. While the ships you presume to be attacking us are indeed Wraiths, they are extremely few in number and in my estimation pose little threat even if we are their target. Do you hunt, Mr. Swann?"

"Huh?" Swann boggled at the ludicrousness of the statement.

"What they are doing is called 'flushing the quarry.' They may not even know where we are. If we bolt now, we completely forsake our ability to hide on this world. I think you give them far too much credit."

A vein started to throb in Swann's forehead. Words crowded his throat so thick and so hot that he choked on them and was perforce rendered silent.

"I am sure that, in your time as a rebel," Vaughn continued, "you have learned to be hypersensitive to the thought of discovery. Besides, I have my orders, and until I hear from Prince Valerian, I will use my own best judgment, and that judgment tells me to stay put."

That did it. A surge of fury dislodged the barrage of words dammed up in Swann's throat, and they came out in a flood. "You idiot! Don't you get it even now? Most of your fleet's been blown to pieces, you've lost people left and right, and you're sitting here spouting bullshit about waiting for Prince Charming and flushing quarries! Vaughn, we're all rebels now! And as a rebel, when I come under attack, *I fight back*! You can do whatever the hell you want."

He slammed down his fist on the console so hard he nearly broke it. Vaughn's impossibly irritating visage mercifully vanished. "Cade! Break cover and start counterattacking! And notify the commander and the captain that they're likely in danger as well and to hightail it out of there to the emergency rendezvous point! No—patch me through to him directly." Swann felt that only he could convey the urgency of the situation.

"Aye, sir!" Marcus and the others on the bridge looked vastly relieved.

"With all due respect," said Narud, sounding not very respectful at all, "I don't think you're in any position to—"

A rough voice sounded deep inside Jim's ear. "Jim! We're under fire from what looks to be a bunch of mercs! Your buddy Valerian's captain is hunkered down but we're busting out. And if they've found us, they might have found you too!"

Narud was still speaking, but Jim had stopped listening the second Swann had started talking.

"Shit," Jim said, interrupting Narud's protesting. "Let's get out of here." At the curious looks he was given, he said simply, "Swann."

"Uh-oh," said Matt, his less colorful version of "shit." Valerian and Narud were smart enough to simply rise, still acting casual, and start walking toward the door. The man that Horner and Valerian had identified as one of Mira's people, Crane, rose and fell into step with them. Another emulated him.

"We've just been tipped off that mercs are attacking the *Hyperion*," Matt said sotto voce. "Warn Mira, and—"

"Somehow," Crane said, "I don't think that's going to happen."

And Jim felt the muzzle of a gun between his shoulder blades.

# CHAPTER FIFTEEN

Valerian gasped. "But—you work for Mira Han!"

"Keep it down and keep moving toward the door," hissed Crane, his eyes darting back and forth. "Nobody has to get hurt here."

Jim and Matt complied, Matt grabbing an alarmed Narud by the elbow and steering him forward. Jim was scanning the room, his mind racing at light-speed, looking for the opportunity. He knew Matt was doing the same. But Valerian, the spoiled idiot, was going to get them all killed.

"You're betraying her—and selling us out, aren't you?" the prince continued, his voice rising. It held an edge of panic, and Jim felt a wave of disgust. The boy was good enough when he was safe and sound on his ship, but he was falling apart once he actually stepped out in the muck. "Aren't you?"

"Shut the hell up," Jim muttered.

"Raynor's got sense," drawled Crane, turning to regard the legendary outlaw. "You don't got no more sense than a—"

Whatever it was that Valerian had no more sense than would remain a mystery. Valerian's face, facile and frightened a heartbeat earlier, grew cold. Swift as a snake he seized Crane's wrist and twisted hard, snatching the gun as Crane cried out and released it, and followed up with a hard kick to the back of Crane's knee. With the same fluid motion, Valerian shoved his right elbow back and into the throat of the second traitor.

Elation and shock surged through Jim. He seized the opportunity the clever prince had given him, snatching the remaining pistol from Crane's belt and dropping him by slamming the butt of the gun against the bastard's skull. He heard the scraping sounds of chairs being shoved back and knew that the time Valerian's ruse had bought them was rapidly running out.

"Let's go!" Jim shouted, and the four of them ran.

It was slow going. The *Hyperion* was like a beast buried alive, struggling to surface and shaking with the effort. Swann was sweating, not from fear, but from an urgent desire to be with his straining engines as they fought to lift the ship free. It had seemed like a good idea at the time, to cover themselves with tons of camouflage, but now Swann wondered how any of them had let themselves be talked into it.

"We lost two engines during the fight and still haven't been able to effect repairs." Annabelle's voice was tense and sharp, and Swann knew she was suffering along with the engines as he was.

"I know, I know," Swann said, "but we've got to get out from under all this!"

"Sensors indicate they'll be blasting their way through right about—"

The ship's consoles lit up.

"Now," Cade finished.

Swann swore. "Come on, baby," he said softly to the *Hyper-*

*ion.* "You're not going to let a few teensy pounds of debris slow you down, now, are you?"

The ship, at last, began to rock. They were getting loose! "A direct hit to our starboard side, through the debris," Cade said. "And I detect more Wraiths incoming." He paused for a moment, then added, "And vikings."

"How many?"

"Brings the total up to eight Wraiths, three vikings," Cade said.

This was not good. Not good at all. One or two Wraiths or vikings against two battlecruisers was one thing. But if you got enough of them—

"Come on, come on," pleaded Swann. The ship rocked again, more freely this time, doing its best to shake off the tons of debris that had effectively buried it. "Any word from the *Bucephalus*?" asked Swann.

"Negative, sir."

"Hail them again. Tell them we're about to bust loose, and ask if they want to come with us or be sitting ducks."

"I'll, uh, rephrase slightly."

"You do that, kiddo. But you make sure he understands that if he doesn't get himself 'flushed' soon, it's gonna be too late."


Nearly all the shots missed them. Only one hit home—a gauss rifle spike ripped clean through Matt's arm. Bright red blood began to spurt wildly. Horner uttered a short, sharp cry, then clapped his free hand over the wound and kept going while Jim pivoted and returned fire. It was the Devil's own luck, Jim realized, and it wouldn't hold. With so much ground between the town and where they left their system runner, they'd never make it to the little ship in time. Which meant, of course, they'd never make it to the emergency coordinates he'd given Swann if anything went wrong.

Which *also* meant that their time in Paradise probably wasn't going to last long.

They'd not be able to get to rescue. Rescue would have to come to them. He'd noticed that one of the buildings near the edge of town had an abandoned look to it; it would have to do.

Narud stumbled and went down hard. The fall was lucky— another spike struck the area where he would have been a fraction of a second earlier. Without breaking stride, Valerian grabbed the scientist, hauled him to his feet, and kept running.

"There!" Jim cried, pointing to the building on the left. "We make our stand there!"

Valerian shot him an appalled look, but didn't slow down. Jim couldn't blame him—the place looked like a good stiff breeze would collapse it. But it was their only option. To keep running out in the open was to simply invite death, and as long as Sarah lived, Jim wasn't about to check out.

They tumbled inside the prefab home and sealed the door. Jim tossed Narud a pistol and nodded to Valerian. "There's a window on each wall. Start defending," he said. "I gotta take care of Matt and arrange for a way out of this place."

Narud stared at the pistol. "This against all of them?" he said, incredulous. "They'll just drop something on the shelter and we're all dead!"

"No, they won't," Jim said. He slipped a first-aid kit out, tore Matt's sleeve off and assessed the wound. The hypersonic spike had passed through the arm cleanly, but the bright color of the pumping blood told Jim an artery had been hit. Jim sprayed a bandage on and applied pressure. "They want us alive, remember? Which means what they can do to us is limited. And that'll buy us some time."

"What happened, Jim?" Matt asked as his friend worked. Blood was seeping out from under the plastiscab bandage and Jim frowned. To distract Matt from what he was doing as he slipped a hand up past Matt's bicep and gripped a pressure point, he answered.

"Got a message from Swann," Jim said, loud enough for the other two to hear even over the firing. "The *Hyperion* and the *Bucephalus* are coming under attack. Your lapdog of a captain is refusing to leave, Valerian," he added. "Swann's trying to get out from under the debris and into open space where he can fight back. We're supposed to meet at the emergency rendezvous."

"If I wasn't so busy firing," said Valerian, suiting action to word as he handled the pistol with a familiarity that surprised Jim, "I'd chew out Vaughn myself."

"If I can raise Swann, I'll tell him you said that," Jim said. "Matt . . . keep that arm elevated." It would help slow the bleeding. Obediently, Matt lifted his arm. He looked like a kid raising his hand in class. "While you're doing that, you think you can get a hold of Mira? She might be able to get help here faster than the *Hyperion*."

"I can try," Matt said. "No idea if the line is secure or not."

"Doesn't matter at this point," Jim said. "They've got to know she's going to be alerted one way or another. Right now, we need numbers more than we need secrecy."

Matt nodded, taking out his fone and entering a code with his good hand. Jim rose, wiped Matt's blood off on his shirt, and moved beside Valerian. "Tell your captain to start hauling ass."


"Captain Vaughn for you, sir," said Marcus, grinning a little despite the direness of the situation.

"Not so smug now, are you?" said Swann the instant Vaughn's face appeared on the screen.

"I, uh, received new orders from my commander, if that's what you mean," Vaughn replied stiffly. His face, however, was showing the strain.

"Sir, three more Wraiths have arrived," Marcus said. Vaughn had the grace to widen his eyes.

"We're almost out," Swann said. "We'll provide cover for your lagging behinds. Now, get going!"

If the ship had been a beast, it would be groaning under the strain. But they were almost clear, and Swann said a silent prayer to the engines that they would hold.

The sudden lurch to freedom took everyone by surprise, but Swann and the rest of the bridge crew whooped as soon as they had recovered their bearings.

The screen had shown nearly nothing, only the vague shapes of bits and pieces of the debris. Now everyone watched as the debris tumbled away, and they rose, massive and slow and the perfect target.

And were fired upon. "Total of eleven Wraiths and six vikings now, sir," Cade said. "Should I return fire?"

Swann stroked his mustache, thinking. He shook his head.

"Nah, not yet. Maximum power stays in the shields for now. Give us some elevation, and once the *Bucephalus* gets her nose out of the ground, we'll start swatting those flies."

The leviathan of a vessel continued to climb skyward, all the while taking fire. The shields held—mostly. The screens focused not on the attacking Wraiths and vikings, but on where the *Bucephalus* was struggling to emerge. "Come on," urged Swann, watching the loose debris still covering the great battleship shifting up and down.

And then Valerian's ship was free too, breaking out of the encasing garbage like a hatchling from its shell, lurching and struggling for a moment longer before she was airborne.

"Okay, then," said Swann. "Target those damned vikings and Wraiths and blast 'em from the sky. Marcus, send Vaughn the co-ordinates for the rescue site just in case he messed that up too. And tell him we're bolting, and unless I miss my guess, we will be encountering a welcoming committee once we leave atmosphere."

Almost faster than a thought, the *Hyperion,* so lumbering when trapped beneath the garbage of the surface, shot upward, firing as she went, climbing toward the openness of space. Swann had been right. More Wraiths awaited them—and a single battleship. The vessel had seen better days, and looked like it belonged on the junk heap that had concealed the *Hyperion* and the *Bucephalus* rather than battling the former flagships. But Swann knew enough about mercs to know that they put their credits where it counted, not in cosmetic care. He was not about to underestimate what the apparently dilapidated battlecruiser was capable of.

"Activate our Yamato cannon. Target the battlecruiser and give it all we got!" he cried. The Wraiths were inflicting the most damage, but without the battlecruiser, they were stuck—they had no ability to make warp jumps. Nor could they dock for repairs.

And Wraiths didn't have Yamato cannons.

Cade lined up the battlecruiser in his sights, and fired. He got in a good solid hit, but the ship was still functional. The Wraiths descended in revenge, diving like maddened hornets.

"Sir, they're targeting the gravity accelerators," Cade said.

"Strengthen the shields," snapped Swann.

"Already done, sir, but with that kind of concentrated fire— Sir! It's the *Bucephalus!*"

Sure enough, the mighty ship had finally broken free of the planet and was now coming to the rescue. Its own cannon was targeting the mercs' battlecruiser, and there were now newer, shinier, top-of-the-line vikings engaged in one-on-one combat with the Wraiths and the mercs' vikings.

Vaughn had come through.

They just might make that rendezvous with the captain and the commander after all.

★ ★ ★

"Oh yes," Mira's perky voice was saying. "I am already aware of the . . . situation and I am sending people to you now. And dear James can put his mind at ease about his friend. She is already on her way to the *Bucephalus*. But, darling, you have got to get away from town! I cannot send in ships for you otherwise!"

"We can't," shouted Matt, screaming to hear his own voice over the firing. He still kept his arm elevated, and the bleeding was slowing, but he knew he had lost a lot of blood. "We're trapped here. We took shelter in one of the abandoned buildings at the edge of town. There was no way we could cross so much open space. Jim says they want us alive, but you know what the odds would be."

"Hmmm," said Mira. Matt was both impressed and frustrated by the fact that she sounded as concerned as if she were deciding which color to dye her hair rather than how to get four people out of a shootout alive. He could picture her, frowning, tapping her chin thoughtfully with a finger.

"Mira, please, you need to hurry—"

"Matthew, you worry too much. Which building are you in?"

"The one on the northwest corner of town. Not too far from the drug den you cleaned up. Same side."

"Is it the very last one on that row of buildings?"

"Yeah, I think so." There was a crash through what was left of the already-broken windows, and something came through. It was small, round, and was starting to emit a pale green gas.

"Shit!" shouted Jim. He covered his mouth with one arm, dove for the small object and threw it back out. Then he bent over and began to cough violently.

"Mira," Matt said, fighting back a cough himself and blinking his tearing eyes, "they just lobbed a gas grenade inside. I'm sure it's just the first. They're trying to render us—" The rest was lost in coughing.

"Matthew, dear one, you must listen. A long time ago I had some escape tunnels put into the four buildings at the farthest end of town. You are in one of those buildings. Start looking for a hatch beneath the flooring!"

Elation flooded Matt, followed by the plummeting sensation of despair. He took a breath to speak, coughed for about fifteen seconds, and resumed in a wheezing voice. "Some of these men firing on us used to be yours," he said. "They'll know about the tunnels!"

"Silly, silly Matthew," she said, her voice warm with amusement. "You think I tell everyone everything?"

Matt started to grin. "Mira, you're amazing!" He turned to his companions. "There's an escape tunnel under the flooring!"

"Mira, darlin', I love you!" shouted Jim, and Matt heard Mira's laughter.

Jim pulled Valerian away and together they started stamping on the floorboards, searching for something that would mark where the trapdoor was.

A second gas grenade was lobbed into the ramshackle building, hissing as it spread its vile contents into the air. Narud grabbed it and threw it back out, but two more came in from the other side. They all started to cough.

Matt was feeling dizzy, and he wasn't sure if it was from loss of blood or the impact of the gas. His legs buckled and he found himself sitting, perplexed, on the floor of the building.

"There," came Valerian's voice. It sounded thin and faint to Matt's ears, as did Mira's voice on the fone.

"Matthew? Keep talking. Has James found the tunnel?"

"I think so," Matt said. He was surprised at how slurred his words were. He was still bleeding. "Mira? I don't think I'm gonna make it out."

"Nonsense." Her voice was brisk and certain. "I am not yet ready to be a widow, Matthew Horner."

And then, somehow, Matt was staring at a pair of boots. Hands reached down, grabbed him none too gently, and he went down a dark hole. He knew no more.

*　*　*

"We lost them."

"What? I gave them to you on a silver platter!" Cooper put all his fury into his voice. The *Hyperion* was engaged in battle; he was alone for the moment.

"We had them trapped in an abandoned building, lobbed in a few gas grenades—then when we busted in, they were gone."

"Gone? How could you lose them in a . . ." Realization crashed over him. "Oh, damn you, Crane, you idiot, there had to be a tunnel in the floor!"

"I, uh . . . I guess there had to have been, yeah."

"And I assume you have no idea where it led."

". . . No."

He glanced ruefully at his small packed bag, stashed out of sight behind the bar. "Okay, this probably won't do you any good, but I'm going to send you the coordinates of the original rendezvous. Knowing Jim, I bet he's changed it a half-dozen times, plus you have no idea where the tunnel goes. I'd send some men to cover the rendezvous point if I were you. The rest of you, get in that building and find out where the tunnel opens out!"

Quickly Cooper sent the coordinates and clicked off the fone. It didn't look like he was going to be rich anytime soon—but a man could still hope.


When Matt struggled to consciousness, his lungs and nasal passages burned, and he felt nauseated. His arm was red-hot agony, but his mind was clear enough to register three things: one, he was alive; two, they had escaped; and three, Valerian was carrying him like a sack of grain slung over one shoulder.

"Put me down," he grumbled.

"Not yet," Valerian said. That was when Matt realized the

fourth thing—Valerian was running, as were Jim and Narud. Where, Matt didn't know; he had a fine view of the ground and Valerian's running legs, but little else.

He started to struggle, then realized all he would be doing would be interfering with his own escape and probably putting them all at risk. Frowning, his head aching from the aftereffects of the gas, he stayed quiet.

"Mira is a fine lady," said Valerian. "Sent us a very nice transport . . . and some fellows to make sure . . . we get on." He panted a little between phrases. "We're almost there."

"And so are the mercs," said Jim.

"We can . . . make it," Valerian said, adjusting Matt on his shoulder. "Hang on, Matt."

From his ignoble position, Matt did exactly that. Valerian broke into a full-out run, and Matt could now hear the sounds of ships overhead. Dust sprang up from misses far too close for comfort. Then there came the sound of counterfire and a voice that made his heart lift.

"Don't you *dare* hurt my Matthew!"

Mira sounded very, very pissed off. And Matt started to feel sorry for the mercs. A few harrowing moments later that felt like centuries, Valerian came to a stop and shifted Matt from his shoulder.

"You need to quit eating pastries," the heir to the empire gasped. His face was bright red and covered with sweat. Matt had no idea how long Valerian had been running, carrying a weight approximately equal to his own.

"I don't eat pastries," Matt said. "Well, not very often. A chocolate éclair now and then, sometimes—"

"Matthew!" Matt first saw a shock of pink, then Mira's grinning face. She sobered once she saw the bloody bandage. "You have very good friends. Now, hurry—the ships have taken damage but we can still make it!"

Matt looked around. Jim, joined by Valerian now that the

prince had been relieved of his burden, was standing in the shadow of a transport, firing at some of the mercs who were on foot. Shadows cast by ships overhead moved quickly on the red, dusty soil.

Mira slipped an arm around him. "Come, come!" she said, ushering him into the vessel. As she eased him down into the seat, he stared at her chest. There was a large, wet, red spot on it.

"You've been hit!" he gasped, surprised at how much pain shot through him.

She smiled gently. "No, Matthew, that is your blood. Your wound is still bleeding. I am fine. But you are so sweet to worry!" She tilted his chin up and gave him a long, passionate kiss. Matt found himself kissing back and blamed it on the emotions roused by skirting death.

Then she was gone, darting off the ship, and Jim, Narud, and Valerian climbed aboard. Jim climbed right for the pilot's seat, and Valerian took the copilot's chair.

"Where are your medical supplies?" Narud asked. "Mr. Horner needs attention."

"Ain't my ship," Jim shot back, closing the doors and preparing for takeoff, "but I'd try under the last seat in the back. How you doing back there, Matt?"

"Alive, sir."

"Good. Narud, you keep him that way. Hang on to the railings and keep your arms inside the bar at all times."

Valerian laughed. And then with an abruptness that made Matt happy that there was nothing in his stomach, they were airborne. Two seconds later, they were under fire. The ship rocked violently, and Matt was glad he was buckled in.

Narud, clutching the medical kit and sitting beside Matt, looked extremely uncomfortable. Matt put his hand over his wound. Mira was right; the wound was clearly more extensive than a plastiscab bandage could handle. It was bleeding afresh, and he put pressure on it. Wincing a little, he said, "We'll make it. Jim's a damned good pilot."

"I'm afraid he'll have to be," said Narud, in a soft, resigned voice. He opened the kit, trying to keep the contents from spilling out, and began rummaging through it.

"This? This is nothing," Jim scoffed. "Watch this." And with only that for warning, Jim pulled the transport's nose up almost vertical. Narud whimpered, just a little. They were so close to the vessel they were evading that Matt locked eyes with its pilot for a moment. Narud scowled and made an angry gesture.

Matt couldn't help it. Maybe it was the loss of blood or the narrow escape or Mira's kiss, but he started to laugh. He recognized it as inappropriate and perhaps even a little hysterical, but why not? Why the hell not? Either they would live or they wouldn't, and whichever it was, it was out of his hands. Narud stared at him, aghast.

"That's my boy," Jim approved from the cockpit. "Better to go out laughing."

Narud turned a shade paler, and Horner laughed even more.

"Swann, this is Raynor."

"Where in the ever-loving galaxy are you, cowboy? We've been fighting off some Wraiths and vikings and who knows what else and are waiting at the rendezvous point."

"I know, but we had to take a shortcut to avoid getting slaughtered. Didn't think you would mind too much."

Rory Swann's language nearly melted the console. "Well, get your butt onto the *Hyperion* while there's still one to get onto the *Hyperion*. And," he added, "a *Hyperion* to get onto."

Matt leaned back into the seat. Blood ran through his fingers, warm and wet. Narud spoke clearly and calmly, making sure Matt met his eyes. "Mr. Horner, the brachial artery has been damaged. A single bandage was insufficient to prevent it from seeping blood. Once we are on board the *Bucephalus*, we should be able to repair it, but I don't have proper tools here.

I'm going to put three bandages on to seal it shut for now. Do you understand?"

"Three for one. Got it."

Jim brought the transport up as quickly as possible, leaving the ugliness that was Deadman's Rock behind. Matt looked out the window while Narud worked. Was it so ugly? That junk had saved them from being hunted, at least for a while. And somewhere down there was a gutsy pink-haired woman who would never, ever be his dream girl, but who was someone he admired and cared about.

Maybe it wasn't so ugly after all.

It fell away from view, the distinct shapes of the building vanishing into the red dust, softened now by clouds. The transport rocked, and Matt saw a flash of light as they were hit, and hit hard. A klaxon started to wail, and the lights dimmed to a blood-red. Matt looked forward, through the main viewscreen.

The *Hyperion* had seldom looked so lovely, but her captain was anguished as he watched the ship taking fire. He did not rejoice in the life lost when a Wraith exploded in a ball of fire, but was glad that the smaller ship was no longer a threat. Jim guided the wounded vessel to the *Hyperion*'s port, circling to find the docking bay. It was opening, slowly. Too slowly.

"We'll never make it!" Narud cried.

"Shut your trap, Doc," Jim said almost blandly. "Such obvious doubt interferes with my miracle working."

They took another shot, this one in the bow. There was the crackle and sputter of the console sparking violently. Jim flicked the extinguisher switch, and a surge of foam put out the flames. He looked over his shoulder at Narud. "There, see what you've done?"

Matt swallowed hard as his eyes met Jim's. The console was completely inoperative. The transport would not slow—nothing in motion in space did of its own accord—but neither were they capable of deviating from their course. If Swann didn't figure out what had happened to them and moved the *Hyperion*—

Another blow. Another fire started to burn in the back.

"What are you doing?" shouted Narud.

"Nothing," said Jim. "Got nothing I can do. Can't navigate, can't communicate, can't fight. It's all up to Swann now."

And to Matt Horner's delight, Jim Raynor laced his fingers behind his head, leaned back in his chair, and started to whistle. Beside Matt, Narud put his head in his hands and moaned, very quietly.

Valerian stared at Jim for a moment, then a smile curved his lips and he emulated Raynor. "When there is nothing to be done," he said, "do nothing."

"You're starting to figure it out, Valerian." Jim's eyes narrowed and he frowned. "Shit. Sitting ducks."


Matt saw it, too, out the window. A Wraith that had seen better days, but was still spaceworthy enough to swoop in and get the transport lined up in its sights. Apparently the notion of "kidnapping" Raynor, Horner, and Valerian—poor Narud was just an accidental bonus—and turning them over to Mengsk had gone out the airlock. One good blast, as vulnerable as they were, would destroy them. Mengsk was seemingly okay with the "dead" part of "wanted dead or alive."

And then the Wraith exploded. Matt craned his neck to see who had fired the shot and saw that it had come from the *Bucephalus*. "Valerian," he said, "maybe you and your people aren't a lost cause after all."

For a long, long moment, nothing happened. The docking bay was open, ready to receive them, but everyone knew that at the speed they were traveling, they wouldn't make it. Another

Wraith would find them. Then, slowly, the docking bay seemed to drift closer. Matt's face split with a huge grin. If the transport couldn't make it in time to reach the docking bay, the amazing Swann would bring the docking bay to the transport. They still weren't out of the woods yet; the door wasn't all that wide, and a slight miscalculation on Swann's part would mean they would crash into the side of the ship, meters away from safety.

But Swann was good. The *Hyperion* moved closer, and Matt held his breath as the transport scraped the side of the entrance, ever so slightly. The doors closed, atmosphere was restored, and the ship dropped heavily to the platform.

"Told you we'd be fine," said Jim.

Two minutes later, both the *Bucephalus* and the *Hyperion* executed a warp jump.

Mira watched the ship take off. All four of the men who had been charged to her care had made it, but Matthew had been wounded. He would survive, though. He was tough. Not tough like her, but tough in his own rather odd and gentle way. For a moment she allowed her gaze to linger on it, until it was nothing more than a bright speck in the sky.

She would miss her husband.

Then she turned her gaze to her enemies, looking from land to air. Mercenaries, hired by her own people—people who had wanted to take what she had. People she had trusted. Already there was a list of names. Mira's mouth set in a hard, thin line, and she lifted a rifle, taking aim first at those her cybernetic eye could see and recognize.

Cross her? Mira Han? Harm Matthew and his friends, who had come in good faith seeking sanctuary?

They would pay for their transgression. Every last one of them.

She started with Crane.

# CHAPTER SIXTEEN

Once he had gotten Matt to the *Hyperion*'s sick bay and proper care—which would, the doctor assured him, include repairing the damaged artery and a transfusion to replace the blood that had been lost—Jim made a beeline for the *Bucephalus* and Sarah. Frederick looked up at him as he entered. There was a look on his face that Jim didn't like. Frederick looked . . . worried.

And more than a little scared.

"Mira's doctors had to tranquilize her," the doctor said without preamble as Jim strode over to his by-now usual seat next to Kerrigan.

Jim shot him a hard look. "Why?"

"She knew," Frederick said. His arms were crossed. He was definitely keyed up. "About the attack."

"Well, of course she—"

"Before it happened, Raynor." Frederick bit the words out. "According to the doctors, she started—well, making things break, screaming that you were in trouble. She got out of bed and fell. I dislike keeping her doped up, but it was the only way I could manage her."

Jim fought to keep his expression neutral. "I see," he said. *So her powers are coming back,* he thought. *Is that a good thing, or a bad thing?*

Sarah murmured, tossing her head. Jim reached out to take her hand. "There, there, darlin', I made it back fine. Just fine. Everyone's all right."

"J-Jim?" Her speech was slurred. It seemed to take a great effort for her to open her eyes, and when she did, the pupils were dilated. "You—you're okay."

"Takes more than a little ambush to keep me from your side," he said teasingly. The funny thing was, it was true.

"Why did you go? I . . . I forget. . . ." She looked up at him anxiously, and Jim thought he'd better tell her.

"Well, we went to notify someone who can help you," Jim began, but another voice, smooth, youthful, and cultured, interrupted him.

"We're going to take you somewhere you can get the treatment you need, Miss Kerrigan," said Valerian.

Sarah stared at him a moment, then started to frown. "You're Valerian."

He smiled. He was still wearing the filthy "undercover" clothes he had been forced to don while in Deadman's Port, but had dropped the act. His voice and body language bespoke his heritage. And Sarah Kerrigan obviously didn't like his heritage.

"I am," he said. "I think our friend Jim here has told you how it is you came to be restored to yourself and resting here in sick bay. But we can't treat you properly here. I contacted an old scientist friend of mine, and we're heading right now to a secret base where the Moebius Foundation has a state-of-the-art laboratory. There, we can—"

"Experiment on me like a rat? No thanks."

"Sarah, I'm not going to let them do that," Jim insisted,

giving Valerian a glance that he hoped would be correctly interpreted as *Get out, let me calm her down.* Valerian lifted his golden brows, but remained where he was.

"You think you can stand up to him? To these so-called scientists?" She was growing more agitated, and Jim supposed he couldn't blame her. "I don't trust you, Heir Apparent. You're a Mengsk. And I know what Mengsks do. Jim, the second we get to this place, you won't be in command anymore. They'll take me and do things to me and lock you up if they don't kill you on sight."

"Valerian's all we've got, honey," Jim said. "And so far, he's been pretty decent. For a priss."

Valerian smirked a little, but it was hollow. Jim didn't need to be able to read minds to know that Sarah's words had wounded him. At the same time, Valerian was a big boy and had to have known precisely what kind of reception Arcturus Mengsk's son was going to receive.

Sarah's eyes closed. "I'm tired," she said, and Jim could tell she was. Fighting the medication even for so short a period of time had wiped her out. He tucked her hand under the sheet, rose, kissed her forehead, and turned to leave with Valerian.

"Her psionic powers are coming back," Jim said quietly as the door closed behind them. He would have preferred not to have let on about that, but as it had been brought to his own attention by the doctor himself, Valerian was sure to hear shortly.

"I see," said Valerian.

"Dunno what she can do yet, but the doctor said she knew that we were coming under attack and started shattering equipment."

"Then I am glad Narud is here to—"

"Not yet," Jim said. "I know he's itching to get his hands on her, but you saw how she reacted to just you. And I trust you a lot more than I do Narud."

Valerian gave him a smile. "Your trust means a great deal, Jim. Thank you for that."

"Don't get all mushy yet," Jim cautioned. "I just said I trust you more than I trust him. I'm going to check on Matt, then come back and see if I can't get Sarah to calm down a little more. It's going to be hard to try to calm her when I agree with her, but I'll do my best."

He stopped abruptly. Valerian turned inquiringly to face him. "Listen, Valerian," Jim said. "I want your word that Narud isn't going to override me when it comes to Sarah's treatment."

"I—he's the professional, Jim, not I. And not you either."

"Don't matter. I know Sarah, I know what she would want, and I can see just a bit more clearly than she does. You've been solid so far, but I need to have your word on it."

He held out his hand. Valerian looked at it for a moment.

"But what if Sarah's life or—"

"I'll make that call, and I'll bear that responsibility. Your word. Or so help me, I will turn on you so fast, take Sarah, and get out of here before you know what happened."

Valerian's expression turned wry. "Well, how can I possibly say no to such a sincere gesture of trust?" he replied. He extended his still-dirty but finely manicured hand and grasped Jim's. "You have my word, James Raynor. I will not throw Sarah Kerrigan to the wolves."

Jim was surprised to see Horner on the bridge already. The young captain was standing gazing at the viewport, his arm in a sling, and when Jim entered, Matt whirled on him. He looked pale and tired, but furious.

"What the hell is this?" he demanded to know.

Jim looked out the viewport. Both ships had taken their jump coordinates from the *Bucephalus,* but things had happened so fast Jim hadn't had a chance to see where those coordinates had put him. Now he did, and he understood Matt's ire.

On the screen was a massive green-blue gas giant. It was surrounded by chunks of spiraling astral rocks, ranging from the size of a planet to that of a dust particle. In between were millions of asteroids that were conveniently battlecruiser-destroying size, and they were crowded together so tightly that the place was known throughout the sector not by its formal name, the Kirkegaard Belt, but as the "Kick-You-Good" Belt.

"It's the Kick-You-Good Belt, Matt," Jim said laconically, his eyes narrowing as he regarded it.

"I *know* that," said Matt. "These are the coordinates Swann got from Captain Vaughn. Why are we here?"

"Well, that is an entirely different question, and one which I aim to ask Valerian right now." He punched a button. "Valerian. Why the hell are we here?"

Valerian's face appeared on the screen. "Because," he said, "the station housing the secret Moebius lab known as Space Station Prometheus is inside that asteroid belt."

Matt simply stared, his mouth slightly open. "You gotta be pulling my leg," Jim said. "There's a reason they call this the Kick-You-Good Belt. It's because if anyone is either insane or simply stupid enough to venture too much farther than where we're sitting right now, they're going to get pulverized. No one's gone in there."

"Ah," said Valerian, "and that belief, which I have gone to great lengths to propagate, is the reason the secret base remains secret. There is indeed a way to navigate the belt. It requires precise coordinates and very careful and patient navigation, but believe me, following this path will bring our two vessels to Dr. Narud's base. It's located in the heart of an asteroid that was hollowed out for this express purpose." He looked a tad too smug for Jim's taste.

"Absolutely not," said Horner. "That might be doable for a smaller ship, Valerian, but we're talking battlecruisers. Two of them, which means our chances of ending up as a permanent part of the Kirkegaard Belt doubles. This place is a ship killer. If you don't believe me, do a quick scan. You'll find the debris of a lot of ships whose captains were foolish enough to try what you're suggesting."

Valerian sobered. "Gentlemen," he said calmly, "I know it looks impossible. But there are many who would have said that recovering Sarah Kerrigan was impossible too."

Jim glanced over at Matt. Matt met his gaze for a moment, then looked away, shaking his head.

"Matt—I had hoped that after our little adventure, you had learned to have a bit more confidence in me and my ability to handle a situation. Jim—you know I think things through. Thoroughly. And just use your logic for a moment—how could a base be established there if such a thing were impossible?"

Valerian had them there. If he wasn't out-and-out lying to them. But Jim's gut told him the young prince wasn't. It was too elaborate a lie, and there seemed to be no reason for it.

"Have you ever taken the *Bucephalus* in?" he countered.

"Ah . . . no, actually. I've always traveled on smaller vessels."

Matt started to throw up his hands in a "there you go" gesture, winced in pain, and aborted the movement.

"But the path is the path. It is large enough to accommodate a battlecruiser—provided that said battlecruiser is extremely careful. Jim—this truly is the only way to get Sarah the sort of treatment she needs. The *Bucephalus* will go first, if you like. To prove my good faith. It's a bigger ship than the *Hyperion*. If we can do it, so can you."

Suddenly Jim smiled. Matt looked at him, puzzled at the expression. "Well, you know, maybe I've just gotten a trifle staid in my old age. Maybe this is just what we need to shake things up a bit."

Matt stared at him blankly for a moment, then wordlessly lifted his good hand and pointed to his wounded arm.

"Matt, the whole reason you got that injury is to get us where we are now. To hook up with Narud and get to Prometheus Station, so that we can take care of Sarah. That's why we asked Mira for the favor and why we ended up accidentally putting her and her whole operation at risk. You want to throw all that away because you're a little unhappy at navigating an asteroid belt?"

Matt sighed. "I hate it when you do that," he said. But Jim could tell that Matt realized his commander was right. He also knew Jim well enough to know that Raynor wouldn't have said it if it hadn't been true. Jim was grateful for such unwavering loyalty.

"Send us the coordinates for this . . . path, Valerian," Matt said wearily. "The sooner we embark, the sooner we'll get there."

Valerian sent the coordinates as requested, then ended the transmission. He turned to Narud, who had been standing out of sight for the conversation.

"You're not a very popular man over there on the *Hyperion*," Valerian said. "Or in my sick bay, I'm afraid."

Narud, unlike Horner, Valerian, or Raynor, had taken advantage of the time to clean himself up. He stood wearing a shirt, trousers, and boots loaned to him by Valerian. They didn't quite fit, but they would have to do for now. At the comment, he merely sighed. "Genius is rarely appreciated in one's lifetime," he said. It was not a joke, and Valerian didn't take it as one. The man was, without question, a genius.

"You must understand their mind-set," Valerian continued. "Think about where Kerrigan is coming from—and Raynor."

"That's exactly what I'm thinking about," snapped Narud. "I

really wish you'd permit me to see her. I can send a transmission ahead to inform my team exactly what to expect."

"You can do that without physically seeing her," Valerian replied. "I'll have Dr. Frederick give you all the data he has on her condition, and you may speak with him freely. It's only a few hours' delay, Emil. You can wait that long. Let Jim . . . soften her up for the whole idea. If anyone can do it, he can."

"Yes," mused Narud, "if *anyone* can . . . it's Raynor."

Annabelle stood in the corridor outside the cantina. Her hand was entwined with that of Travis Rawlins. They'd been enjoying a drink at the cantina, deep in conversation, when he'd gotten the summons to report immediately to the *Bucephalus*. Annabelle had overheard Travis's orders, and had paled when the words *Kirkegaard Belt* had been spoken.

"I've got to go," Travis said quietly. He stood close to her. She could feel his warmth, his solidity, and knew if she looked up she could see the kindness in his dark brown eyes.

"I know," she said.

Neither of them moved.

"You should talk to Chief Engineer Swann," Travis said. "About putting weapons on the *Fanfare*."

"Nah, it's a dumb idea."

"No, I think it's a great idea. It might be too impractical to arm all of them, but even just one—who knows how many lives could be saved?"

"What would a navigator know about dropships?" Annabelle said teasingly.

"Not much," Travis admitted, "but he knows a good thing when he hears about it. Or . . . sees it."

Annabelle stared at him for a moment, then down at her boots. "Well," she said at last, her voice wildly unsteady. "You should be going."

"You'll need to let go of my hand," he said gently, even though he himself made no move to disentangle himself.

"I know that too," Annabelle replied. "But for some reason, I don't seem able to." She risked a look up, and her heart jumped. "Funny, huh?"

He shook his head and stroked her cheek with his other hand. "Not really. I . . . find myself in the same position."

Annabelle was used to being in the company of men and generally enjoyed it. She was part of a team; she had a role. She belonged. She thought of Rory as a gruff uncle, Jim and Matt as big brothers, and the rest of the engineering staff as comrades. But now she was very much aware that she was a woman, and Travis was a man, and he smelled . . . really good.

And he was about to navigate their way through the most notorious asteroid belt in the sector. With the biggest battle-cruiser ever built.

"I'm pretty good at what I do, Annabelle," Travis said, a hint of a smile on his handsome face.

"Of course you are! I didn't mean to— It's just that—"

He silenced her with a kiss that was as sweet and exciting as it was completely unexpected. What was she doing? Falling in love with a man she barely knew? And yet from the moment he had taken her hand when she thought people were dying by the thousands, she'd opened up to him like a flower blooming. She felt as though she had been waiting for—

"I've been waiting for you all my life, I think," Travis said softly, pressing a kiss on her temple.

"Oh," said Annabelle, her voice a bare whisper. She mentally kicked herself. What a stupid thing to say: "*Oh.*" But somehow she couldn't think of anything else. She clutched his hand like a lifeline.

He laughed, his breath warm and sweet on her face. "Don't worry. I'll get us through this asteroid belt just fine. But I want something in return. Talk to Swann."

"Oh, I don't think—"

"Please . . . promise? You'll never know till you ask, right?" She nodded. "That's true."

"And . . . since you never know till you ask . . . will you have dinner with me when we dock?"

She smiled, feeling her heart on her face, wide open and happy. Everything suddenly seemed possible. "You got a deal," she said.

Her hand felt achingly empty as he left.

# CHAPTER SEVENTEEN

Jim faced a hard decision—whether to stay on the *Hyperion* with Matt as the vessel attempted to navigate the asteroid belt, or to return to the *Bucephalus* to be with Sarah for the duration of the journey.

"You don't need to stay here, sir," Matt said. "The crew won't navigate any better with your presence, and . . . I know you'd rather be there."

"It ain't about what I want; it's about what's best. Sarah's pretty upset at the idea of arriving at this place, and I don't blame her. On the other hand, the crew's pretty upset about getting there."

"Again, respectfully, I say that your presence will make more of a difference to Kerrigan than the crew. It's not as if you're copping out and leaving them." He grinned a little. "In fact, you'd be in the lead vessel. That might tell the crew just how confident you really are."

"I ain't that confident," Jim confessed.

"Of course you're not. But it'll look like you are."

Jim allowed as how Matt had a point, clapped the younger man on the shoulder of his uninjured arm, and went to the *Bucephalus*. Before he went to sick bay, however, he stopped off at the bridge. Valerian and Narud seemed surprised to see him.

"So I've been thinking," Jim said. Narud muttered what may have been a disparaging comment about how Jim's "thinking" was a remarkable event. Raynor ignored him. "We should make a joint announcement, heard on both ships. For my part, I'll tell them that I'm over on the *Bucephalus,* the lead ship, and that I have every faith in your navigator—" He raised his eyebrows inquiringly in said navigator's direction.

"Travis Rawlins, sir."

"Oh, so you're Travis. Annabelle can't shut up about you. No, don't look embarrassed, son. Annabelle has a good head on her shoulders, and I trust her judgment."

"Er . . . thank you?" Travis still sat straight in his chair, but glanced over at Valerian for reassurance. The prince nodded and lifted a hand, indicating that there was nothing to worry about.

"That I have every faith in Travis Rawlins to get us to this station safely. And what you should say is something about when the station was built, how many times ships have successfully traversed the path to and from the place, and download into the computer databanks any visual proof that said station actually exists."

"Absolutely not," Narud said. "This station is highly classified!"

Jim turned to Narud. "Okay, then. Perhaps you'd care to deal with a mutiny?"

"You can't possibly think that your crew would do such a thing," Narud scoffed.

Jim had scratched his beard thoughtfully. "Well, I do and I don't. I don't think they'd have one of them weapons-toting,

equipment-smashing type of mutinies. But I sure could see
them simply stopping work and quitting. Ain't no one in my
crew conscripted or forced to stay if he or she doesn't want to."

This was clearly aimed at Valerian, who bridled slightly at
the implication. "I will remind you, Jim, that Sarah is on our
ship. If your crew chooses to 'stop work,' as you put it, you'll
lose them. Because my crew will obey *my* orders."

"I ain't taking a swing at you because I know what you're
really saying," Jim said. "But you know as well as I do that everyone on both ships is scared shitless of traveling through *that*."
He stabbed a finger in the direction of the viewscreen—and the
countless number of asteroids it displayed. "And you know
they'll all feel better if they get some reassurance from the people who've done this before that they ain't gonna wind up plas-
tered against a space rock."

"I agree that an announcement would hearten the crews of
both vessels," said Valerian. "Dr. Narud, I respect your desire to
keep Prometheus Station as covert as possible. I funded this
base, and I will use my own best judgment as to what to release
to the crews. After all, shortly they will be beholding at least
some of it with their own eyes. I think Raynor is suggesting that
they simply want assurance that the place exists, not how many
computers we have. Isn't that correct?"

"That's about the size of it."

Narud scowled, but knew when he was outmatched. He
nodded reluctantly. Jim nodded once, then hurried to sick bay.
Sarah was awake. There was color in her face, and he saw that
she was halfway through a meal.

He couldn't suppress a grin. "You know what makes me
happy, don't you, darlin'?"

She shot him a look, and her eyes were cold. "You don't
know what makes *me* happy." She shoveled the food into her
mouth almost mechanically. And then Jim realized what was
going on. Sarah was doing everything she could to recover her

strength in case she had to fight against people she perceived as her captors.

"I do know," Jim said quietly. "Sarah—do you trust me?"

She swallowed, not replying at once. Then she softened, ever so slightly. "I do."

"Then trust me to know what I'm doing, and that I'm going to do right by you. They are not going to hurt you."

"I said I trust *you,* Jim. Not Valerian."

"Let me worry about Valerian and Narud. You keep eating."

"There's a lot of fear on this ship, Jim. I might not have to worry about Valerian and Narud, if what people are thinking about the asteroid belt is true."

"Well, honey, you do have a point. We're just going to see what happens. Guess all will be solved if we end up smears on a rock, huh?"

And he was pleased to see that despite her determination to keep scowling, she ducked her head and tried to hide a smile.

He'd promised he'd "work on her." He knew that Valerian and Narud assumed that he would be attempting to talk her into seeing Narud before she absolutely had to.

He would let them assume that.


It was six hours of nail-biting, sweat, prayers, and curses. Everyone in both ships knew about the Kick-You-Good Belt. They all knew the stories. And they could all even see the debris of other ships that had had the audacity to try what they were now attempting.

Annabelle kept trying to distract herself, but she kept sneaking peeks at their progress. At one point Swann came up to her and said roughly, pressing some creds into her hand, "You're relieved of duty. Get your butt to the cantina. Have a drink on me. Talk to Cooper about how worried you are about that navigator fella."

She blushed. "I *am* worried, Rory. But please don't single me out like this. I can handle it."

He gave her a glare. "Of course you can. You're one of my engineers. I'd be saying the same thing to Milo over there if it was his girl who was in charge of navigating these two monster ships through a nasty asteroid belt."

Annabelle regarded him skeptically, but saw in his eyes that he was telling the truth. "Thank you. But I think work's what I need."

He peered at her, then nodded, smiling a little. "And *that's* why you're one of mine. If work's what you need, then get back to it. You don't get paid to loaf around."

She hesitated, recalling the last—*no, don't put it that way, Annabelle*—the most recent conversation with Travis. She felt a sudden clarity. Travis would do it. He wouldn't be navigator of the Dominion flagship if he weren't the best. With newfound confidence she said to Rory, "Actually, there was something I wanted to talk to you about. If things are quiet enough so that you're shooing me off to go get a drink, maybe you'd let me try this instead."

"Go on, kid. I'm all ears."


Valerian displayed none of the concern he felt about the journey. The crew was worried enough; they needed to see him behave as his usual calm, almost blasé, self.

"Your man is going very slowly," Narud said.

Valerian looked at him. "This ship has been damaged enough as it is. I don't want to have another hole in it."

"Every minute that we delay is a minute that I am not treating Sarah Kerrigan," Narud said. He sighed in annoyance. "I wish you would let me see her."

"With all due respect, Dr. Narud, you won't be able to make a thorough diagnosis with the equipment on board. You can do amazing things, but every artist needs a palette. Let Jim talk to her."

"You seem to be romanticizing that outlaw."

"On the contrary," Valerian said. "Any false ideas I might have had about Raynor or his people have quite fallen away." He didn't add that they had been replaced with something more important—an accurate, informed opinion of the man. And the more that Valerian learned about Raynor and his Raiders, the more he knew his decision to challenge his father had been the right one.

Slowly Rawlins steered the great ship through the looming threats. Now and then there was a faint shudder and sometimes a scraping sound as he went a bit too close to a chunk of rock, but Valerian could hardly blame him for that.

"Coming up on the coordinates for the station, sir," Rawlins said after what felt like an eternity.

"About time," said Narud.

"Well done, Mr. Rawlins," said Valerian. "That was masterful."

"Thank you, sir."

Valerian and the Moebius Foundation he ran had agreed that the work they performed, and the main station at which they performed it, needed to remain the galaxy's best-kept secret. It was to that end that Valerian had placed the station inside the so-called "impenetrable" Kirkegaard Belt. It was unlikely anyone would dare enter, and if they did, unless they knew the route, they wouldn't get far.

And it was also to that end that Valerian had come up with the idea of not just building a station, but secreting it inside an asteroid. The site was thus doubly secret. Generally, once someone knew about it, they were taken there and didn't leave. Only Narud and a few of his most trusted people ventured forth.

"Sir?" said Rawlins in a slightly puzzled voice. "According to the coordinates Dr. Narud gave us, it should be this asteroid, Number 3958. But I'm detecting no signs of any space station."

Valerian and Narud exchanged a slightly amused glance. "Please ring the doorbell, Doctor," Valerian invited.

Narud inclined his head and stepped up to the console. He opened up a channel. "This is Doctor Emil Narud. I am here with the *Bucephalus* and the *Hyperion*. Please prepare for docking and employ protocol response 221-C."

And suddenly, like a hologram materializing, it was there. A schematic appeared on the screen beside Rawlins, and information began to run in a column to the side.

"That never stops being entertaining," said Valerian. It was the third level of secrecy—cloaking, both to the senses and to technology. He punched a button. "Attention, crew of the *Bucephalus* and the *Hyperion*. Your faith in me and my navigator has been rewarded. I invite all of you to behold . . . Space Station Prometheus."

"Do you want to see it?" Jim asked.

"No," said Sarah, "but I bet you want me to."

"Well, you gotta see it at some point." Jim reached over for a small viewscreen and played around with it for a moment. "I gotta admit, I'm kinda curious as to what Valerian's been sinking all his creds into that's got him so—whoa."

The last word was a soft breath, and Jim's eyes widened. He was not much of a connoisseur of beauty, nor did he particularly indulge in luxuries. But as he turned the screen so that Sarah could see, even she had her breath taken away—in a good way.

Space Station Prometheus was, as had to be expected of Valerian, aesthetically exquisite. If ever a space station could be dubbed a "work of art," it would have to be this. The materials that comprised it had to be the normal plascrete and neosteel that other, lesser constructs were made of, but somehow, the thing looked otherworldly.

"Xel'Naga," Sarah said, and Jim nodded. It was made by terrans, but the swirls, curves, hues, and lighting reminded him of the beautiful and mysterious artifacts that had brought Kerrigan back to him.

There were three main rings, two small and one larger at the center, protectively encircling an elongated sphere that looked like a silver-blue tear poised eternally waiting to fall. There was nothing hard-seeming or spiky—all was harmony and grace.

As they watched, a ramp began to extend from the main drop-shaped sphere. A translucent screen formed about it, creating a clear tunnel as atmosphere generators did their jobs.

A voice crackled from the monitor.

"Mr. Raynor? Miss Kerrigan? It's time to depart. Space Station Prometheus has officially put out the welcome mat."

# CHAPTER EIGHTEEN

The transport bearing Raynor, Sarah, Valerian, Narud, Dr. Egon Stetmann, and a few other Raiders docked at the extended ramp. Jim had ordered them along for two reasons—one, he thought it prudent to have a couple of friends around, and two, the place looked amazing, and he thought some of the crew might enjoy seeing it. The pilot confirmed what Jim already had concluded—that there was an adequate, albeit temporary, artificial environment. They would be able to walk down the platform and directly into the space station as if they were strolling on a sidewalk back on Mar Sara.

Jim had wanted Sarah to be carried in on a stretcher, or at the very least a convalchair, but she had refused. "I go into this of my own will, or I don't go—on my own two feet, or I don't go," she had said. Jim knew her well enough to recognize the *I'm done negotiating with you* tone in her voice. He was, to be honest, simply relieved she was willing to even set foot on the station at all.

Dr. Narud had approached her with a kindly mien, extending his hand. "Miss Kerrigan," he said, "I am so pleased to see you."

She hadn't taken the hand, and Jim, supporting her with an arm under her elbow, felt her go rigid. "I wish I could say the same."

"Dr. Narud is anxious to begin helping you, Sarah," Valerian, the diplomat, had said smoothly. "I'm relieved you are finally at a facility where you can receive proper treatment."

She had eyed him too, then taken a seat on the vessel and had said nothing more to Narud or Valerian. At one point, though, she leaned over and whispered in Jim's ear.

"There's something wrong with Narud. I've met him before."

"Well, you weren't exactly who you are now, darlin', but you did meet him. I'm not surprised he feels familiar."

She shook her head impatiently, groping for the words. "No, not that way. I don't remember him specifically. Not 'met' as in . . . it's hard to explain. . . . He feels familiar, but not as himself. Psionically."

Jim nodded, but he was a bit worried. Sarah's abilities were only recently starting to come back to her, and they were clearly not under complete control. She'd been through a terrible ordeal, her memory was spotty at best, and she was, rightly, suspicious.

Problem was, given her current state, Jim wasn't sure if she was being suspicious with reason or paranoid without. Nonetheless, he didn't like Narud either, and needed no extra urging from Sarah to watch the man like a hawk.

It had been an awkward, but fortunately brief, flight. Now they stepped out onto the gleaming white platform. A soft sigh escaped Egon's lips, the sort of sigh a man breathes when he's fallen in love. "It's . . . so beautiful already," he said. A few meters away, the smooth surface of the teardrop station began to slowly iris open.

"There are, of course, some tests I'd like to run before we can even properly begin treatment," said Narud.

Jim started to reply when the door opened completely, revealing the Prometheus Station welcoming party. Jim had expected to see a gurney and doctors.

He saw armed guards.

He thought two things simultaneously.

One: Sarah was right. And two: Why hadn't he brought a weapon?

"What the fekk is this?" he snapped, whirling to protectively move Sarah behind him.

"If the lady would come quietly, we can begin the tests that—" Narud began.

"Like hell!" snapped Sarah, stepping out from behind Jim. She sure didn't look weak or frail. Her color was up from her anger, and her body was temporarily fueled by it. "I will not submit to becoming a test subject for your lab!" She pointed over the edge of the platform. "I'll dive right off this if your men try to lay a single hand on me. I swear it!"

"She'll do it too," Jim said.

"Jim," began Valerian. "Please. You don't treat patients without first determining exactly what is amiss with them."

"Prince Valerian is quite right," said Narud. "I think it would be best if—"

"Platform," said Sarah. "Gravity."

"I don't give a damn what you think, Doc," snapped Jim. "You heard the lady. What she needs right now is basic, decent human care and plain and simple medical aid. Not a damned thing more. We clear?"

There was a clattering sound as the guards, in perfect unison, raised their clean and shiny weapons and took aim at Raynor. There was an answering clatter as the Raiders did the same thing.

Jim couldn't suppress a grin. He found himself oddly at peace with whatever was about to go down. The tension stretched out for a long moment.

"I," said Narud, "am a poor host, I'm afraid. I instructed the guards to utilize protocol 221-C. This is standard procedure when admitting newcomers."

"Damn stupid way to say hello," said Raynor.

"Most of our visitors are not outlaws and understand the necessity for precaution. Nonetheless," he said, and waved to the captain of the guards to lower the weapons, "I do apologize. I am sure you will appreciate the . . . uncertainty of the situation in which we find ourselves and the fact that I care greatly about the safety of people entrusted to my care. A sentiment I am certain you understand, Mr. Raynor."

"Yeah," said Jim. "You gonna stand there jawing all day or are you going to take her to sick bay?"

Narud gestured. A second group emerged, a man and a woman clad in white pushing a gurney. "That's better," Jim said. He turned to Valerian and looked at him for a moment, then at his Raiders.

"I'm going to sick bay with Sarah. What's going to happen to them?"

"They will have supervised access to the station," Narud said.

"Supervised?"

"Jim, it's a top-secret research facility. Dr. Stetmann," he said, turning to a now-pale Egon, "would you like strangers tromping around in your lab without your presence?"

"Well—er—no," stammered Stetmann, "but I confess"—and he laughed a little—"I'm champing at the bit to have a look at your lab, Dr. Narud."

"I think that can be arranged," said Narud, smiling. "Again, I do apologize. As I said—it's standard operating procedure that was inappropriate in this case. I do hope you'll forgive me. I've been so defensive against the outside for so long, it's become a habit. There's a dining area, a recreational area, a library—your people are free to explore those areas and more. With or without an escort—their choice. But for certain areas, I'd like one of my people to accompany them. Is this acceptable?"

Still holding Sarah's elbow, Raynor felt her start to slump slightly. The adrenaline and outrage that had fueled her were ebbing, and he had no more desire than she did for her to look weak in front of these people.

"Okay. You know where to find us." He turned to Cam Fraser. "You get treated in a way I wouldn't like, I want to know about it."

"You got it."

The doctors reached out for Sarah, presumably to help her onto the gurney. Raynor placed himself between them, shook his head, and lifted her himself. Holding her hand, Raynor walked beside her down the long hallways to the sick bay. There was art on the walls, not quite as lavish as that which Valerian displayed, but lovely and tasteful nonetheless. The lighting was on the dim side but efficient, the carpeting thick and plush. There was soft music piped in from somewhere.

"So tell me, Dr. Narud," Egon was saying animatedly, "I of course know that you're an expert on the zerg. I am but a newcomer to that *exciting* field and I was wondering, what is your opinion on the prevailing theory that—"

Jim tuned out the science talk. His mind went back to another type of conversation altogether, in another corridor, years ago.


## 2500


Sarah was walking so fast that Raynor found he had difficulty keeping up with her as they strode down a corridor in the

*Hyperion.* "Slow down there, hoss," he said. "My legs are older than yours. And you can't outrun something just because you don't want to hear it."

"I don't want to hear it because it's bullshit," Kerrigan snapped.

"It ain't," Jim insisted. "Sarah, I'm telling you, we're jumping from the frying pan into the fire here. I ain't saying he's going to do it, but you have to open your eyes. Arcturus Mengsk has the potential to be every bit as terrible as the Confederacy. The man is out for himself. He's trying to overthrow the government not because he feels it's the morally right thing to do, but so that he can step into power when everything starts falling apart. Don't you see?"

She stopped and, biting her lower lip, turned to him. "I see that he's not what I once thought he was. But I also believe he's the best chance we—that anyone—has of overthrowing the Confederacy. He's done some ruthless things. I know that. But I can't believe you think that he's as evil as the Confederacy, after all the things they've done. Think about the Ghost Academy, Jim. The place that murdered your son. Think about the cans made of toxic material that slowly killed your mother. The Confederacy did that, not Mengsk!"

He put a hand on her shoulder to halt her. She jerked away, green eyes blazing, but didn't keep moving forward.

"Darlin', listen to me. You know that Mengsk will do whatever it takes to achieve his goal. You *know* that."

She nodded. "I know. His goal is to overthrow the Confederacy and its corruption."

"His *goal* is to create a power vacuum. Then he'll step up as the savior."

"Lesser of two evils, Jim. Much lesser."

Jim ran his hand through his hair, exasperated. "Okay. I will agree that he liberated you from a horrible life. I agree that he busted me out of prison. Why do you think he did those things,

Sarah? He did it because we would be useful to him. He counted on us being so grateful that we would turn a blind eye to everything else he was doing. He's used you, honey. And me. Sons of Korhal, the Confederacy of Man—two sides of the same ugly coin. I've watched him, Sarah. I've watched his reaction to gaining power, and it ain't pretty."

She softened, letting the anger go. "If Mengsk is driven, it's because he has a vision of a better universe for everyone. And yes, 'everyone' includes Arcturus Mengsk. And unlike other people, he actually has the ability to make it happen." She lifted a hand to stroke his face. Swiftly he covered her hand with his own.

"It's just . . . you mean a lot to me, Sarah. I know things have happened fast, but it's true. And I couldn't bear the thought of anything bad happening to you."

Slowly, she removed her hand. "I know," she said quietly. "But I can't just sit on the sidelines. I have to put myself at risk, just as you do." Sarah looked down, a stray lock of red hair falling over her eyes. "I can't help but think that maybe we shouldn't have gotten involved."

"Don't say that," he said. "Don't ever say that."

## 2504

But the words had been spoken and could never be unsaid. And there had been many times over the last few years that Jim had wondered the same thing. He wasn't wondering it now. He hadn't been able to stop Arcturus from the despicable act of betrayal that bastard had performed on a woman who had chosen to stand by him, even when her faith was shaken. But he sure as hell had been able to do something about it. That Kerrigan was alive and seemingly human and holding his hand as he walked beside her was due to him. And he was humbly grateful that Fate—and, yes, Valerian Mengsk—had put him in a position to help her.

They turned a corner and stopped in front of a large door with an elaborate pad. The doctors all stepped in front of it and had their fingerprints and retinas scanned, spoke proper codes, and the door, like the entrance to the station, irised open.

Jim whistled, soft and low. The area was a paean to technology all on its own. It all looked so new and glittery, and he couldn't even guess at the applications for half of the tools. Even so, it lacked the forbidding coldness of much technology. If it was not the worn, well-known handles, buttons, and knobs of the *Hyperion*, it was at least approachable.

The bed on which he gently placed Sarah had a blinking console on one side and a chair on the other. Above the bed was a monitor that was currently dark. Two nurses manifested seemingly from nowhere, moving quickly and quietly to enter data on the console and begin hooking Sarah up to the monitor overhead.

"Tell me what you're doing," he said, and one nurse gave him such a genuinely pleasant smile that he mitigated the harshness of his voice partway through the sentence.

"Of course," she said. "We're going to monitor all her brain and body activities and painlessly take blood and tissue samples. We'll be giving her a topically based infusion of nutrients that will also hydrate her. And if you're well enough, Miss Kerrigan, I've been told that you've been invited to join Dr. Narud for dinner."

"Let me see the chart," he said. She handed a small device to him. He tapped the screen, looking through it, and saw nothing that contradicted anything the nurse had said.

"Okay," he said, and sat down beside Sarah. An awkward silence stretched as the nurse prepared Kerrigan. Then the woman leaned down and with the same genuine smile she had given Jim, said, "Miss Kerrigan, you should be fine for the next few hours. Please press this button if you need anything at all. In the meantime, I encourage you to relax." Her smile widened. "Don't tell Dr. Narud, but some of us have been known to crawl into these beds rather than our own to grab a little shut-eye—they're particularly comfortable."

The smile faltered as Sarah didn't smile in return, just nodded curtly. The nurse quietly stepped away.

Jim covered Sarah's hand with his own and cleared his voice. "Listen, Sarah. I— I . . ."

Her fingers on his lips stilled them. "Jim. Shhh. I know."

He kissed her fingers and gave her a crooked smile, changing the subject. "So . . . you said something back on the *Bucephalus* about Narud." He kept his voice low.

Sarah's gaze unfocused for a moment, then alertness returned to her green eyes. "They're not paying attention. We can talk, for now. And yes, I did. I'm feeling stronger, Jim. This station—it feels like the lab where they experimented on me. Back in the days of the Confederacy."

"Well," Jim said cautiously, "it *is* a lab. You might be feeling that way no matter what lab you were in."

"I thought about that, believe me," Sarah said. "But it's not my imagination or my memory problems. There *is* a familiar psionic resonance coming from Narud. I don't trust him. I simply *do not.*"

"Me neither. The question is . . . what are we gonna do about it? You aren't recovered, darlin'. You're too smart not to know that." He touched the tentacle strands that now served her for hair. She flinched, ever so slightly. "He's the only chance we got to find out exactly what happened to you and how to bring you all the way back. For what it's worth, Valerian has proven himself pretty trustworthy. Ain't stumbled yet, and there's been plenty of opportunity for it."

"You trusted his father too."

"At first, yeah," Raynor said. "But so far Junior really does seem different, darlin'. How far that will go, though, and what it means, I don't know."

And that was it, really. There was too much they didn't know, too much they couldn't be certain about. And so they stayed in silence, hands clasped, trusting in each other.

Because they could be certain about that.

# CHAPTER NINETEEN

When Jim and Sarah had gone, Narud turned to Valerian. "While she's being properly attended to, I'd very much appreciate it if you could show me that lovely, lovely artifact."

"Oh yes!" enthused Egon. Valerian gave the young scientist an indulgent smile, ignoring the fact that it was he who had been addressed, not Egon. "We carried the collected pieces aboard the *Hyperion*," Stetmann continued in his obliviousness, "but Prince Valerian has it on the *Bucephalus* for the moment."

"Actually, Dr. Stetmann," said Narud, "Prince Valerian has arranged for you to have a private, albeit supervised, tour of one of our labs, if you're interested."

Egon's eyes looked as large as saucers. "I, uh—why, yes, of course, that would be wonderful!"

Four more people were emerging from the station onto the platform, two men and two women. One of the women, tall, with jet-black hair, pale skin, and gray eyes, stepped up to Egon and extended a hand.

"Dr. Stetmann? I'm Dr. Chantal de Vries. It's my pleasure to show you around one of the laboratories."

Judging by Egon's expression, thought Valerian, it was hard to tell if the young man was more pleased at the prospect of seeing the lab or accompanying the striking-looking woman. No doubt a happy combination of both.

"Nice to meet you," Stetmann said, managing not to stammer, though the tone of his voice climbed slightly higher as he shook her hand. "I'm very excited. About the lab. I mean, I've done my best to study the zerg with the facilities I have, but—"

She smiled. "Come on. I'm going to show you things that'll knock your socks off."

She didn't quite slip her arm through his, but she didn't have to. Egon followed her with a quick, happy pace that reminded Valerian of a puppy.

Well, Valerian mused, at least one of Jim's crew was going to enjoy the visit. He turned back to the others. Narud was already making introductions; the remaining three, Doctors Nancy Wyndham, Joseph Reynolds, and Adrian Scott, were shaking hands with the Raiders.

"The doctors have instructions to take you anywhere you'd like," said Narud, "with the exception of a few off-limits places. Please—enjoy yourselves. I . . . would like to make up for your less-than-friendly initial reception."

Valerian could feel the tensions abating, and was glad of it. So much mistrust—and as one who had grown up surrounded by the miasma of same, he both understood and regretted it. As they walked toward the entrance, Narud looked at Valerian and smiled. "One more thing—would you be willing to authorize some repair units aboard both your vessels?"

It was not as strange an offer for a science station to make as it might seem. Arriving at Prometheus was a risky venture even for the most experienced pilots, and Valerian had made sure that only the best repair equipment and personnel were available if needed.

"Of course," he said. He clicked on his comm. "Matt, this is Valerian. I'd like to send some repair teams aboard the *Hyperion*. Any objections?"

"You kidding?" came Matt's voice. "At this point Swann is scrounging repair tape and chewing gum. Please, send as many people as you want."

"They'll be returning shortly on the transport then. Valerian out."

He turned to Narud. "Now," the doctor said, in a voice of barely contained excitement, "the artifact."

Valerian grinned. "Now the artifact," he agreed.

The xel'naga artifact, the end result of years of searching and study, hovered almost complacently in the bay of the *Bucephalus*. The lab's interior was of a hue that once was called "gunmetal blue," the light soft and easy on the eyes. The artifact was a short black column, three-sided, with an almost magical azure light seeping from the edges where the pieces had been joined together. No one could look at it and be unmoved, not even the most cynical of the Raiders or the most firmly resoced of the marines. And certainly not a scientist who had devoted the last few years of his career to studying the zerg and the xel'naga.

Below the gently moving alien construct was its sarcophagus-like transportation casing. Like the force field currently enveloping the device, the casing was made of a material that, everyone hoped, effectively contained any energies the artifact might passively emit.

Valerian was proud of what he and the Foundation had achieved, and stood by, smiling gently, as Narud stared.

"As I promised, it's yours," said Valerian. "I'm sure you'll learn even more about it when you have the chance to study it yourself."

The door hummed open, and Raynor entered. He stepped inside, folding his strong arms across his broad chest, saying nothing.

Narud ignored him. "So beautiful, for a weapon," he said.

"Weapon?" asked Jim. "So you know that's what it's for?"

"The fact that it reversed the infestation that transformed Kerrigan into the Queen of Blades is obvious proof of that," said Narud, condescension tingeing his voice. Four bolts emerged, whirring, from the top of the casing that had borne the artifact—the weapon—to Char with such astonishing results. The casing top slid apart, then flipped open. The artifact rotated, slowly, gently, so that it was now parallel to the open box, and was just as slowly and gently lowered onto cradling metal arms inside.

"To the xel'naga, who extensively modified both the protoss and the zerg, being able to destroy their DNA would naturally be a weapon," continued Narud, his gaze fastened on the artifact as the casing closed over it. The gentle blue illumination vanished, and the lab suddenly looked grayer, more military. "That terrans found a way to employ it for a positive end result had nothing to do with the designer's intent."

Jim grunted noncommittally. "Well, it's all yours now," he said. "Don't do anything I wouldn't do."

Narud smiled. "I appreciate that you have a great deal of emotion connected with this device," he said. "Please be aware it is in the most respectful of hands. Thank you, Prince Valerian. I'm going to have this transported to the lab on Prometheus, and while I'm there, check up on your enthusiastic young scientist."

"Thank you again for allowing him access," said Valerian.

"He's a good kid," said Jim. "Smart and learns quick."

"Perhaps then there might be a position open on Prometheus for him, if you and he so desire," said Narud. "And please—I'll be having a dinner to welcome you on the station at 2000 hours. Prince Valerian, of course, I hope you, Mr. Raynor, and Sarah Kerrigan will attend."

"Nurse already invited us. I'll see how Sarah feels at the time."

"Thank you. I still feel rather bad about your initial impression. That was entirely my fault, and I hope you'll give me a chance to make a better one."

The door opened again, and two marines in full combat uniform entered. Before Jim could say anything, Valerian said, quickly but casually, "Thank you, gentlemen. There is the artifact. Please escort it safely."

Jim relaxed, subtly, and Valerian sighed inwardly. He couldn't blame Jim for being suspicious, but the constant mistrust was growing rather tiresome. The marines approached, grasped the handles on the box, and departed, carrying the mammoth thing as if it weighed nothing at all.

"See you at dinner, Prince Valerian. Mr. Raynor, I hope I will see you and Sarah as well." He seemed to want to extend a hand, but, perhaps realizing it would be ignored, merely nodded to both of them and followed the marines.

When the doors closed behind him, Jim said, "Why do I dislike the idea of that man with that artifact?"

"Jim," said Valerian, "the Moebius Foundation was responsible for gathering the—"

"*I* was responsible," said Jim. "My crew and I were the ones who stuck our necks out to get those things."

"You were paid well," said Valerian, ignoring the heated tone in Jim's voice. "And in the end the artifact gave you something infinitely more precious than money. Didn't it?"

Raynor's brow furrowed and he said nothing.

"The Moebius Foundation is mine. Not my father's. And I am my own man—not my father's. Emil Narud is a master scientist, and I believe with all my heart that he will be able to help Sarah make it all the way back to being human."

Jim's gaze met his evenly. Valerian didn't look away. After a moment, Jim nodded, and said, "Well, at least we'll get a good meal out of this."

"You're sure you don't want to come?" Jim asked Matt for the second time. "Swann's more than capable of overseeing the repairs."

"Of course he is," said Matt. "But I really have no interest in the station, sir. I'd much rather stay here."

Honestly, so would Raynor. While he was certain that Narud and Valerian would be clad in formal finery, Jim had opted for simple but clean. Even at his best in this life, he'd been either a farm boy or a marshal, and neither required a uniform that had anything fancier than a star for jewelry. He had taken the time to shower, shave, and trim his hair and beard, but that was his only real concession to what was certain to be the formality of the occasion.

He shrugged. "Suit yourself. I'll bring you back a doggie bag."

"You do that. Couldn't convince Kerrigan to go?"

Jim shook his head. "She wasn't having any of it. I'm not sure yet if she'll even submit to more than the basic medical care. And I'm not sure I want her to. I hope to learn more this evening that'll make things clearer one way or the other. Heard anything back from Egon?"

"Nope," said Horner. "I thought maybe you had."

"Probably still drooling like a kid in a candy store at one of the labs," said Jim. "Narud threatened to hire him away. I'm sure he'll be at the dinner. Maybe I can offer him a raise to stay with us."

Matt smiled a little. "Twice nothing is still noth—"

"Shut up or I'll punch that wounded arm of yours. See you in a couple hours."

★  ★  ★

Jim went first to Prometheus's sick bay, determined to try one more time to get Sarah to attend the dinner. If nothing else, he was sure the quality of the food would be good for her. The nurse who had been tending to her looked rather put out. As Jim entered, she preempted him by saying, "I told her she and I were a similar size. I had a lovely dress she could have borrowed."

"I don't wear dresses," Kerrigan said shortly. Jim thought back to the green sundress, but said nothing. She might have worn a dress once, but that meant nothing now. She gave him a quick and challenging look. "Come to twist my arm?"

"Wouldn't dream of it," he said. "Come to see if you had changed your mind."

"No way."

"I told Matt I'd bring him back a doggie bag. You want one too?"

That actually got a smile out of her. "I'm fine, Jim," she said. Jim hesitated, then leaned over and kissed her gently on the lips. She froze at first, then returned the kiss softly. As he pulled back, he whispered, "I'll be back as soon as I can—and I'll tell you everything I've learned about Narud."

She was smiling when he left.


The door to what was modestly called the all-purpose room irised open, and Jim immediately felt even more like a fish out of water than he had on the *Bucephalus*.

The light was soft but not dim, and the music was soothing. It was similar to the same inoffensive but uninspiring music he had heard throughout the station. A young woman approached him, smiling, and offered a tray of fine glassware filled with sparkling wine. Jim accepted a glass and took a sip. It was no doubt high quality and wretchedly expensive, but all it did was make him wish that he was in the cantina, drinking a beer and listening to his beloved jukebox.

Valerian was, as Jim had anticipated, dressed to the nines. He had eschewed his military attire for something comparatively simple, a black jacket with matching trousers, polished boots, and a dark blue ruffled shirt. A gold pin in the shape of a wolf's head adorned the black silk cravat. His hair still had the one unruly golden lock. Jim hoped he never would be able to tame it. Valerian would be too picture-perfect otherwise.

"I am sorry Miss Kerrigan opted not to attend," he said, "but am very glad you did, Jim."

"Thanks." He wasn't trying to be rude, really. He just felt out of place and wanted this to be over with.

Narud approached, clad similarly to Valerian but not quite as elegantly. The only thing that stood out was a rather peculiar piece of jewelry that looked, like the station, to be of xel'naga design.

Of course, Valerian spotted it at once. "Is that a piece of a xel'naga artifact, Doctor? It looks like one."

"Heavens no," said Narud. "Just a little tribute I had designed hoping to honor Miss Kerrigan."

"I want one. I'm sure I can make it all the rage."

Narud chuckled. "I'm sure you could. It's just a piece of costume jewelry, Your Highness, but if you wish, I'll see if I can have another one made." He turned to Jim. "Welcome, Mr. Raynor. It's good to see you, but I'm sorry you came alone. I so wanted Miss Kerrigan to be here."

"Well, people in Hell want ice water," said Jim. He knew his smile was a smirk. He didn't care.

Narud didn't miss a beat. "And I don't see your Captain Horner either," he added, looking around.

"I don't see Egon," said Jim. "Where is he?"

"He apparently was so enraptured with his tour of the labs— and, quite possibly, with Dr. de Vries—that he has opted to spend more time observing."

*Instead of attending an intimate dinner where he could pepper a captive Narud with questions?* "I'll see if I can't talk him into coming," he said, reaching into his pocket and fishing out his comm. He was watching for any sign of a negative reaction from Narud, but the man merely smiled pleasantly.

"Go right ahead," he said. "Perhaps you can succeed where I have failed."

"Egon Stetmann," came Egon's voice.

"You're missing out on free food, Egon, and a chance to bend Narud's ear till it breaks."

"Oh, I know that, sir. But I'm having such a great time here! You don't . . . I mean I don't have to leave . . . do I?"

The voice was plaintive. Reassured that Egon, whatever he was up to, was unharmed and obviously happy, Jim said, "Nah. Your loss though."

"Oh, I hardly think that, sir. Anything else?"

"Not that I can think of. I ain't gonna lose you to these brainy boys, though, am I?"

"Not at all. Though I'm sure I'll have a lot to share with you when I come back!"

Jim clicked off the comm and pocketed it. "You were right," he told Narud. "Just so long as I get my chief scientist back at the end of the day."

"Oh, I don't know," said Narud, attempting levity. "A bright young fellow like that? We may have to kidnap him. Until that time, though," and he indicated a well-dressed young man approaching with a tray of something small and delicate and pastry-like that smelled savory and delicious, "please enjoy yourselves."

As it turned out, Egon wouldn't have missed that much, at least not at the beginning. Narud was much more interested in listening than in talking for the first part of the meal. He pressed them for the details of where they had located the pieces of what would become the "weapon" and when Raynor had first begun to be curious as to what the purpose was. How the weapon had worked, and in what condition they had found Kerrigan.

Jim managed to put away a sizable amount of the appetizers, the shellfish soup, and more of the wine despite being peppered with questions. But as the main course was served—a generous and mouthwatering portion of what looked and smelled like a prime cut of skalet steak—he said, "You know, I can't help but feel like instead of sitting in a comfy chair eating good food, I should be having a light shone on me and needles shoved under my fingernails. Care to lighten up on the inquisition, Doc?"

Narud had the grace to look embarrassed. "Please forgive me," he said. "I'm just so eager."

"I completely understand," said Valerian. "Jim is an intelligent man, but he doesn't share our passion for science, I'm afraid."

"I do when science gets me what I want," Jim said, cutting into the steak and putting a forkful in his mouth. *Sweet mother of mercy, it was delicious.* The phrase had belonged to Tychus; the big man would have been on his third helping by now. If only things had been different.

"But Mr. Raynor is right," said Valerian. "Please—surely you've had time to analyze the data we've given you on Sarah Kerrigan and run a few tests on her of your own." Before Jim could react, he added, "You were present when they drew blood and tissue samples, Jim. They've done nothing else to her."

*Yet,* thought Jim, but his mouth was still full of skalet, so he stayed silent. Narud turned to him, his expression one of professional concern.

"Let me share with you what we do know, Mr. Raynor," Narud began. "These tests that Valerian mentioned are extremely preliminary, and once we've convinced you and Miss Kerrigan to permit others, we'll know more. There is still a great deal of zerg mutagen in her system. I'm sure you were aware of that when you saw her . . . hair, for want of a better term."

Jim had swallowed the bite of steak and now gritted his teeth.

"The hair is a visible sign, but there are many other parts of her that also must be infected. It could be her brain, her abilities, her kidneys, or liver—anything and everything could be touched in some way."

"I thought the artifact would take care of that," said Jim.

"Mr. Raynor, surely you can appreciate how—well, how *alien* this alien artifact is," said Narud earnestly. "We've only even been aware of the existence of the zerg, the protoss, and the xel'naga for a few years."

"Valerian said you were the expert," said Jim.

"He is," said Valerian, "but even an expert can't know everything, not yet."

Narud rubbed his temples and sighed. "Sarah Kerrigan needs to be thoroughly examined for the good of humanity and for her own well-being," he said. "You're tying my hands and preventing me from achieving either of those goals. We don't know what that mutagen is doing to her. Let me speak bluntly. Every minute we waste arguing about it could be another minute closer to losing her—or loosing her upon humanity."

Suddenly the delicious food tasted like rations. Jim had a sinking feeling that Narud was right. He couldn't deny the evidence of those Medusa-like tendrils in place of Sarah's soft, flowing red hair. And if that was the mutation they could see—

But what about what Sarah had said? About how Narud felt familiar to her? Was it just her spotty memory or was something else going on? Jim did care about humanity, but he knew in his heart he cared about Sarah just a little bit more. He wanted what was best for her.

But right now, he realized sickly that he had no idea just what that was.

# CHAPTER TWENTY

Sarah lay in the sick bay bed. Jim had arranged for her to eat the same meal they were eating, and she had to admit, it smelled good. Really good. On a more practical note, she knew she had to build up her strength. Sometime, from some place, a fight was coming, and she had to be ready.

So she made her nurse smile as she tucked into the skalet steak and mashed tubers with some kind of berry sauce. While she ate, she thought about the situation.

Clearly there was some zerg mutagen still left in her DNA. Anyone with eyes could figure that one out. And she couldn't help but wonder if that was only the tip of the iceberg. If she and everyone else could see this, what else was going on inside her body—hell, maybe inside her mind—that they *couldn't* see?

So yes, on one level, she agreed with them. She did need to know exactly what had happened to her—and what the artifact had and hadn't done. At the same time, it seemed to her that her very cells were screaming a warning about Emil Narud. She knew him. She . . . Sarah shook her head, forcing herself to take another bite. It was as if she had known him—and forgotten him—but still, on some level she couldn't quite access, she remembered him. And the memories, if indeed that was what they were, were far from pleasant.

Sarah Kerrigan had a wealth of unpleasant memories. Her mother, her father, a small, sick kitten . . . being the queen of the zerg . . .

. . . the hydralisk—Kerrigan's hydralisk—had gone for the mother first. Using its scythe-like arm to almost casually slice the woman's skull into two neat pieces. As brain and bone and blood spattered, the little girl screamed even louder, the sound piercing and lost.

*"Mama! Your head! Your head!"*

*"Her head came apart. . . . Her head came apart. . . ."*

And then it felt like a shadow fell over her soul.

She choked on the meat and spat it out, gasping for breath, skin covered with gooseflesh.

Something was wrong. Something was very wrong.

Her stomach clenched with apprehension as adrenaline poured into her system. For a terrible second, she felt like she would vomit up the fare, but by sheer will she kept it down.

She could almost taste the—malice, she supposed it was—the glee. And it was personal, personal in a way the attack on Jim, Horner, and Valerian hadn't been.

Her head whipped up and she stared at the door.

They were coming.

Egon Stetmann wondered when he would outlive his usefulness.

He hadn't expected a thing. Which, of course, he should have. But he had walked into the spider's parlor under the blithe assumption that the fraternity of science had its own code of honor, and that assumption was why he was now bound and stashed underneath a desk in a supply closet like an extra box of test tubes.

He'd been too eager, of course. He was always too eager. He'd been so agog at the vast discoveries that surely lay beyond the door to the laboratory that when his drop-dead—*oh, hah, there's a term for you, Egon*—gorgeous escort—*oh, and there's another one; it's just pure comedy gold here on Space Station Prometheus*—had shoved a slugthrower in his side and directed him to speak into a recording device, he hadn't even been frightened. Just confused. Well, at first anyway.

"Why are you sticking that thing in my side?" he'd asked, utterly baffled.

De Vries had rolled her eyes. "It's called a threat, idiot," she'd said. And, of course, the word that had immediately registered wasn't *threat* but *idiot*, and, of course, like an idiot, he'd said, "Hey, now, I was on the fast track on the Tyrador III research fa—"

At which point he had nearly thrown up, because she had slammed the business end of the weapon into his stomach, hard, and said, "Shut up and say something."

At this point, he had recovered his wits sufficiently that he didn't point out what an oxymoron those two phrases were but merely said, "Okay. What do you want to know?"

"I don't want to know anything. Just talk."

"Uh . . . okay . . . this is Egon, and I'm . . . talking. . . ." he'd said, his voice creeping higher as he had started to fully realize the direness of his situation. "I'm not sure what I'm talking about, but this is me, and . . . these are words, and—"

"That's enough."

"Enough for what?" He couldn't help himself; the words had left his mouth before he could censor them.

She smiled. Stetmann wondered what it said about him that even though he was scared stiff—*oh, hey, you got 'em rolling in the aisles, Egon old pal*—he still found her attractive. "I needed a sample of your voice. I'll feed it into the adjutant's data files, and if anyone attempts to contact you on this"—she had reached inside his coat pocket for his comm—"I'll be able to convince them you're safe and sound."

"That's—smart," he'd said, defeated.

"I have three degrees," she'd said.

"So, uh . . . now what?" He'd stood up straight and tried to look brave. "Are you going to execute me?"

She had laughed, a very unladylike snort that was somehow the epitome of insult. "Narud wants you alive. Probably to pick your brain of what little helpful information you might have."

"Oh." Well, that was good, at least.

"Count your blessings, Dr. Stetmann. You're better off than Sarah will be," de Vries had said, and that was all he knew. He awoke God knew how much later to exquisite pain in his head. He tried to move and suddenly vomited, quite violently, and winced, feeling that he had just added insult to injury.

*Think.* He had to think. It was what he was good at. The room was dim, but light came in through cracks around the door. That it wasn't one of the oh-so-spiffy irising doors that he'd seen thus far was heartening. It meant that this wasn't a particularly important room, and that he might actually be able to break out of it. Well, yeah, except for the tied-hands-and-feet thing, which he was just now discovering.

His eyes had been closed long enough so that the dim light was sufficient for him to see. He was under a desk, with boxes at his head and feet. Steeling himself against the pain, Egon did his best to scoot out into the middle of the room. Gracelessly, lurching spasmodically with his hands tied behind his back and his ankles bound, he managed it. Once, he sneezed violently at the dust and froze, convinced that someone was going to come and finish the job de Vries had started, Narud be damned. The minutes ticked by and finally his heart slowed down. Another good sign—no one was posted outside guarding him.

He was in the middle of the small room now, lying on one side. He'd even managed to avoid soaking himself in the puddle of his own vomit. Egon looked around as best he could from his position and confirmed his guess that he was in a supply closet.

*What sort of things were in a science base's supply closet? Needles . . . tubes . . . containers of all varieties . . . No knives or—*

No knives. But broken glass was pretty sharp. And tubes and containers were still usually made of glass. It was still the most reliable material for the delicate work that went on in a lab. It was cheap and almost completely nonreactive. With an effort, looking no doubt like a flopping fish, he sat up. The desk beneath which he had been thrust was piled high with boxes. On the opposite side of the small room was a shelf with more small boxes. The light was insufficient for him to read from this distance. He'd have to stand, somehow.

Egon currently sat with his long legs stretched out before him. Now he bent them back to his side and wrenched himself into a kneeling position, "walking" over to the shelves. The boxes were labeled with their contents, but he found nothing useful on the first or second shelf. He craned his neck and sighed. He had two choices—try to get to his feet from his current position or try to maneuver his bound wrists so that they were in front of him, not clasped at his back.

His legs were really, really long.

Egon sank back, momentarily daunted by the effort it would take. He wasn't limber or fit. He was just a scientist.

*For a smart guy,* he told himself, *you sure were pretty stupid. You walked into that trap with a KICK ME sign on your back. You failed as a smart guy. Now you have to be a tough guy. Like Jim.*

Raynor would no doubt have already been out of the bonds

and have blasted his way through the station. Nobody knew where Egon was. Probably no one even knew that he was in trouble. Something that de Vries had said came back to him now: *"Count your blessings, Dr. Stetmann. You're better off than Sarah will be."*

What did she mean by—

Oh no. They were going to take Kerrigan. Experiment on her. Maybe kill her. Maybe kill Raynor too. And as far as Egon knew, right now he was the only one who was aware of it.

He whimpered, just a little, just once. And then Egon Stetmann grimly sat back down on the cold floor and began slowly, painfully working his tightly bound hands down his body and trying to pull his gangly legs through a very, very small gap.

Matt Horner despised rations just as much as the next person with taste buds did, but he despised sitting in awkward, formal situations with people he didn't trust even more. He amended that almost immediately. Of course he trusted *Jim*, and he was beginning to seriously consider Valerian as someone worthy of cautious trust as well.

But he didn't like Narud, and he would have given a lot of credits to not be there at the dinner tonight. Fortunately, he'd been able to decline without paying anyone.

The repair team was, according to Swann, "getting right down to brass tacks," whatever that meant. Horner assumed it meant they were doing a fine job, going by the pleased tone of the chief engineer's voice. "And our own Miss Annabelle has an idea she's cooking up. If it works, we'll tell you about it. If it doesn't, I never mentioned it."

"Uh . . . okay," Matt had said.

He figured he could relax for a couple of hours. The ship was safe, for the moment, as were Jim and Valerian and Sarah. As an extra bonus, even Rory wasn't grumbling. He sat back in his chair, adjusting his arm carefully, took a deep breath, released it, and closed his eyes. His arm hurt.

"Captain Horner?"

His eyes snapped open. "What is it, Marcus?"

"I'm getting readings that—well, I don't know what Narud's boys are doing in engineering, but I'm guessing they might have messed things up."

"What are you seeing?" Matt was on his feet and peering over Cade's shoulder before he had even asked the question, intent on seeing for himself.

"Well, this is apparently what's on the outer rim of the asteroid field," Marcus said.

There were blips on the screen. Lots of them.

"It—it can't be ships," said Horner, a sinking feeling growing in the pit of his stomach.

"Well, sir, that's what it looks like, which is why I wondered if—"

"Horner to Swann," Matt said, interrupting Marcus. "Narud's boys doing anything other than making repairs? Anything that might be interfering with the sensors?"

"I don't think so, but I'll poke around a bit. I'll get back to you."

"You do that."

Matt began to pace, thinking hard, his eyes darting back to the screen. It didn't look like a malfunction. The little blips didn't move in any uniform pattern. Some stayed where they were, others moved slightly, and then they were joined by still more blips—

He made a decision. If it was an error, he'd apologize. Hell, he'd host a dinner on the *Hyperion* to make up for insulting Narud's people. But he couldn't take the chance.

"Horner to Swann."

"Hell, kid, give me a moment to—"

"Stop the repairs. Now. Just do it."

★  ★  ★

Annabelle, despite being engrossed in her new project, had overheard the initial conversation. She'd developed a sudden, keen interest in ship navigation over the last few days, due to her sudden, keen interest in Travis Rawlins. There was a way that they could check to see if it was a ship malfunction or an actual threat—and that way made her smile, just a little.

She clicked her comm on the proper channel, attempting to raise Travis on the *Bucephalus*. Normally he answered immediately, because she wasn't stupid enough to contact him in the middle of anything resembling an emergency. This time, though, he didn't pick up.

He could be busy. He could have left the comm in his quarters. He could be bored with her and ignoring her. But Annabelle suddenly knew that something was wrong. Horner's voice penetrated her thoughts.

"Stop the repairs. Now. Just do it." Matt's voice was deep and intense.

"Fer the love of—all right, all right." Swann punched the button and turned to one of Narud's people. "You heard the captain. You're to stand down, all of you. I don't know what kind of bug he's got up his ass, but he's the captain."

"This is outrageous," protested one of them. "We came here in good faith to lend you a hand. You think we're responsible for phantom images on . . ."

Annabelle tuned him out. Following a hunch, she kept the schematics of the *Fanfare* up on her display while quickly tapping in a command to access the current level of the energy cells. She hoped she was wrong, both about this and about not being able to contact Travis on the *Bucephalus,* and at first the signal looked completely normal. She was about to breathe a sigh of relief when—

The measurements, represented by orange bars, should be fluctuating slightly. Instead they were completely static.

Which meant that she was looking at a fake image.

Rory was still yelling at the engineer from Prometheus, who was yelling back. Her heart racing, Annabelle quietly contacted Horner herself.

"Engineering to bridge," she said, keeping her voice low. She glanced over at the two arguing engineers. It didn't look like either of them had noticed.

"Annabelle? Where's Rory?"

"Arguing with one of the engineers from the base," she said. "Matt—there's nothing wrong with your sensors. Someone is draining the energy from the power cells. And—and I think they're also blocking contact with the other ships. I can't contact Travis."

Matt believed her at once. For one thing, he could hear the yelling in the background, and for another, Annabelle was as steady and levelheaded a crewman as he could hope to have. If the "engineers" sent to "help" were blocking her from contacting Travis on the *Bucephalus*— "Contact Raynor at once," he ordered.

Static. The communications officer turned to him helplessly. He didn't need to say a word.

"Marcus, what's the status on those ships outside the belt?"

"They're— Sir," Marcus said, turning to his captain, "they're entering the Kirkegaard Belt."

"How many?"

"*All* of them."

# CHAPTER
# TWENTY-ONE

The meal had progressed to dessert, but the conversation had not progressed at all. Narud was still pushing his point, Jim was still digging his heels in, and Valerian was still trying to mediate. The dessert was very good—a berry cobbler of some sort that smelled as good as heaven and tasted as sweet as sin.

"Oh, and Valerian," said Narud, "I've had some port brought in for you specially. You do prefer tawny ports to ruby, do you not?" The servers brought an old, dusty bottle and three small glasses.

"Indeed I do. How thoughtful of you to remember." As the drinks were poured, Valerian said to Jim, "My father and I have similarities as well as differences. We both enjoy a fine port. He prefers the ruby ports, I the tawny."

Jim accepted the drink readily. He figured if this dinner was some sort of elaborate way to poison him, it'd have been done earlier in the meal. And he was never one to turn down a good drink—or, usually, even a poor one.

He took a sip. It was almost as good as the dessert. "Huh. Cherries and caramel, kinda."

Valerian raised a blond brow approvingly. "You have a discerning palate, Mr. Raynor."

"Odd, since I'm used to drinking the cheap stuff," said Jim, feeling no sense of shame at the statement. He was rarely ashamed of the truth. He took another sip. He could get used to this.

"I'm glad you're enjoying it, Prince Valerian," said Narud. He nodded to the server. "Please—clear the table and bring in the ruby port."

"But the man said it was his father who. . . ."

And then Jim knew, a fraction of a heartbeat before the doors irised open and three armed, but unarmored, guards appeared. Valerian gazed at them in utter confusion. Even as his senses sharpened and his mind went into high gear on how to get out, Jim felt a strange pang of sympathy for the kid.

"You son of a bitch," said Raynor to Narud.

"Emil—what—?" Valerian couldn't even seem to form a complete sentence, he merely turned to stare at his "friend" with an open mouth and shocked, wide gray eyes.

"Mr. Raynor has figured it out," said Narud. He smiled thinly. "I regret to inform you, Your Excellency, that your father will be here in a few moments. With," he added, "what's left of the entire fleet at his back."

Valerian still looked completely stunned. He looked over at Jim, his eyes wide. Jim looked back at him steadily.

*You ain't a telepath like Sarah,* Jim thought, *but you're no fool either. You've been around me and Matt long enough. Read my eyes. Figure it out, Valerian. You be ready, damn you. Or we're both dead.*

Jim gave a shrug and reached for the bottle of port. "Well, since this is likely the last nice thing I'm going to have, might as well have another—"

He leaped to his feet and threw the port at the first guard, who ducked, but not fast enough. The bottle grazed the man's temple.

Valerian jumped up the second Jim sprang up to throw, charging at the guard nearest him with two of the very fine, very sharp steak knives. The guard, who had been completely fooled by Valerian's feigned helplessness, raised his gun a half second too late. He dropped, gurgling, as blood gushed from his mouth. Two knives were embedded hilt deep in his throat. Valerian seized the dropped weapon and turned to fire on the third guard. He riddled the guard's body with steel-tipped spikes.

*Good boy,* Jim thought, grabbing a chair to follow the path of the bottle. This man, though, had been expecting the attack. He dove out of the way, rolling and coming up firing.

"You fools!" snarled Narud. "You think you'll escape? Prometheus is my station, and it's crawling with my people and Mengsk's!"

Jim dove under the table. He gritted his teeth, braced his feet firmly, and visualized Tychus Findlay lifting the jukebox so long ago as he straightened his legs and heaved the table upright. It was massive, but not so large that it didn't turn over. Narud, who had still been sitting, sprang up and stumbled backward.

Jim leaped for him—

And landed hard on the floor on nothing.

Narud had vanished.

"What the—" Laughter greeted him, smug and satisfied, from over by the door.

For an instant, Jim couldn't comprehend what was going on. Then he remembered the xel'naga-inspired "pin" Narud was wearing.

*"Is that a piece of a xel'naga artifact, Doctor? It looks like one."*

*"Heavens no. Just a little tribute I had designed, hoping to honor Miss Kerrigan."*

Sarah Kerrigan—ghost. The goddamn pin was a Moebius reactor.

"Valerian! He's got a cloaking suit—by the door!"

"A bit busy at the moment," grunted Valerian. Jim looked up to see that more guards were streaming into the room. He scrambled for the weapons from the dead guards and motioned to Valerian to join him behind the table. It wasn't much protection, but it was a little better than simply standing up and presenting one's chest as a target.

"How many?" asked Jim.

"I counted six," Valerian said. His body was taut, focused, and each move was exactly what was needed, no more. Jim spared a nanosecond to be impressed.

"We can pick them off as they come in the door," said Jim. "We gotta get out of here."

"Fine suggestion. Care to elaborate?"

Two more guards stuck their heads into the door. Jim and Valerian each took one, and the guards fell with their heads impaled.

"Don't know yet. We gotta get Sarah and Egon too."

"She's dead already," whispered a silky voice at his ear. Jim whirled and started firing, but Narud had already slipped away again. Raynor willed his heart to slow, willed the red curtain of anger that clouded his judgment to evaporate. He'd seen Sarah in action. He knew what to look for—a slight shimmering, caught at the edge of one's vision. Easy to shrug off as a trick of the light or one's imagination—if one didn't know better.

Jim knew better. "Keep firing," he said to Valerian. "Hold the door. I'm going for Narud."

He let his gaze go soft, inviting the blur out of the corner of his eye to appear again. His body raged with impatience, but he forced a cool head and steady breathing. He allowed the sound of weapons fire, so urgent and demanding of attention, to fade into background noise. Only calmness would gain him the desired result—and oh, he badly desired to destroy Narud, he who would dare harm Sarah Kerrigan.

And there it was. A slight distortion of space, a little blurring of the gentle sky-blue color of the wall. He whirled to his left and started firing, but again, nothing happened.

Even so, he smiled. "Didn't get him," Jim said to Valerian. "But I got the next best thing. A way for us to get the hell out of this room."

Matt knew exactly what had to happen and when and how if the *Hyperion* had even a slim chance of making it out of this alive. "Annabelle, listen carefully. I'm sending in backup. Don't say anything to anyone. I'm betting those guys are armed to the teeth. Let Rory keep arguing. Can you quietly get some help and start trying to undo whatever it is they've done to the power cells?"

"I—sure. I'm on it." He could hear her falter, just for an instant, then recover. Like a Raider should.

"You were right about the *Bucephalus*. We're cut off from it and the station. If your navigator friend is as sharp as you say he is, he'll notice the ships too."

"Oh yeah, I'm sure he will." She wasn't. Neither was Matt.

He contacted security and had several very irate crew members armor up and head for engineering. He sent out another call to the *Bucephalus,* which went unanswered.

"Marcus, you monitor the *Bucephalus*. Let me know if it starts prepping for battle."

"Sir," said Marcus, "do you think that the *Bucephalus* might be in on this?"

"It's possible," said Matt. "If Valerian's a traitor."

"But—you don't think he is?"

"Let me put it to you this way," Matt said. "The only one I trust is Jim right now. But that doesn't mean I'm going to attack the *Bucephalus* if they're in the same situation as we are. You kill your enemies, not your allies." *You just have to know which is which,* he added silently. He was taking an awful risk not turning on the *Bucephalus* and blasting it while its shields were down; that was the safe course of action. But he knew in his heart that it wasn't the right one.

Not yet, anyway.

"Sir, they're putting their shields up and prepping for battle," said Marcus. "But we've not been targeted."

Matt nodded. "Estimated time of that . . . armada's arrival?"

"Approximately seventeen seconds."

"How the hell did it move so fast?" he wondered aloud. "Of course they know the route, but it took us hours."

"They've been blasting some of the smaller asteroids and towing the pieces away," said Marcus quietly. "They've even pulverized some of them."

"Oh," replied Matt. "That . . . would do it." Hell with following the route. The ships had simply made their own shortcuts.

Eight seconds.

Three.

Two.

One.

Sarah had called for the nurse. No one had answered. She was completely alone in Prometheus's sick bay, having been too wrapped up in her own thoughts of guilt and worry to have noticed the nurses had all quietly departed.

Alone.

And they were coming for her.

She disengaged herself from the drips and dressed in the jumpsuit she had asked to have brought to her awhile ago, determined that she wasn't going to die in a hospital gown. She was sorry she had eaten. The delicious meal sat heavy and churning in her belly. It would slow her down when—

When what?

She was so abysmally far from the top of her game it was laughable. Suddenly she remembered standing alone, out of ammo, knowing she had been abandoned. Knowing they were coming—not just dozens, but hundreds, perhaps thousands of zerg, descending upon her. Once, Mengsk had saved her. But that day, he had left her to die.

Something had stilled and slowed inside her. Bitter anguish had turned to dull, sad acceptance. Fighting was futile. She couldn't win, not against so many zerg.

She couldn't win now. They were coming, and they would take her, and that was all there was to say. Maybe they wouldn't torture her. Maybe—

And then it was there, sharp and clear and brutal, like harsh sunlight glinting on a knife blade. She recognized it for what it was at once, and the very familiarity of it suddenly galvanized her.

Alpha waves. They were sending a cloaked ghost. Set a thief to catch a thief.

*No!*

The door opened, and without even thinking, her body and mind snapping into action, she lifted her hand, focused her psionic energy, and blasted the invisible foe into a wall. There was a crunch and a shimmer as the corpse, now visible, slid down the white surface. He had not come alone, of course. Four guards rushed in, but before they could fire, she froze their motion and, snarling, turned their brains to soup. They dropped, dead in an instant, fluid leaking out of eyes, ears, noses, and mouths.

For the briefest of instants, Sarah realized that not only had her abilities returned but they also had come back stronger than before. She had always been good—no, the best—at what she did. Killing. But now she had suddenly become a demigod. For a second, the revelation troubled her, and then her thoughts went elsewhere.

*Jim!*

He was in immediate and deadly danger.

They all were—

The base rocked, as if it was little more than a child's plaything and the child had grown irritated with it. What the hell could possibly do that to a space station inside an asteroid? Had someone rigged the place to explode?

And then suddenly she knew, and her body went rigid with hatred. The base was under attack.

"Oh, no you don't, you son of a bitch," she growled, feeling rage swell up inside her, fill her face with blood, shoot adrenaline through her veins. "Not this time. Not *ever again.*"


Egon was rather proud of himself. He'd managed to stay calm, locate a box of test beakers, break one, and was now using the sharp fragment to saw at his wrist bonds.

Suddenly the floor beneath him shuddered. Boxes trembled on their shelves for an instant before tumbling down on him. Egon lifted his still partially bound hands to ward off the boxes and yelped as the sharp piece of glass dug into his palm. Then it was over.

"Jeez," he breathed, repeating the word over and over again. Just as he'd calmed down a little bit, the sharp, angry wail of an alert klaxon sounded. Then a calm, recorded voice began to announce, "Attention. Space Station Prometheus is under attack. Await further instructions. Attention . . ."

He groped with a bloody hand for the piece of glass and continued working on the bonds. Finally they snapped, and he turned to his feet. The shard, slicked with fluid, was slippery, but he managed to free himself. Well, at least from the bonds. He still didn't know if the door would open.

He rose clumsily, his feet numb from the tightness of the bonds, grasped the door handle, and hoped hard.

It didn't turn.

Despair, temporarily kept at bay, washed through him. He was still trapped. Trapped on a science station, locked in a small supply closet, and no one knew where he was. If Jim and Valerian were still here, they were prisoners too. He and they would be turned over to Mengsk, who had to be the one behind this attack, and they'd be experimented on or tortured or killed.

That is, if anyone ever actually *found* him. More likely he'd die here, alone, slowly, of dehydration, or else be blown to smithereens.

The door handle turned.

He froze for an instant, then looked for a place to hide. There were boxes all over the place, but nothing large enough to hide his gangly frame. Grimly Egon decided he would not go down without a fight this time. He grabbed one of the smaller boxes, wincing at the pain in his cut hand, and lifted it over his head.

The door slammed open. Egon had only the briefest glimpse of a silhouette against the light of the corridor when the box flew from his fingers.

A hand reached forward, grabbed his coat lapel, and pulled him into the light.

He stared at a face that was beautiful in its fury, crowned by hair that was not hair but looked like draped serpents.

"Stay close behind me," said Sarah Kerrigan, her voice low and intense and as frightening as the expression on her face. "I'm only rescuing you once."

# CHAPTER
# TWENTY-TWO

The "engineers" sent to "repair" the *Hyperion* and, presumably, the *Bucephalus,* had inadvertently done some good. Needing to maintain their cover while they sabotaged the power cells, they had actually made some repairs. It was the only reason that the *Hyperion* was able to withstand the attack from three battleships and the Wraiths they bore.

Engineering was hard at work undoing the damage and restoring communication between the two ships and Space Station Prometheus. There didn't seem to be any problem receiving communications from the *White Star,* though.

"This is Emperor Arcturus Mengsk," the loathed and familiar voice had said as soon as the fleet appeared out of the asteroid field. "Surrender and you will escape destruction."

"Mengsk," Matt had said, not even bothering to pretend respect by using a title, "this is Captain Matthew H—"

"Oh, I know your voice by now, Matt," said Mengsk. "I know where your boss is . . . and where his little girlfriend is too. There are people aboard your vessel and the *Bucephalus* who have done work for me, and I'd prefer not to blast them into pieces. Or you, for that matter. You are outgunned and barely limping along. So surrender and save us all a great deal of time and trouble."

"Gosh, that sounds just fine, but somehow I don't think my boss would want me to do that," Matt said, and nodded to tactical. With no further warning, they unleashed the full power of the Yamato cannon on the *White Star*.

And since that volley, things hadn't slowed. Not Mengsk's angry threats, nor the retaliatory attack, nor the onslaught on the station. That seemed to be the main target, and Matt thought sickly, why wouldn't it be? Both Kerrigan and Raynor were on the station.

He was certain it was Valerian who had tipped off his father. Matt hadn't really wanted to believe it; Valerian had come perilously close to winning his trust. But the *Bucephalus* was just sitting there, not moving to attack either side, and Matt Horner thought viciously of Vaughn and his unwillingness to act. He wasn't surprised that the worm didn't have the guts to even join Mengsk in the attack.


"I said *offline,* sir," said Elias Thompson, the chief engineer of the *Bucephalus*. He sounded both irritated and frightened, a combination his captain completely understood. "When I say offline, I mean we can't fire!"

"They're going to blast that space station and our prince with it back to the twenty-first century if we don't help the *Hyperion!*" snapped Vaughn. His plan had been to join the *Hyperion* in the attack against Mengsk—who clearly had no intention of reconciling with his son, if he was so hell-bent on attacking Space Station Prometheus with such vigor—the instant it had started. Vaughn intended to send in his fighters and cover them, so at least the poor devils—there were so few vessels left—had some kind of backup from the *Bucephalus.*

The problem was that the engineers and weapons experts sent to help them had been intent on doing exactly the opposite. No matter how frantically the engineering team worked, people were dying. And he knew what Matt Horner must be thinking.

Vaughn rubbed his eyes with a trembling hand. "Send in the fighters," he said.

"Sir," said Travis, "with all respect, without any cover from us—"

"I know. But we've got to do something. Thompson, how much longer?"

"Till what? Till we can fight, or we can move, or we can contact Valerian?"

"Any or all."

"I've got no idea, sir. We're doing the best that we can."

*As are we all,* thought Vaughn. He opened the comm so he would be heard throughout the ship. "This is Captain Vaughn. All personnel with experience in flying any smaller craft are to report to the docking bay at once. We don't have much to throw at Mengsk, but we're going to give it all we've got. The *Bucephalus,* if it must go down, is going to go down fighting."


Cooper knew he had to get out of here. Now.

It wasn't supposed to happen this way. The men from Space Station Prometheus were supposed to have completely screwed over engineering and then taken hostages. Then they would have escaped to join Mengsk and brought the amiable, grinning, friendly bartender that everyone underestimated with them.

But that bastard Horner had been too sharp. Somehow, and Cooper didn't know how, he had been tipped off that something was wrong down in engineering. Cooper's contact had been mysteriously silenced in the midst of a sentence. Now Mengsk had finally arrived and was attacking both the station and the *Hyperion.*

No one was about to come into the cantina now, not in the middle of an attack, so Cooper simply grabbed his bag and left. His mind was racing. His only contact had been with the men sent to sabotage the ship. He had spoken with Arcturus Mengsk several hours earlier, as well as with Narud, but now he couldn't seem to raise either of them. Uttering a blistering oath, Cooper flung the comm away as he raced down the corridors.

His only thought was that at some point they'd be sending out ships to do one-on-one fighting. They'd be surprised to see him, but he knew how to handle a Wraith, and he figured he could pull the ol' "I need to help any way I can!" routine, and they'd let him in. After a very short time they'd have to, because all the more experienced pilots would be just so many pieces of flesh floating in space.

It was a desperate attempt, and didn't stand a good chance of success. Unless he was extremely careful, the very people he was working for would destroy him, and if he was too obvious, then the Raiders would make short work of him. He had to look convincing but not threatening. Sweat broke out under his arms, and he swallowed hard.

*This is not supposed to be happening,* he thought for the hundredth time. *Not supposed to be happening.*


"Sir," said Marcus, "I detect several small ships launching from the *Bucephalus.*"

Matt frowned and leaned forward. *What the . . .* "Why aren't they fi—" And then he knew. "Dammit. Get some cover on those fighters! Now!"

"At once, sir," said Marcus.

"And Swann—I've got to have communications restored!"

"'Sabotaged' generally means things have been messed up," retorted Swann. "Doing the best I can!"

Matt's thoughts were racing but calm. Jim was on that station, which meant that he, Matt, had to figure out a way to keep everyone alive long enough to bring the commander home. He now had an obligation to the *Bucephalus* as well. She hadn't run when she could have, and was choosing to send people into the fray when she had no way to properly protect them. That spoke volumes to Horner, and he wasn't about to let those people die needlessly if he could help it.

The station was still being slammed with attacks. Horner had to distract Mengsk, had to get that attention focused back on the *Hyperion*—while somehow still protecting his own ship and those pilots sent on a suicide mission. If only there was some way to—

"Swann!"

"Oh, for cryin' out loud, what now?"

"The tampering—we can't warp, right?"

"Not yet. I got the whole team working on it along with me."

"You and two of your best move off that task. Here's what I want from you instead."


Narud was very clever. Jim would give him that. Jim would probably even agree with Valerian's earlier statement that the scientist was a genius. But people who were geniuses tended to know it, and be overly fond of demonstrating it, which, ironically, sometimes made them stupid.

Narud had been stupid. He'd been so intent on showing Jim and Valerian how damned clever he was that he had inadvertently revealed how he'd escaped. Narud had been cloaked.

And so had the doorway through which he'd run, in a sense.

"Hologram. Come on!" Jim cried, and charged at the seemingly solid wall. Valerian had hesitated only an instant, then provided cover as the two took a leap of faith and raced for the holographically "cloaked" opening. Jim extended his hand, in case Narud had closed the door behind him. It was a good precaution, as the scientist had done exactly that. Jim groped for the handle, turned it, ran through the open door, and once Valerian had followed, closed and locked it. He turned to the Heir Apparent, grinning.

Valerian's face looked like it was chiseled in stone. Only spots of color high on his cheekbones and the intensity of his gaze revealed that he was a living being.

"What is it?"

Valerian started, then shook his head. His golden hair had come free of its usual small ponytail and spilled over his shoulders. "Nothing."

And then Jim understood. "You've—that was the first time you—"

"No. But that doesn't make any difference. Those were men, Raynor. Human beings. And now they're just corpses."

"I'm sorry you had to do it, Valerian. I really am. But the shitty irony of this kind of life is, if you want to do the right thing, you gotta be willing to get your own hands dirty. You *did* do the right thing. What you had to do. And you did it well."

There was a look in Valerian's eyes that Jim recognized. In battle he had seen it time and again—the look on the face of someone who has taken a life. A wish that there had been another way.

"I wish that too," Jim said quietly. "Every damned time. But we better get a move on."

They were in a dimly lit corridor, clearly some infrequently traveled back passageway. There was only one place to go—forward. Jim checked his weapon, then started to run lightly down the carpeted hallway. He reached for his comm. "Dammit," he said. "They've blocked the signal."

At that moment, there was a deep, reverberating boom, and the station rocked. They stumbled slightly and turned to look at each other.

"He's attacking the station," said Valerian bitterly. "The scientific knowledge that will be lost—"

"Mengsk don't give a rat's ass about that," Jim snapped. "He just wants us all dead. Me, Sarah, you. You know anything about the layout of this place?"

"I helped design it."

"Sweet mother of mercy, a break," Jim breathed. "Where are we in relationship to sick bay?"

Valerian's aristocratic brow furrowed. "If I remember correctly, that room is surrounded by a variety of work corridors. So that repair teams or service personnel can get where they need to go without interrupting anything. There's a hub several meters up ahead where it widens into a larger area with several offshoots."

"And one of those will take us to sick bay?"

"Yes."

"But you don't know which one?"

"Er . . . no. Jim, my focus these last couple of years hasn't been on memorizing the layout of the station."

Jim bit back a retort, mainly because Valerian had a point. "Maybe there'll be a map."

"Crazy young maverick," muttered Swann as he worked with Earl and Annabelle on Horner's request. "Chances are slim to none this'll work. Only someone who knows nothing about engineering would hatch a plan like this."

The plan hatched by the crazy young maverick currently captaining the *Hyperion* was indeed radical, but Annabelle knew that Rory thought it actually was possible, or else he wouldn't have agreed to even waste time trying. Her heart had soared when he told her; anything that could protect both the *Hyperion* and the *Bucephalus* was something she could get behind. She still hadn't been able to talk to Travis and ascertain that he was all right. She pushed the thought of his kind face out of her mind and focused with renewed intensity on the project at hand.

The more they looked at the situation, the more possible it began to appear. "Well, hey, boss, maybe we should get more people who know nothing about engineering to propose ideas," quipped Earl.

"Shut your trap," growled Rory, but there was no real malice in the words. He, too, was starting to brighten a bit. "Maybe this really *can* work. . . ."

# CHAPTER
# TWENTY-THREE

"Holy hell, there *is* a map."

Jim couldn't believe it, but as he and Valerian slowed to a stop near the entrance of the corridor and moved forward cautiously, he saw a small atrium in the center of a domed area. The space was like the hub of a wheel, with at least five corridors, counting theirs, going off in different directions. There were three benches, some plants in pots, and a small fountain that bubbled in an incongruously cheerful fashion next to a large holographic representation of Prometheus Station. Unfortunately, they were too far away and in the wrong position.

"Now," Valerian said, "to get to the thing without getting shot."

"It seems deserted," said Jim, putting emphasis on *seems*. "I would think that any personnel would be hightailing it to escape pods at this point."

"Most likely," Valerian agreed. "You go first."

Jim shot him a nasty look, and Valerian grinned. Jim sighed, then stepped forward; he was more experienced at this sort of thing than Valerian. He held his gun, taken from one of the late guards, in front of him, moving slowly, and peeked out around the edge of the corridor. He braced himself for the sudden roar of weapons firing, preparing to duck back to safety, but nothing happened.

"Seems clear," he said. Together he and Valerian sprinted for the holographic map.

Valerian touched a small button on the podium, and the hologram reconfigured itself, zooming in to where they now stood. "There's the corridor we came out of," he said. "And— the second to our right leads to sick bay and some area that's not identified. Probably one of the more sensitive laboratories."

"How many labs are there?" asked Jim, wondering if they would be able to locate poor Egon. Hoping they would be able to find him . . . and find him alive.

"Twenty-seven," said Valerian. "I know what you're thinking. Even if we know that Egon was taken to a lab, we don't have time to—"

"Sarah first," said Jim. "We get her to safety. Then Egon. I don't leave any of my crew behind."

Valerian smiled. It was oddly gentle. "Then neither shall I."

Jim nodded once, then turned and started racing down the hallway toward sick bay, Valerian right beside him.

Narud stood in the main security center of Space Station Prometheus, which was, for the moment, the single safest place to be. The room was all screens and small, blinking lights, and no fewer than seven armed guards stood awaiting his command. Narud knew he couldn't linger. He would need to depart, and shortly, but he had to make sure that his adversaries were dead. They had very inconsiderately refused to die when they were supposed to, and were now running around loose on the station.

His eyes were fastened on the feed that showed them in Atrium #4. It was very close to the security center; Valerian and Raynor had obviously followed him. He frowned slightly. He had wanted to make a dramatic exit, thinking they would be killed immediately afterward. Instead, they'd seen his cloak.

"Send a unit after them," said Narud. "I want their bodies riddled with metal. They can't be allowed to live, and they seem to have more lives than many a cat I've known."

"Of course, sir," said the security head. "Vrain, Osgood, Warren, Mitchell, Tseng—you heard Dr. Narud." The four men and one woman nodded and headed for the door.

Once they had gone, Narud leaned forward and pushed a button. He smiled a little to himself. His guards were good, but he had decided that another weapon was even better.

Several meters past sick bay, a door, heavy and locked with redundant security measures, slid open. Mammoth guns, designed to blast anything that moved, were turned off.

And two shadows, lumpy and grotesque, moved out into the corridor.

"We tripped . . . something," Valerian said, his breath coming quickly as they ran. "Those lights . . . weren't flashing . . . before."

Considering there had been a whole bunch of flashing lights and blaring sirens before, Jim wondered how Valerian was able to pick out the new ones while running at full speed, but he believed the Heir Apparent. Instead of replying, he pressed his lips together and forced his legs to increase their pace. He was not leaving without Sarah.

He lurched to a clumsy, sudden halt as Valerian grabbed his arm and yanked him back. Jim wrenched free and turned, scowling. "What the—"

"Do you hear that?"

Jim looked at the prince blankly. "What, something other than the fifty-two different klaxons wailing?"

"Shh!" It was a ludicrous statement, but Jim fell silent, straining to hear—whatever it was Valerian heard.

And then he did.

It was a sharp, high sound, more felt than heard, and Jim had an idea what was making it. His blood ran cold in his veins, and his hair stood on end.

Valerian blinked, almost in a daze of horror. "I knew Narud had been working on them," he murmured. "But he told me the research was preliminary. . . . I didn't know he . . ." As if abruptly awoken, Valerian literally shook himself and grabbed Jim's arm.

"Hybrid," Jim snarled.

"Run," said Valerian.

"Now wait a minute. Sarah's back there, and I—"

"Sarah will live or die on her own, Jim," Valerian shouted. "And we *will* die if we don't run *now!*"

The awful sound, boring through Jim's brain, was coming closer. And suddenly fear seemed to pierce him, as if the sound had drilled a cold, terrified hole into his heart. The sound sensation was joined by a slamming, slithering noise as the things came closer.

He remembered the hybrid, and he knew Valerian was right. Jim ran.


"You ready down there yet, Swann?" Matt asked.

"You asked me that ten seconds ago," Swann's voice growled. "And the answer is still no."

Matt bit back a retort. Swann was doing the best he could, which was damn good, and he knew what he was asking of the chief engineer was challenging. But he was watching the screen blossoming with explosions as one by one, the unprotected Wraiths and vikings launched by the *Bucephalus* were blasted into oblivion. Each one hurt him worse than his still-painful injury.

"Okay, kiddo, let's get this show on the road," said Swann. "Last chance to change your mind."

"Do it," ordered Matt.

The massive battlecruiser had been moving, positioning itself to both defend and attack as needed. Now the *Hyperion* slowed and then came to a full stop, hanging seemingly dead in space. Matt knew that once the import of this registered on Mengsk, they would become the main target rather than the space station itself.

He was counting on it.

Two seconds later there was a crackle on the comm. For a horrible moment Horner was afraid that Rory had miscalculated, that he had tried to do too much, too fast, and they were actually now as dead in space as they appeared.

Then Marcus cried excitedly, "Sir! It's working!"

"Switch to *Bucephalus* view," ordered Matt.

Marcus obliged. Matt felt almost weak with relief as he saw a blue halo enveloping the *Bucephalus* and the remaining Wraiths. Swann, following Matt's seemingly insane idea, had diverted all power from the ship's engines to the shields. That extra power had enabled the *Hyperion* to extend its shielding capabilities to protect Valerian's ship and the little vessels it was sending out to defend it. It had not come without a cost. Not only was the *Hyperion* stuck right where it was until power was returned to the engines from the shields, but the shield itself was also much weaker than usual. There was only so much energy to spread around, and the larger the area covered, the less effective the shield.

But it was buying time for the beleaguered *Bucephalus* and the Wraiths. Even as Matt watched, the Wraiths that had been little more than fish in a barrel began to inflict some serious damage on the ships that had, moments before, been obliterating them.

"Swann, it worked! You're amazing!" shouted Matt.

"Yeah, let's all remember this next time we're distributing some credits," Swann said. "Oh, and I got a special bonus gift for you. Gimme about twenty seconds and you'll be able to talk to the *Bucephalus* and, I hope, our cowboy boss down on the station."

The *Hyperion* rocked from a blow that was, now, much more damaging than it ought to have been.

"Matt?"

Jim Raynor's voice had seldom been more welcome to Matt than now, though it was hard to distinguish his voice from the myriad background noises, all of which sounded dire. "Sir! What's going on?"

"Long story." Jim's voice was clipped and breathy. Matt guessed they were either fighting or running. "How's the *Hyperion*?"

"Still around, sir, as is the *Bucephalus*. We'd lost communication with each other until just now, and the *Bucephalus* can't fire. We're currently defending both ships."

"You can't hold out for much longer." It was a statement, not a question. "Valerian's talking to the *Bucephalus*. You guys aren't going to make it if you hang around for a few stragglers."

"Sir, you, Valerian, Egon, and Kerrigan are hardly ordinary stragglers. You get off that station and we'll—"

The console exploded in a series of sparks. Cade ducked back, lifting his hand to shield his face for a moment. There was a hum as the backup systems came to life.

"Matt, I'm giving you an order. If we make it off the station, we'll find some way to get to you on our own. But you and the *Bucephalus* are taking a pounding."

There was a new sound Matt could hear over the clanging. Gunfire. And some sort of strange, high-pitched keening sound that Matt instantly remembered with loathing and fear. For a long, tense moment, there was no further word from Jim.

"Commander?"

"We're okay," said Jim, panting, his voice giving the lie to the words. He was alive, but he was definitely not okay. "You need to get out of there with my Raiders, Matt. Those thousands of lives are more important than any other single life. You're the Raiders now. You gotta stay alive so that they can continue."

"Sir, I—"

"Don't make me die for nothing, Matt. I'll haunt your ass, I swear I will."

Matt couldn't manage a smile at the humor. Jim was right. If they lingered too much longer, Mengsk and his fleet would destroy both battlecruisers and then the station. He would have eliminated his chief enemy and everything Jim had done to stand against him. There would be surviving pockets here and there, but Matt knew that the rebellion would die here, if he continued to fight.

There seemed to be no other option but to retreat—and leave Jim, Valerian, Sarah, and Egon to their fates.

"Jim?"

"Go, Matt, now!"

Matt closed his eyes briefly. "Contact the *Bucephalus*," he said, his voice bitter. "Tell them we're getting out of h—"

Before he could finish the word, the *Hyperion* took a hit. The ship rocked violently, and everything went black.


The things were closer now. Of course they were. They were protoss-zerg crossbred monstrosities, things that never should have existed outside of nightmares. Jim was certain the creatures were toying with him and Valerian, and that made him hate them even more.

Movement up ahead drew his eye. "Shit," he said. "Guards. Start firing!"

"With the hybrid—"

"Do it!"

The guards were trained professionals, and Jim and Valerian were their targets. But they were also human, and Jim knew what he would do if given a choice between two humans running at him and—however many of those things.

That would give him and Valerian a chance.

Sure enough, the guards weren't looking at them. They were staring, jaws agape and eyes wide, at the hybrid barreling down behind the two men. Their weapons were up and they were emptying them about a meter over Jim's head. Jim and Valerian fired and the guards fell. Not breaking stride, Jim leaped over the still-twitching bodies and kept running. He heard the hybrid pause, heard the unspeakable sounds of armor crunching and flesh tearing. The guards had bought them time.

Jim knew he shouldn't look back. But he had to.

It was a mistake.

There were two of them. They were huge, filling the corridor, and were as different as they were horrifying. One looked like a giant insect, with six slender, protoss-like legs supporting a long, angular body. Two appendages, a cross between a mutalisk's scythe-arms and a protoss's fine limbs, worked busily at one of the guards, who hadn't had the good luck to die quite yet. The hybrid lifted him, opened its mouth horizontally, and took a huge bite.

The other was squat, with the long skull of a protoss and the jaws of a zergling. It had a bony protrusion like a fan behind its head. Parts of its body and its companion's were limned in glowing blue radiance.

They were nothing like the hybrid he had encountered before, nor even like each other. Jim supposed that was because these were Narud's pets. "Great," he muttered. "Each one's its own special snowflake."

And then Jim heard something even more hated than the sight of the hybrid.

"Mr. Raynor. My estranged son. My colleague Dr. Narud assures me that there is a frequency that will calm the hybrid and render them docile. And, of course, I can call off the guards. All you need to do is surrender to the justice of the Dominion for your crimes. And," Arcturus Mengsk continued, "give me that bitch Sarah Kerrigan."

Valerian's hand on his arm, yanking him around roughly, broke Jim out of his horrified daze. "Come on!" Valerian shouted, shaking him. "We're not going to let him win!"

Hybrid loose, Narud escaped, Sarah trapped, the *Hyperion* damaged and coming under devastating attack—

Jim Raynor thought that Arcturus Mengsk might already have won.

# CHAPTER
# TWENTY-FOUR

*"All you need to do is surrender to the justice of the Dominion for your crimes. And give me that bitch Sarah Kerrigan."*

Sarah stopped so quickly at the sound of the despised voice that Egon almost ran into her. She stood, every muscle rigid with hatred, her breathing quick and shallow. She had known the moment the station had come under attack who was behind it, but to hear his voice again after what felt to her like years, so long, after everything that had happened—

*"Boys . . . ? How about that evac?"*

The descent of the zerg upon her as she turned to face them.

Her body being twisted and reshaped inside the chrysalis.

And worst of all, the joy she had taken at killing while she had been the Queen of Blades.

The joy of murdering a mother in front of her child's eyes—and then killing the girl seconds later, along with those who would've helped her.

All of this could be laid at his booted feet. All of it.

And now he was coming for her.

She threw back her head, mouth open in a wordless banshee scream, her body contorted in rage and agony, her fists clenched and digging little red crescents into her palm.

No, no. Mengsk was not coming for her. *She* was coming for *him.*

"Uh, Sarah?" Egon's voice behind her was laced with concern and more than a little fear. She ignored him.

"Mengsk!" she screamed, the shout tearing at her throat. She could almost imagine it raw and bleeding. Sarah knew he was simply broadcasting throughout the station, not caring about any response he might be eliciting. Arrogant bastard. Talking just to hear his own voice. "You left the job undone! *You left me alive!*"

She could feel it bubbling up inside her, like lava pushing against the surface, eager to break free. It was hot and violent and sweet, and she closed her eyes and invited it in. Let it come. Let it fuel her. Let it serve her as she destroyed her foe.

Suddenly everything took on a new clarity. She opened her eyes and felt like a blind woman who was truly seeing for the first time. She could sense the faintest ripples of air, hear Egon's heartbeat, wild and frightened as a rabbit's, as if she had pressed her head to his chest. Licking her lips, she could even taste the station.

And she was suddenly giddily aware of her enemy's minions up ahead.

From standing stock-still, Sarah broke into a run. She could sense her lungs as they took in air, oxygenating her blood, feel that renewed blood moving through her body. She was a perfect machine, functioning as never before.

There were eight marines as she rounded the corner. They were in full combat suits, moving quickly, their metallic arms easily bearing weapons nearly as large as the men they would be attacking.

"Mengsk!" Sarah shouted. "Mengsk! Watch this!"

At the first sound, they turned and lifted their weapons.

They never fired a single shot. The visors of their helmets were suddenly spattered with red, and they dropped where they stood.

Sarah tuned out Egon's shocked cries and pressed on.

"Sir?" Marcus Cade was peering at Matt. "Should I get a medic? How do you feel?"

"How long have I been out?" asked Matt. He lifted a hand to his throbbing head and it came away wet and red. He'd struck his injured arm, too, and it hurt like hell.

"Only a few seconds."

"Then I'm fine," said Matt. "We've got more important things to worry about. How badly was the ship damaged?"

Cade winced a little. "It was pretty bad. Rory's not happy. We're not in good shape, sir."

Matt nodded and thumbed his comm. "Swann, were you able to transfer the power back to the engines?"

"Yeah. Hell of a lot easier than doing it the other way."

"How mobile are we?"

"We ain't gonna be zipping around the galaxy footloose and fancy-free anytime soon, but she could move."

At the very least, Matt thought, the *Hyperion* and the *Bucephalus* could distract Mengsk and lure him away from the station. Maybe Jim could find his way to a ship and escape.

Sometimes one needed to tell oneself little lies.

"Cade, fire one more volley on the *White Star* directly, then let's head out the way we came. Vaughn, you hear me? Your navigator ready?"

"Rawlins has the course laid in, and our engineer has just informed me the engines are back online, if somewhat damaged," came Vaughn's voice. "We can run with you, *Hyperion*; we're just not sure how far."

"Understood. Stand by. Marcus, fire on my command." He punched a button. "This is Captain Horner. All vessels, return to the *Hyperion* and *Bucephalus*. We're getting out of here pronto."

He watched as the ships kept firing a few moments longer, then turned and began heading back as they had the chance.

"What the— Sir, one of the Wraiths has broken formation and is heading right for the *White Star*!"

Matt leaned forward. "Who's in that ship?"

Cade checked quickly. "Um . . . huh. Sir, that's Cooper."

"Bartender Cooper?"

"Yeah. Apparently he showed up and said he couldn't sit by when he had the ability to fly and fight."

"That's . . . pretty noble of him, but he needs to come back," said Matt. On the surface, it did seem noble, and far be it from Matt Horner to deny anyone a moment to show courage. "Patch me through." At Cade's nod, he continued. "Coop, this is Matt. You can't do much against that ship. Come on home. We're getting out of here."

Silence.

Matt frowned slightly. Something wasn't right about this. Why wasn't Cooper responding? "Can he hear me?"

"Yes, sir."

Something was gnawing at the back of his mind. He moved and his wounded arm twinged slightly, and then it all fell into place. He, Jim, and Valerian had all assumed that it had been someone on Mira's team who had betrayed them. And, of course, it had been. But Crane and the other malcontents hadn't been alone. They'd known too much—more than what could have simply been picked up by listening to Mira.

"I'll miss the mai tais," he murmured. *But not the treachery.*

"Sir?"

"Let him go," Matt said. "It's a better death than he deserves."

Marcus looked at him, completely at a loss.

"I'll explain later," Matt told him.

"Sir, he's a Raider; we can't just—"

"Those are my orders, Marcus. And no. He's not a Raider. Not anymore. For now, has everyone else reported in?"

"Yes, sir." Marcus still looked unhappy, but he knew and trusted Matt. He would not protest anymore.

"Then let's give the *White Star* one final parting shot."

The Yamato cannon's final attack left its mark. Matt regarded the blaze for a second before issuing the order.

"Let's go." Matt wasn't ashamed that his voice broke, just a little, on the last word.

The *Hyperion*'s front thrusters fired, and the great battleship suddenly went into reverse. For a moment the *White Star* and the other Dominion vessels kept firing where they were.

"Come on," Matt whispered, "you don't want us to get away. . . ."

And then the *White Star* started moving. The other ships, two left now, followed. "They're giving chase and moving away from the station," said Marcus, trying and failing not to smile.

"Good," said Matt. "Now all we have to do is navigate one of the most treacherous asteroid fields with about twenty-five percent shields, half our engines, and Arcturus Mengsk on our tail."

Sarah slammed to a halt a second time, this time reeling from what her mind was sensing.

*Zerg!*

Something that was both protective and horrified surged up in her. The next instant, she was confused.

*Protoss?*

They sensed her, too, and there was no recognition or affection from them. Only hunger and hatred and joy in killing. And then two other presences brushed her mind. Jim! She had found him! He was alive, but emotions were racing through him intently and swiftly—fear, concern, determination, hatred—

*I'm not leaving her to those . . . things.*

"Jim," she breathed.

"The commander's here still? He's alive?" Egon's voice was welcome. The onslaught of the red-hate thoughts of the hybrid aliens and Jim's careening emotions had threatened to combine into a tidal wave that nearly pulled her under. She was instead thrust back into the present, a present where her own red-hate was the only thing that was stable and strong enough to bear her.

There was a doorway up ahead, a grim square that had nothing of the elegant irising of most of the doors Valerian and Jim had seen on Space Station Prometheus. Jim, out of breath from running at top speed for too long, merely pointed. If they could get enough distance, they could get through the door and slam the controls down on the other side.

If they could get enough distance.

Hope, sharp and keen as a knife, spurred both men on. Jim didn't look back this time to see how close they were. Either they would make it or they wouldn't. His lungs and legs were burning as he forced them to work harder, harder, *get me through there, just give me this break, we can double back to find Sarah*—

They raced through and halted so abruptly they almost fell. Jim turned, sweat pouring from him, and realized that yes, yes, there was enough distance. He hurled himself toward the panel and struck it hard with his palm.

Nothing happened. The control panel had been deactivated. Narud and Mengsk had taken every precaution to ensure that their prizes would not escape alive.

Jim threw back his head and roared. Not with fear, not with grief, but with rage at his helplessness. Moving jerkily, his limbs quivering with the demand he'd placed on them, he swung up his rifle and began firing. Beside him, wordless, Valerian did the same.

It was futile. But he had to do it. The hybrid barely seemed to blink as they surged forward, slaver dripping from jaws and mandibles, scenting the prey within reach, eager for the kill.

The bony protrusion seated behind the skull of the squat hybrid suddenly cracked right down the middle. So did the skull below it. The monster spasmed as it fell, and before Jim's shocked gaze the thing's brain . . . *exploded.* As if a switch had been thrown—and perhaps it had in some respect—the blue illumination that had limned parts of its body was instantly extinguished.

The second hybrid, however, was still alive, and furious at the death of its companion. Faster than so huge a creature should be able to move, it whirled on its six too-slender legs to face its opponent. Its sideways jaws opened as it issued a cry of challenge. Jim's gun clattered to the floor as his face contorted in agony. He clapped his hands over his ears, but the gesture didn't do anything to shut out the sound *inside* his head. His eyes squeezed shut, seemingly of their own volition.

A hand on his shoulder shook him. "Jim! Look!"

Jim opened his eyes and equal parts joy and horror shot through him.

*Sarah!*

Clad only in a simple jumpsuit, she was almost more frightening to behold than the hybrid with which she battled. He had seen her face wearing all kinds of expressions: wry humor, irritation, anger, love. But he had never seen this expression before—not even on the face of the Queen of Blades.

In this moment, Sarah Kerrigan was no longer lover, friend, ghost, or even a part-zerg mutation.

She was what Arcturus Mengsk had once called her: an avenging angel.

She had no weapons; she did not need them. As Jim watched, she was a blur of motion. The hybrid lunged at her, screaming that terrible psionic cry, its scythe-like arms, glowing blue, whirling as it descended upon her. She would be sliced to ribbons. But Sarah was not there. She leaped upward, somersaulting to land on the thing's back. She stayed there less than a heartbeat, but it was enough. Grasping one of its legs with each hand, she threw back her head and uttered a cry of rage. The limbs tore easily from the body, spewing ichor. Sarah threw them up in the air as she vaulted from the hybrid's back. Like thrown javelins, both legs, bearing a single razor-sharp claw on the end were impaled in the thing's neck. It squealed, its remaining limbs scrabbling against the floor. Blood seeped around the wounds, glowing pale blue.

Sarah leaped again, landing in front of the thing. Gleefully, thinking its chance had come, it extended its head. The horizontal jaws opened wide enough to engulf Sarah's head. Instead of darting away, Sarah lunged forward, grasped each jaw in her hand, and pulled, uttering a visceral cry of hate.

There was a horrible *crack.* And then Sarah finished the job.

Like an insect blasted with a lethal spray, the thing writhed and squirmed, legs flailing, emitting that awful squeal the entire time. Then it lay still.

Silence.

Sarah still stood, holding a piece of jaw in each hand. She stared at the thing, her breasts heaving as she panted, gasping for air. Her eyes didn't blink.

". . . Sarah?"

No response.

"Darlin'. . . it's okay. You got 'em. They're dead."

She blinked and turned her head slowly in his direction. Blood, ichor, and brain matter had spattered her. Her face relaxed as their eyes met, then hardened again as she gazed at Valerian.

"Mengsk," she said, in a deep, angry voice, and began to move slowly, with a dreadful sense of purpose, toward Valerian.

# CHAPTER TWENTY-FIVE

"Sarah, don't!" Forgetting what danger he himself might be in, Jim darted forward and grabbed Sarah's arm.

She turned to him, green eyes blazing. "He's a Mengsk, Jim! He can't be trusted!"

"Just like telepaths can't be trusted?" Jim said. He kept his gaze locked with Sarah's, vaguely aware that Egon had just hurried up to him and that Valerian hadn't moved. "Just like outlaws can't be trusted?"

"You know what I mean. Let me go."

"No, I won't. I won't let you do something you'll regret."

"Commander," said Egon hesitantly, "something happened when she heard Mengsk's voice. . . . I'm not so sure that's, uh . . ."

"Not so sure it's still me, Egon?" Sarah snapped. "Oh, it is. It truly is."

"Then you don't want to kill this man," said Jim. "He's not his father. Time and again he's shown that to me."

"He's shown nothing to me."

"Then you just gotta trust me on this, don't you?"

Jim held in his mind all that Valerian had done. All the promises he had kept, all the danger he had faced. This boy was his daddy's get, for certain, but he was his own man. Sarah's eyes bored into his, and he knew she was reading his thoughts. For a second, he thought she saw those green eyes shimmer with tears, then she looked back at Valerian. Reading his thoughts now, Jim realized. Her tight jaw relaxed, just a little.

"No," she said. "You're not Arcturus. Not yet, anyway."

"From you, Miss Kerrigan, I shall take what I can get." He gave her a slightly crooked smile.

Jim turned to Egon. "I see Sarah found you," he said. "I'm glad you're alive."

"Me too," said Stetmann. He glanced at Sarah, his brow knitting, and Jim wondered what exactly the young scientist had witnessed when Sarah had heard Mengsk's voice over the loudspeaker. Jim clapped him on the shoulder, startling the boy slightly, then stepped up to Sarah. Gently he wiped a smudge of something thick and purple-black from her cheek.

"Thank you, Miss Kerrigan. You came in the proverbial nick of time," said Valerian.

"We don't have much of that left at this point!" Jim reminded them.

"No," said Sarah. She nudged one of the hybrid corpses with a foot. "Mengsk wants to make absolutely certain none of us leave this station alive. On top of firing at the station and having Narud let loose his pets, he's ordered some marines to track us down as well. I ran across eight. I'm sure there are more."

Egon paled and looked down, and Jim didn't need to ask what Sarah had done to the marines. "Well then, we better not linger. Let's head to the docking bay."

"And pray there's at least one ship still there," said Valerian.

"No," said Sarah. "Not yet. We've got to get the artifact. It's far too dangerous to leave in Narud's hands. He can't be allowed to escape with it."

They all groaned slightly, but none of them protested. They all knew she was right. "Egon," asked Jim, turning to his friend, "do you know where they might have taken it?"

"Dr. de Vries wasn't really interested in telling me anything useful," Egon said. "She just wanted to get me out of the way. I don't know anything about it."

"I do," said Valerian. "I know exactly where he would have stored it."

"You need the map again?"

"No," said Valerian, and smiled a little. "It's not *on* the map. Come on!"

"How long do you plan to keep this up, kid?" asked Swann.

"As long as it takes," said Matt.

The *Hyperion* and the *Bucephalus* were taking a pounding. It wasn't possible to keep this up. They were buying time, that was all they were doing. Jim didn't realize how banged up both vessels were when he issued his order. He—

Matt blinked. It was a risky choice, but anything was risky now. There wasn't a safe option available. "Get me Vaughn," he said.

"Vaughn here," came a voice, both exhausted and tense.

"I've got a plan," said Matt. "Here's what you need to do."

Five minutes later, everything was in order for Matt's gamble. Swann had warned him against it—"You could stall out the engines with a stunt like this"—but Matt knew it was the only choice he could live with. Or die with.

"Everyone ready?"

There was a chorus of *ayes,* and Matt took a deep breath. "Vaughn, keep them busy."

"Will do, Horner."

"Okay. Cade . . . jump!"

*   *   *

"What the— Sir, we've lost the *Hyperion*," said a very nervous navigator aboard the *White Star*.

"What do you mean, 'lost'?" Mengsk stepped forward, hovering ominously.

"I mean, sir, that she's just—gone. There's no trace. She must have jumped."

"Jumped? Where? We're in the middle of an asteroid field. A jump would be suicide. Helmsman, stay on target with the *Bucephalus*. This has got to be some kind of trick. Varley, find out where they went."

"Aye, sir." The navigator kept hitting buttons, calling up images, trying to find some answer for his emperor. Then he paused, his eyes going wide. "Uh, sir? They just came out of warp. And it looks like—like they jumped . . . *behind* us!"


Valerian seemed to know where he was going. Apparently he was more familiar with the location of the extremely secret laboratory than he was with how to get to sick bay. Jim supposed he shouldn't be surprised.

The lab was located deep within the center of the station. As they descended, taking what felt like endless amounts of stairs— "We don't dare use the lifts," Valerian had warned—the hammering Prometheus was taking seemed more distant. Valerian led the way. Luck was with them in that Narud hadn't seen fit to block Valerian's high-level security access. Sarah paced him impatiently. Jim and Egon brought up the rear, the young scientist huffing and puffing with exertion.

"You need to work out more," said Jim.

"Apparently . . . I do . . ." gasped Egon. His face was unhealthily red. They ran down another corridor, and Valerian slowed.

"This is it," Valerian said. He put his hand up to the scanner. It dutifully made a note of his fingerprints, voice patterns, and retina.

The door slid open. The room was dark. "Lights," Valerian called. The room was illuminated. They stood and stared directly at the platform. An empty platform.

"We're too late," Sarah breathed. "He took it. He *took* it!"

Valerian looked shattered. "I made this possible," he said softly. "I gave this weapon to him. And now—"

"Stop wallowing, Valerian," snapped Jim. "Narud stole the damn thing. What you did was give Sarah a shot at being a human being again. And saved my hide a few times."

"We can still stop him," said Sarah. Her expression was distant. She hadn't been listening, with either ears or brain, to what had just been said. "There's only one way off this station. I was wrong to detour here. We should have gone there and tried to cut him off!" She looked furious, but Jim knew it was with herself and her miscalculation.

"Then let's go back there, darlin'," said Jim. Scarcely were the words out his mouth than he heard a voice in his ear.

"Commander?"

"Matt?" Jim frowned. "I thought I told you to get the hell out of here."

"I did, but I came back."

They had all turned around now and were racing back the way they had come. "That wasn't the plan."

"Well, it is now. We're trying to divide the Dominion forces. The *Bucephalus* is leading them on a chase. Two of them are following; the *White Star* is probably going to figure out what I did and come after me. I'd rather have you all safely on board before then."

"Ditto," said Jim. "We're heading to the docking bay now. Meet you there."

This time, the stairs all led *up*. Egon didn't complain, but Jim feared for the scientist's blood pressure. But there was nothing to do—there was no time for anyone to stop and catch his or her breath, no time to do anything but hurry, hurry and pray they weren't too late.

Sarah led the way this time, setting a pace that was nearly impossible for the rest of them to follow. She took the stairs two at a time, and as they were about to head into another corridor, she stopped and lifted a finger to her lips. She motioned for them to go back down. Jim realized at once that marines were about to descend on them.

"Hide under the stairs," he hissed to Egon and Valerian. They followed, obeying his orders. Jim waited for Sarah to join them, and then, an instant too late, realized what her plan had been.

He heard the sound of the carnage before he saw it. There was the unmistakable sound of gauss rifle fire pinging off walls and railings, echoing insanely in the stairwell. Sarah screamed something, he couldn't tell what, and there was a horrible cry of a human being in torment that was suddenly cut off. Jim and the others raced back up the stairs, weapons ready to fire, but paused. Neither he nor Valerian wanted to hit Sarah, but she was moving so swiftly, there was no clear shot. Two of the marines—in hardskins—were already down. Jim couldn't see their faces; blood and goo obscured the visors. Another marine was firing wildly as Sarah straddled his chest, reaching down to trigger the suit's emergency lockdown. The man fell, but Sarah was on a fourth before he even hit the floor. This one she hurtled over the stairs. Jim felt a strange twinge of pity.

There was only one left. Sarah whirled, clenched her fists, and shouted something unintelligible. The woman's head exploded, and the hardskin tumbled down.

Sarah turned to look at him. The tendrils that served her for hair were moving, either from their owner's recent vigorous activity, or of their own volition. Jim didn't know, nor did he want to. He swallowed hard. Valerian and Egon said nothing.

"What are you staring at?" Sarah challenged. "Let's go. We've got to stop Narud!" She raced ahead.

Jim tried to shield his thoughts from her, but he knew the horror and chagrin seeped through anyway. He only hoped she was more focused on looking for more marines to slaughter than on reading his mind.

"You think we'll be able to stop him?" asked Egon as they hurried through the door.

"I think Sarah can stop just about anything," said Valerian. "And she would know if he had left the station."

Jim was embarrassed that he hadn't reasoned it out for himself.

The wailing of the klaxons and the sounds of vessels firing on the station were so much white noise to him now. His focus was on Sarah, racing through doors, leaping over debris, catching her balance with astounding, effortless grace as the rest of them lurched and stumbled with each hit. They were almost to the docking bay when she suddenly tensed and shouted, "No! No! He's going to get away!"

Had it been only a few hours ago that Jim, Egon, Sarah, and Valerian had approached the extended bridge with its own atmosphere to dock at the exquisite Space Station Prometheus? It felt like another lifetime ago. They followed Sarah to the door. She skidded to a halt, tilting her head, thinking . . . and listening to thinking. They all halted as well, catching their breaths, Jim and Valerian cradling their rifles. Jim realized that they had all tacitly agreed to Sarah being their de facto leader.

"He's still here, but we're going to have to fight our way through," she said. "Everyone ready?"

She looked at each of them in turn. All of them, even Stetmann, nodded. Sarah turned to the door and punched the controls.

The door opened onto hell.

# CHAPTER TWENTY-SIX

Jim was already running, yelling and firing before he even fully realized what they were up against. And when he did, he didn't slow. There would be no point.

There was a transport at the end of the ramp, and four marines were maneuvering the box containing the artifact toward it. Narud was already aboard, waving in a "come on!" gesture. Between them and Narud and the artifact were about a million marines.

And one hybrid.

The thing went right for Sarah, and she for it, each doubtless recognizing the most dangerous foe. This one had no legs, but still moved with shocking speed on its serpentine lower body. Bat-like wings, disturbingly reminiscent of those belonging to the Queen of Blades, stretched outward. Two sets of pincers reached for Sarah, huge enough to snap her in two if they closed upon her.

They didn't. She nimbly leaped out of the way, a gymnast in

a competition that granted life to the winner, and landed like a cat. She reached out her arm and the hybrid stumbled backward, covering its head with two of the pincer-arms before renewing its attack.

Jim, Egon, and Valerian concentrated on the human element. There was no shelter on the broad walkway. They had to rely on the element of surprise and the chaos—and the distraction that the battle between Kerrigan and the hybrid was providing, even to the likely resoced marines. It was all but impossible to shut it out; the screams of the creature, both psionic and audible, bored into one. The fugitives had the double-edged benefit of having become quite familiar with hybrid and how they fought. The marines hadn't.

It was the only advantage they had, and Sarah knew it. As Jim and Valerian fired, rushed about, and fired again, she darted and dove so that she was actually *leading* the hybrid, toying with it and turning it against the hated Narud and his allies.

Jim couldn't hear Narud over the cacophony of battle sounds, but he could see that the artifact was almost loaded. So could Sarah. She paused for a second, anguished as she stared at Narud.

"Sarah!" Jim shouted.

The hybrid had seized the instant of inattention and the pincer was descending. At the last moment, she leaped away, but not without cost—the thing had taken a chunk out of her thigh.

And at that second Jim felt a metal spike sear his own arm and grunted in pain. The limb was weakened, but he could still manage his weapon and began firing again.

It was hopeless. Jim knew it, and knew the others did too. They were outnumbered at least four to one, outgunned, and Sarah could not help them against the marines.

*Hell, we all gotta die one day. Seems as good a way to go out as any,* Jim thought.

The transport doors closed. It lifted off. They had failed to stop Narud. All that was left to them now was to rid the galaxy of one more hybrid and take as many of Mengsk's marines down with them as they could.

Then, with no warning, there was fire in the sky above Space Station Prometheus. Jim's gaze flickered upward and a huge grin started to spread over his face. Narud's transport was coming under attack.

By the *Hyperion* dropship *Fanfare*. How the hell Swann had been able to modify a dropship so that it could fire weapons in so short a time Jim didn't know, and right now didn't care.

"Bless you, Swann. And you, too, Matt, you disobedient bastard," Jim muttered. The sight of the ship gave his battered body renewed energy, and out of the corner of his eye he saw that Valerian and Egon were also grinning like idiots. They still probably wouldn't make it, but they had something they hadn't had a minute before—hope.

The *Fanfare* was firing furiously at Narud's ship, but the transport had moved almost out of range. Even as Jim watched, there was a flash, and it was gone. Another flash, and Jim's heart sank as quickly as it had risen a moment ago.

The *White Star*.

But the Raiders aboard the dropship seemed to have more optimism than their leader. Instead of defending themselves from the battlecruiser, they took aim at a more immediate threat. Sarah, obviously sensing their intent, leaped away right as the dropship blasted the hybrid to a pulp. Then it started mowing down the marines.

"Go, go!" cried Jim. Valerian and Stetmann seemed all too eager to obey, but Sarah didn't move. She stood, spattered with gore, and clenched her fists. A sudden wave rolled off her. Like dominoes, the marines dropped. The wave went all the way up to the dropship as Sarah cleared a path paved by human ruin. She stood for a moment longer, swaying, and then collapsed.

Jim threw down the gun and raced toward her. Valerian and Egon were already running toward the dropship. Jim was hard on their heels, gritting his teeth against the pain while holding Sarah as best he could as he swiftly followed the path she had made, despite the ghoulishness. The ramp was lowered and eager hands reached to take Sarah from him and pull him to safety. He half jumped, half fell in. Valerian hauled him the rest of the way.

The ramp was raised and the pilot lifted off immediately, even while many of them were still standing. Jim tumbled into a seat. Valerian and Egon scrambled for seats beside him.

"Sarah?" Jim asked the medic, Lily Preston. The medic blocked his view of the person beside Sarah. As Lily moved to take her own seat and the dropship climbed, Jim realized that there were two people in the vessel who were sitting down, but very, very still. One of them was Sarah.

The other was Annabelle Thatcher.

"Oh, please, no," Jim breathed.

"Sarah's unconscious," Preston said in reply to his query, "but she seems to be all right. Just exhausted from . . . from the attack."

Jim nodded, grateful for the news even as he felt sickened by what had happened to Annabelle. The engineer's hazel eyes were wide open. Blood was pouring out of her ears, nose, and mouth and trailing down her face like crimson tears. There was no sign of any other injury.

Preston didn't need to say it, but Jim said it in his mind. *The attack on the marines that she couldn't properly control. The attack that had blown up Annabelle's brain. Oh, Annabelle . . . I'm so sorry. So goddamn sorry.*

Annabelle had to have been in the far part of the cabin, closest to Sarah's psionic attack. There was a panel in the back that was open, revealing glowing lights and wires. She had probably been working on something when . . .

"Why was she even *here,* dammit?" asked Jim, pain lacing his voice. "It should have been just you and the pilot, Lily. Engineers aren't part of the standard team. Why her?"

"The weapons that a dropship isn't supposed to have? Her idea. Designed and installed them herself." With a calm that seemed callous but was only the medical professional's protection against emotional devastation, Preston sat beside Sarah and regarded Jim evenly. "She had to come with us in order to operate them manually. There wasn't time to properly integrate them into the system."

Again Jim nodded mechanically. He couldn't take his eyes from the body. From Sarah's latest kill, inadvertent as it was. The woman who had made it possible to attack Narud's ship and destroy one of the hybrid had bought their lives at a terrible price.

Beside him, Valerian said, "Travis will be devastated."

So was Jim.


"This is the *Fanfare* to the *Hyperion;* come in, *Hyperion!*"

"Read you loud and clear, *Fanfare.* Did you get the cargo?"

"Yes, sir, but not without a casualty. We lost Annabelle."

Matt closed his eyes for a moment. "I'm sorry to hear that. I'll tell Rory myself."

"Yes, sir. We should rendezvous in about six minutes. Coming in hot."

"Sir," said Cade, "incoming ships behind us."

Ships fore, ships aft—the fragment of an old poem came into Matt's head: "Cannon to right of them, cannon to left of them, cannon in front of them, volley'd and thunder'd." Odd, what came to mind in moments of crisis. He vaguely recalled that the poem hadn't ended well for those facing cannons from any side.

Up ahead, the *White Star* was hot on the tail of the *Fanfare.*

Behind the *Hyperion,* another battlecruiser and several other smaller vessels had appeared out of warp.

"Start firing aft," he told Marcus. "Horner to docking bay. We've got the *Fanfare* coming in in about six minutes. Prepare to receive and we'll be getting out of here immediately afterward."

*If we make it that long.* More attacks volley'd and thunder'd. There came another flash of light.

"What now?" asked Matt wearily. "Another Dominion battleship?"

"No, sir, it's—"

And then Matt was treated to the shocking sight of fire blossoming on the *White Star* as a familiar voice reached his ears. "This is Captain Vaughn of the *Bucephalus.* Seems my navigator can't bear to be parted from that fetching engineer of yours. He thought you might need a hand."

Matt felt a sharp pang. "Indeed we do, *Bucephalus,*" Matt said simply. "We've got your commander and ours on that dropship coming in at top speed. And tell Travis . . ." Matt steadied his voice. "Tell Travis that Annabelle might just have been the one to have saved them all."

There was a good chance that it was true. And if it wasn't, dammit, it should have been.

"You worry about the dropship; we'll handle the *White Star,*" said Vaughn. "Our weapons are back online and I am itching to use them to their fullest."

Matt needed no second urging. The *Hyperion* turned, maneuvering so that the docking bay was as close to the *Fanfare* as possible. A few tense seconds later, Horner heard the welcome words, "I've got them, Captain!"

"Then let's get the hell out of here."

"Er . . . exactly how were you planning on doing that, sir?" asked Marcus.

Matt realized he had no idea.

★ ★ ★

*The smell of blood freshly shed, its taste coppery and tangy. The terror contorting the faces and saturating the minds of those who fell. She knew them all, through her beloved zerg, they who were part of her soul and body and mind. The thrill of the new genetic material, the birth of the new thing adapted from it. The joy of unity, unity so great that humans could not conceive of it. No pain or trauma in the sharing of minds here. Only power, for one and for all, only purpose, to move forward, destroy, and conquer.*

*And she herself, so beautiful, long rustling "locks," wings to stretch and admire, or with which to attack. Energy unending.*

*Purpose. Belonging.*

*Belonging that she had had when freed by—*

*Arcturus!*

Her eyes snapped open and her breath caught in her throat. Dimly she was aware that she was in the sick bay of the *Hyperion,* but she did not care.

He'd not given her unity and peace and belonging. He'd given her hell. His talk of her as a weapon was true. Except once, she had been merely a single, solitary blade. Deadly, yes, but limited.

Arcturus Mengsk had made her into a nuclear bomb.

*"All you need to do is surrender to the justice of the Dominion for your crimes. And give me that bitch Sarah Kerrigan."*

It was time to stop running. It was time to turn and fight. There would be a reckoning for what Arcturus Mengsk had done.

And he would not emerge alive from the conflict.

# CHAPTER TWENTY-SEVEN

"Sir?"

This was Matt's ship. They were looking to him for the answers. And his mind was a blank. As if to hurry his thinking along, the ship shuddered underneath another barrage.

"Sir, the *Bucephalus* is requesting instructions on how to proceed."

"Noted," said Matt, simply to say something. He stared at the screen, hoping inspiration would hit. The first time they had entered, following the very careful pathway to the station, it had taken six hours. Now he wasn't even sure there was a pathway anymore. Mengsk had pulverized so many asteroids there was just a cloud of—

"Stardust," he said quietly.

Arcturus Mengsk chuckled as he saw the two battleships dart into a cloud of dust: all that remained of one of the troublesome asteroids that, not very long ago, the *White Star* had blasted into dust, pebbles, and various sizes of rocks. Did they really think pulverized asteroid matter would conceal them? It was so naïve it was almost cute, like a child covering his eyes and thinking himself unseen to others. Still . . . Mengsk frowned slightly. Jim Raynor hired better people than that. Smarter. It was one reason the outlaw had been so successful in eluding capture—the man was many things, but he wasn't stupid. Neither was Captain Vaughn, commander of the *Bucephalus*. What made them think—

"Fire into that dust cloud. Now!" he barked.

The helmsman obeyed. There was the illumination of laser fire . . . and then nothing. No glorious and expected and, damnit, logical explosion.

The *Hyperion* and the *Bucephalus* weren't there.

"What's going on?" Arcturus demanded. "Where the hell are they?"

His helmsman looked both desperately unhappy and frantic. "Sir, I—we can't find them."

"They're two battleships hiding in dust clouds, son. What do you mean you can't find them?"

"We—they irradiated the dust particles as they passed through them. It's obscuring our sensors. We can't penetrate it. Compensating . . ."

"Hurry."

"Yes, sir, we—there it is." He put it on-screen. They could now use their systems to "see through" the dust cloud . . . and they saw nothing.

The battlecruisers were successfully hiding long enough to make short, erratic, and unpredictable jumps from cloud to cloud. The mighty Dominion was at least a minute behind them. And there were literally dozens of clouds. There was no way Mengsk could find them before they had enough of a head start to make a long-range jump.

The little rebel sons of bitches were kicking stardust in his face.

Sarah was on the bed in Jim's quarters. He sat beside her, facing the door. She had turned her face to the wall. The door chimed and Jim called, "Come on in."

Valerian, Matt, and Swann entered, looking first at Jim, then at Sarah, and back to Jim.

"Shouldn't she still be in sick bay?" asked Swann. "After—"

"Take a seat, fellas," interrupted Jim, indicating three chairs. "Once she woke up, she wasn't about to stay there. So I asked her to come here." He looked at each of them sharply, making it clear that this line of questioning was going to stop. Sarah remained silent, anger radiating from her tightly curled-up form.

Matt and Valerian exchanged glances. Swann perched uncomfortably at the edge of the elegant chair, eyes on the floor. Valerian raised a golden eyebrow. Matt shrugged, indicating the Heir Apparent could proceed.

"Jim, I've no wish to belabor the obvious, but I think it imperative that we all realize that after what you, Egon, and I witnessed Sarah do, she absolutely must be tested." He paused, doubtless awaiting a furious rebuttal from Kerrigan, but none came. He continued. "She's still unspeakably dangerous. We watched her—"

"I was there, Valerian; I saw it," Jim said, an edge to his voice.

"I agree with Valerian," said Matt, surprising Jim slightly. "Egon told me some of what he saw. And what she did to—I mean, what happened to Annabelle—"

"Nah, you were right the first time, kid," Swann said, his voice raw. Everyone had known and liked Annabelle, but Rory had worked closely with her. The pain of her death—especially in such a manner, by friendly fire—had cut deeper than Jim had expected. Sarah curled up even tighter, and his chest ached at the gesture. "What she *did* to Annabelle."

"Rory, I know you know Sarah didn't intend for that girl to come to harm."

"Tell that to Earl and Milo," replied Swann. "Tell that to Travis Rawlins."

"I will, and I know Valerian and Matt would too, because it's the God's honest truth."

"I know, Jim," said Matt, "but how does that make it any better to know that Sarah herself can't even control it? We're not out of this yet. Our ships are battered nearly to pieces and we're still wanted criminals. The next time there is a situation like this—and you know there *will* be a next time—what's going to happen then? What's she going to do? *She* doesn't even know!"

Jim could sense her stiffening, withdrawing into herself even further. She hadn't said anything after awakening in sick bay other than, "I'm leaving."

"It was an accident," Jim repeated.

"I know, sir. But Annabelle's dead. I . . . I can't lose anyone else—not like that."

"Jim, you are a good leader," said Valerian quietly. "I know you care about Sarah. But you have a responsibility to those who follow you, who put their faith in you. Sarah, willingly or not, is a threat. You need to assess that threat properly in order to protect both her and your crew."

They were all right, and Jim knew it. He didn't want them to be, but they were. Silence stretched, long and uncomfortable, punctuated only by Sarah's quick, angry breathing.

"Okay," Jim said finally. "I'll talk to her."

The other three looked unhappy with the words but nodded. It was the best they were going to get, and they seemed to know it. They rose and began to walk toward the door. Valerian simply nodded at Jim. Rory paused as he left, looking searchingly at his commander.

"Do the right thing, cowboy," was all he said.

Matt, too, started to leave, but Jim rose. "Matt?"

"Sir?"

Jim stood beside him. "You disobeyed orders, son. You know that."

"Yes, sir. Permission to speak freely?"

"Always."

"You're alive to punish me for it."

Jim smiled slightly. "That's true enough," he said. "You were supposed to get the hell out of there. But . . . I'm kind of glad you didn't."

Matt smiled, and for a moment, he looked just like the youthful idealist Jim had met years ago, his eyes shining, his face losing its lines as he smiled gently.

"I couldn't leave you behind, sir. Ever."

"What course should I set?" asked Matt as he caught up with Valerian.

"Permit me to be amused that you're asking me," said Valerian.

"I figure you've got the funds and the connections," said Matt, shrugging slightly. The two men fell into step.

"I do," said Valerian. "My recommendation to Mr. Raynor is that we head for the Umojan Protectorate. I have the coordinates for a top-secret orbital platform that will be able to effect repairs to the *Bucephalus* and the *Hyperion* efficiently, swiftly, and covertly."

"How covertly?"

Valerian gave the other man a thin smile. "Not even my father's finest spies know about it, if that's your concern."

"It is, and are you sure?"

"Quite."

"Let's hope your bartender doesn't know about it either."

"Beg pardon?"

"I'll explain on the way."


Jim had given Sarah his quarters, sharing a room with refugees from the *Herakles*. For the duration of the trip Sarah had refused to speak to anyone. Finally, when they were beginning docking procedures, he went and knocked on the door.

Sarah opened it. She had showered and dressed in one of his shirts and a pair of pants, cinching the belt tightly at the waist. She wore her own boots, though. Jim noticed that she had cleaned off the spattered blood of hybrid and human both. She stood at the door, gazing at him.

"Can I come in?"

"Your quarters," she said. "Do what you want."

"Well, they're your quarters right now, darlin', and I don't come in unless I'm invited."

Sarah was turning away from him, and he saw her shoulders tense slightly at the usage of his term of endearment. "Come in, then."

He took a seat in one of the chairs as she sat down on the edge of the bed. Sarah looked . . . worn. Not weary, for she had obviously slept, nor ragged, as she had showered and changed into clean clothes, albeit his. But just . . . worn. Both older and childlike. She had been pushed to her limits on the station, and it had taken a deep toll. He didn't want to have this conversation.

"I know you don't," she said, "but we're going to have to have it, so let's get it over with."

Blunt it was to be, then. Fine with him. "Okay. It's got to be clear to everyone including you that you've still got zerg mutagen in you, and we've got to learn everything we can about it in order to help you. You're a smart woman, Sarah, one of the smartest I've ever known. You sure as hell are smarter than this farm boy. So I know you know that I'm right."

He expected an angry rebuttal. Maybe some furniture tossed around a bit. Instead, her shoulders slumped slightly.

"I . . . I'm not sure how I feel about that, honestly."

He rose and sat down next to her on the bed, tentatively reaching for her hand. She let him take it.

"They're just going to study you. Figure out how to get all that zerg shit out of you and get you all the way back to being Sarah Kerrigan. They're going to help you."

"I've heard all this before, Jim, and you know it."

He winced slightly. It stung. It was true. He searched for words to convince her, realized she probably was reading everything in his mind anyway, and stayed silent.

For a long time they sat there, hand in hand on the edge of the bed.

Sarah took a deep, shuddering breath, then turned to him. She had made her decision. Her eyes searched his for a long moment.

When she spoke, her voice was soft and oddly gentle. "For you, Jimmy. I'll do this for you."

She squeezed his hand tightly, tightly, her strong fingers almost breaking his. The pain was glorious. But Jim Raynor knew that it wasn't the pain that made his eyes sting and his throat tighten.


They sat together on the small system runner that Jim piloted toward the platform. Valerian's assurances that the place was undiscovered seemed to be holding this time. There were no surprises, no battlecruisers appearing out of nowhere, no too-polite master scientists. Just a simple-looking station that was likely anything but, and a quiet, sad pall of defeat that hung over everything.

Too many had died. Mengsk was still out there, and so was Narud, and so was the devastating alien artifact. Sarah had once again become something she had hated, and a cheerful life had been snuffed out—not because of Sarah's hated enemy, but because of *her*.

Jim firmly believed that Sarah would be well taken care of—that they would find out how to permanently remove or suppress the zerg that still lingered inside her. He knew Sarah didn't believe it, and he desperately hoped he was right.

He hoped a lot of things.

They reached the station, docked, and were met by a scientist who introduced herself as Maddie Wilson. No guards, no weapons. It was a good sign.

They held hands as they followed Dr. Wilson down a corridor and into a lift. She turned to Jim and Sarah. "I know you've both been briefed, but just to remind you, you're going to be completely isolated. The room is going to be extremely secure. We will be observing you through screens and can communicate with you."

Wilson gave what looked to be a sympathetic smile. "If you'd like to talk to someone about what you're experiencing, all you need to do is say so. Understand that you are safe here, even though it might feel otherwise."

Sarah was silent. The lift came to a gentle halt. Wilson led them to a room at the end of a long hallway and keyed in a code. "Here we are," she said.

Raynor squeezed Sarah's hand, leaned over, and whispered in her ear, "I love you."

Sarah turned to look at him, her face softening into a smile that held love, sorrow, and resignation. "I love you too," she whispered back. Then she took a deep breath and they stepped inside.

Jim could see that one wall appeared to be nothing but a window, opening onto what seemed like endless floors below.

As they watched, silently holding on to each other, they saw a small shape. It drew closer, turning and shimmering. It looked like a bubble, the sort that children blew with soap to entertain themselves, but was nothing so innocent. It grew larger as it approached, finally floating over to press itself over the window, which dissolved.

Sarah squeezed his hand one last time. To Jim's surprise, it was he who had a hard time letting her go. He watched, silent, as she stepped forward into the bubble. As it pulled back, sealing her in, she began to float, weightless in its interior. She turned over, slowly, and moved toward Jim, placing her hand on the bubble's surface.

Swiftly, he pressed his hand against hers, feeling it through the thin layer.

Down Sarah and the bubble floated. Jim watched, pulling back his hand, as she grew smaller and smaller, drifting farther toward the bowels of the station, past levels of busily working scientists who, if they spared her a glance at all, only looked at her with curiosity either detached or hungry. She wasn't Sarah Kerrigan to them, with all her anguish and joy, laughter and brokenness. She was a test subject. Something to poke and prod and research. For all Valerian's claims that they would help her, and Jim believed him, the path to Sarah's healing would be a cold and impersonal one.

But at least she had that chance. Arcturus had tried to take it away from her—using Tychus as his tool. Tychus was gone, by Jim's own hand. There was no chance now of redemption, or camaraderie. Jim felt a small, sad smile curve his lips as he recalled Tychus's headstrong, bluff, take-no-bullshit attitude. It didn't hurt so much anymore. Jim could have done nothing else and have been who he was. He wasn't even angry at Tychus. Just at the man who had used his best friend.

He thought of Annabelle, lying broken and bleeding. She had been such a cheerful soul, reliable, intelligent, devoted to the Raiders. Her idea had saved them—and Sarah, uncontrolled, had killed her. Jim felt Annabelle's loss most keenly, but there were so many others. Each one of the . . . yes, billions . . . of victims had a story. And a life that had been cut short because of the Queen of Blades.

But *not* because of Sarah Kerrigan. Sarah, whom he loved, whom he knew bone-deep. Sarah, the assassin who grieved. Sarah, who had trusted him to bring her here—to be tested, probed, analyzed.

"Oh, darlin'," he said softly, "I'm sure hoping I did the right thing."

There was nothing in the chamber but Sarah. No thoughts of others, about waffles or terror, a loose thread in a jacket or the rapture of love. Just her. Alone. Completely alone.

No, not quite. She had brought her memories with her, her choices every step of the way every moment of her life. Her decisions to refuse or cooperate, to be yielding or stubborn. To kill or to spare.

She knew that during the course of this "testing," if that was truly all it was, she would have to face each of those moments, those choices. Jim hadn't understood that. He was an intelligent and . . . good man, but there was so much he didn't understand. Couldn't understand.

But she loved him. And she knew he believed, and so she believed in him. Part of her did hope that he was right, that Valerian would help restore her to her old self—as much as anyone who had undergone what she had could be restored. She recalled her words to Zeratul, bitter and resigned: *"Fate cannot be changed. The end comes. And when it finds me, I shall embrace it at last."*

Maybe she had been wrong.

Firmly she pushed the hot anger, the electric-shock memories, and the cold, sick guilt aside. Even the revenge, like a savage animal she held to her heart that ripped at her even as she clung to it, could wait. She would have to face all these things but not yet. Not just yet. For now, she kept her gaze locked with Jim Raynor's, remembering the first time he had kissed her, the first time their bodies had joined in lovemaking. The tenderness of his touch, and the stunning purity of his soul beneath all the things he had done and the things that had been done to him. She clung to that purity, letting it calm her. Letting herself believe for a moment that there could indeed be a way out of this.

Jim's bearded, beloved face drew farther and farther away. And then Sarah Kerrigan was alone with her thoughts and memories of love.

Of love and the desire for revenge.

And she could not have said which one was the sweeter.

# ACKNOWLEDGMENTS

As always, I'd like to thank my editor, Ed Schlesinger; my agent, Lucienne Diver; and the good Blizz folks: Cameron Dayton, Micky Neilson, and Sean Copeland, among many others.

# STARCRAFT TIMELINE

### c. 1500

A group of rogue protoss is exiled from the protoss homeworld of Aiur for refusing to join the Khala, a telepathic link shared by the entire race. These rogues, called the dark templar, ultimately settle on the planet of Shakuras. This split between the two protoss factions becomes known as the Discord.

(*StarCraft: Shadow Hunters*, book two of *The Dark Templar Saga* by Christie Golden)

(*StarCraft: Twilight*, book three of *The Dark Templar Saga* by Christie Golden)

### 1865

The dark templar Zeratul is born. He will later be instrumental in reconciling the severed halves of protoss society.

(*StarCraft: Twilight*, book three of *The Dark Templar Saga* by Christie Golden)

(*StarCraft: Queen of Blades* by Aaron Rosenberg)

### 2143

Tassadar is born. He will later be an executor of the Aiur protoss.

(*StarCraft: Twilight*, book three of *The Dark Templar Saga* by Christie Golden)

(*StarCraft: Queen of Blades* by Aaron Rosenberg)

**c. 2259**

Four supercarriers—the *Argo,* the *Sarengo,* the *Reagan,* and the *Nagglfar*—transporting convicts from Earth venture far beyond their intended destination and crash-land on planets in the Koprulu sector. The survivors settle on the planets Moria, Umoja, and Tarsonis and build new societies that grow to encompass other planets.

**2323**

Having established colonies on other planets, Tarsonis becomes the capital of the Terran Confederacy, a powerful but increasingly oppressive government.

**2460**

Arcturus Mengsk is born. He is a member of one of the Confederacy's elite Old Families.
(*StarCraft: I, Mengsk* by Graham McNeill)
(*StarCraft: Liberty's Crusade* by Jeff Grubb)
(*StarCraft: Uprising* by Micky Neilson)

**2464**

Tychus Findlay is born. He will later become good friends with Jim Raynor during the Guild Wars.
(*StarCraft: Heaven's Devils* by William C. Dietz)

**2470**

Jim Raynor is born. His parents are Trace and Karol Raynor, farmers on the fringe world of Shiloh.
(*StarCraft: Heaven's Devils* by William C. Dietz)
(*StarCraft: Liberty's Crusade* by Jeff Grubb)
(*StarCraft: Queen of Blades* by Aaron Rosenberg)

(*StarCraft: Frontline volume 4*, "Homecoming" by Chris Metzen and Hector Sevilla)
(*StarCraft* monthly comic #5–7 by Simon Furman and Federico Dallocchio)

## 2473

Sarah Kerrigan is born. She is a terran gifted with powerful psionic abilities.

(*StarCraft: Liberty's Crusade* by Jeff Grubb)
(*StarCraft: Uprising* by Micky Neilson)
(*StarCraft: Queen of Blades* by Aaron Rosenberg)
(*StarCraft: The Dark Templar Saga* by Christie Golden)

## 2478

Arcturus Mengsk graduates from the Styrling Academy and joins the Confederate Marine Corps against the wishes of his parents.

(*StarCraft: I, Mengsk* by Graham McNeill)

## 2485

Tensions rise between the Confederacy and the Kel-Morian Combine, a shady corporate partnership created by the Morian Mining Coalition and the Kelanis Shipping Guild to protect their mining interests from Confederate aggression. After the Kel-Morians ambush Confederate forces that are encroaching on the Noranda Glacier vespene mine, open warfare breaks out. This conflict comes to be known as the Guild Wars.

(*StarCraft: Heaven's Devils* by William C. Dietz)
(*StarCraft: I, Mengsk* by Graham McNeill)

## 2488–2489

Jim Raynor joins the Confederate Marine Corps and meets Tychus Findlay. In the later battles between the Confederacy

and the Kel-Morian Combine, the 321st Colonial Rangers Battalion (whose membership includes Raynor and Findlay) comes to prominence for its expertise and bravado, earning it the nickname "Heaven's Devils."
(*StarCraft: Heaven's Devils* by William C. Dietz)

Jim Raynor meets fellow Confederate soldier Cole Hickson in a Kel-Morian prison camp. During this encounter, Hickson teaches Raynor how to resist and survive the Kel-Morians' brutal torture methods.
(*StarCraft: Heaven's Devils* by William C. Dietz)
(*StarCraft* monthly comic #6 by Simon Furman and Federico Dallocchio)

Toward the end of the Guild Wars, Jim Raynor and Tychus Findlay go AWOL from the Confederate military.

Arcturus Mengsk resigns from the Confederate military after achieving the rank of colonel. He then becomes a successful prospector in the galactic rim.
(*StarCraft: I, Mengsk* by Graham McNeill)

After nearly four years of war, the Confederacy "negotiates" peace with the Kel-Morian Combine, annexing almost all of the Kel-Morians' supporting mining guilds. Despite this massive setback, the Kel-Morian Combine is allowed to continue its existence and retain its autonomy.

Arcturus Mengsk's father, Confederate senator Angus Mengsk, declares the independence of Korhal IV, a core world of the Confederacy that has long been at odds with the government. In response, three Confederate ghosts—covert terran operatives with superhuman psionic powers enhanced by cutting-edge technology—assassinate Angus, his wife, and their young daughter. Furious at the murder of his family, Arcturus takes command of the rebellion in Korhal and wages a guerilla war against the Confederacy.

(*StarCraft: I, Mengsk* by Graham McNeill)

## 2491

As a warning to other would-be separatists, the Confederacy unleashes a nuclear holocaust on Korhal IV, killing millions. In retaliation, Arcturus Mengsk names his rebel group the Sons of Korhal and intensifies his struggle against the Confederacy. During this time Arcturus liberates a Confederate ghost named Sarah Kerrigan, who later becomes his second-in-command.

(*StarCraft: Uprising* by Micky Neilson)

## 2495

After living an indulgent, self-destructive lifestyle as outlaws, Jim Raynor and Tychus Findlay are cornered by authorities, and Raynor's criminal years come to an end. Although Tychus is apprehended, Raynor manages to escape. Raynor retires on the planet Mar Sara and marries Liddy. Their son, Johnny, is born shortly after.

(*StarCraft: Devils' Due* by Christie Golden)

(*StarCraft: Frontline volume 4*, "Homecoming" by Chris Metzen and Hector Sevilla)

## 2496

Jim Raynor becomes a marshal on Mar Sara.

## 2498

Despite Jim's reservations, Johnny Raynor is sent to the Ghost Academy on Tarsonis to develop his latent psionic potential. In the same year, Jim and Liddy receive a letter informing them of Johnny's death. Unable to cope with her grief, Liddy wastes away and dies soon afterward.

(*StarCraft: Frontline volume 4*, "Homecoming" by Chris Metzen and Hector Sevilla)

## 2499–2500

Two alien threats appear in the Koprulu sector: the ruthless, highly adaptable zerg and the enigmatic protoss. In a seemingly unprovoked attack, the protoss incinerate the terran planet Chau Sara, drawing the ire of the Confederacy. Unbeknownst to most terrans, Chau Sara had become infested by the zerg, and the protoss had carried out their attack in order to destroy the infestation. Other worlds, including the nearby planet Mar Sara, are also found to be infested by the zerg.

(*StarCraft: Liberty's Crusade* by Jeff Grubb)

(*StarCraft: Twilight*, book three of *The Dark Templar Saga* by Christie Golden)

On Mar Sara, the Confederacy imprisons Jim Raynor for destroying Backwater Station, a zerg-infested terran outpost. He is liberated soon after by Mengsk's rebel group, the Sons of Korhal.

(*StarCraft: Liberty's Crusade* by Jeff Grubb)

A Confederate marine named Ardo Melnikov finds himself embroiled in the conflict on Mar Sara. He suffers from painful memories of his former life on the planet Bountiful, but he soon discovers that there is a darker truth to his past.

(*StarCraft: Speed of Darkness* by Tracy Hickman)

Mar Sara suffers the same fate as Chau Sara and is incinerated by the protoss. Jim Raynor, Arcturus Mengsk, the Sons of Korhal, and some of the planet's residents manage to escape the destruction.

(*StarCraft: Liberty's Crusade* by Jeff Grubb)

Feeling betrayed by the Confederacy, Jim Raynor joins the
Sons of Korhal and meets Sarah Kerrigan. A Universal News
Network (UNN) reporter, Michael Liberty, accompanies the
rebel group to report on the chaos and counteract Confederate
propaganda.
(*StarCraft: Liberty's Crusade* by Jeff Grubb)

A Confederate politician named Tamsen Cauley tasks the
War Pigs—a covert military unit created to take on the
Confederacy's dirtiest jobs—with assassinating Arcturus
Mengsk. The attempt on Mengsk's life fails.
(*StarCraft* monthly comic #1 by Simon Furman and Federico Dallocchio)

November "Nova" Terra, a daughter of one of the
Confederacy's powerful Old Families on Tarsonis, unleashes
her latent psionic abilities after she telepathically feels the
murder of her parents and her brother. Once her terrifying
power becomes known, the Confederacy hunts her down,
intending to take advantage of her talents.
(*StarCraft: Ghost: Nova* by Keith R.A. DeCandido)

Arcturus Mengsk deploys a devastating weapon—the psi
emitter—on the Confederate capital of Tarsonis. The device
sends out amplified psionic signals and draws large numbers of
zerg to the planet. Tarsonis falls soon after, and the loss of the
capital proves to be a deathblow to the Confederacy.
(*StarCraft: Liberty's Crusade* by Jeff Grubb)

Arcturus Mengsk betrays Sarah Kerrigan and abandons her on
Tarsonis as it is being overrun by zerg. Jim Raynor, who had
developed a deep bond with Kerrigan, defects from the Sons of
Korhal in fury and forms a rebel group that will come to be
known as Raynor's Raiders. He soon discovers Kerrigan's true

fate: instead of being killed by the zerg, she has been transformed into a powerful being known as the Queen of Blades.
(*StarCraft: Liberty's Crusade* by Jeff Grubb)
(*StarCraft: Queen of Blades* by Aaron Rosenberg)

Michael Liberty leaves the Sons of Korhal along with Raynor after witnessing Mengsk's ruthlessness. Unwilling to become a propaganda tool, the reporter begins transmitting rogue news broadcasts that expose Mengsk's oppressive tactics.
(*StarCraft: Liberty's Crusade* by Jeff Grubb)
(*StarCraft: Queen of Blades* by Aaron Rosenberg)

Arcturus Mengsk declares himself emperor of the Terran Dominion, a new government that takes power over many of the terran planets in the Koprulu sector.
(*StarCraft: I, Mengsk* by Graham McNeill)

Dominion senator Corbin Phash discovers that his young son, Colin, can attract hordes of deadly zerg with his psionic abilities—a talent that the Dominion sees as a useful weapon.
(*StarCraft: Frontline volume 1*, "Weapon of War" by Paul Benjamin, David Shramek, and Hector Sevilla)

The supreme ruler of the zerg, the Overmind, discovers the location of the protoss homeworld of Aiur and launches an invasion of the planet.
(*StarCraft: Frontline volume 3*, "Twilight Archon" by Ren Zatopek and Noel Rodriguez)
(*StarCraft: Queen of Blades* by Aaron Rosenberg)
(*StarCraft: Twilight*, book three of *The Dark Templar Saga* by Christie Golden)

Juras, the brilliant inventor of the protoss mothership, awakens from a centuries-long sleep to discover that Aiur is under

threat from the zerg. Not knowing the zerg's true intentions or the reasons for their assault, the scientist struggles to decide whether or not to attack the strange aliens.
("Mothership" by Brian Kindregan at us.battle.net/sc2/en/game/lore/)

The heroic high templar Tassadar sacrifices himself to destroy the Overmind. However, much of Aiur is left in ruins. The remaining Aiur protoss flee through a warp gate created by the xel'naga—an ancient alien race that is thought to have influenced the evolution of the zerg and the protoss—and are transported to the dark templar planet Shakuras. For the first time since the dark templar were banished from Aiur, the two protoss societies are reunited.
(*StarCraft: Frontline volume 3*, "Twilight Archon" by Ren Zatopek and Noel Rodriguez)
(*StarCraft: Queen of Blades* by Aaron Rosenberg)
(*StarCraft: Twilight*, book three of *The Dark Templar Saga* by Christie Golden)

The zerg pursue the refugees from the planet Aiur through the warp gate to Shakuras. Jim Raynor and his forces, who had become allies with Tassadar and the dark templar Zeratul, stay behind on Aiur in order to shut down the warp gate. Meanwhile, Zeratul and the protoss executor Artanis utilize the powers of an ancient xel'naga temple on Shakuras to purge the zerg that have already invaded the planet.

On the fringe world of Bhekar Ro, two terran siblings named Octavia and Lars stumble upon a recently unearthed xel'naga artifact. Their investigation goes awry when the device absorbs Lars and fires a mysterious beam of light into space, attracting the attention of the protoss and the zerg. Before long, Bhekar Ro is engulfed in a brutal conflict among terran, protoss, and zerg forces as each group fights to claim the strange artifact.
(*StarCraft: Shadow of the Xel'Naga* by Gabriel Mesta)

The United Earth Directorate (UED), having observed the conflict among the terrans, the zerg, and the protoss, dispatches a military expeditionary force to the Koprulu sector from Earth in order to take control. To accomplish its goal, the UED captures a fledgling Overmind on the zerg-occupied planet of Char. The Queen of Blades, Mengsk, Raynor, and the protoss put aside their differences and work together in order to defeat the UED and the new Overmind. These unlikely allies manage to succeed, and after the death of the second Overmind, the Queen of Blades attains control over all zerg in the Koprulu sector.

On an uncharted moon near Char, Zeratul encounters the terran Samir Duran, once an ally of the Queen of Blades. Zeratul discovers that Duran has successfully spliced together zerg and protoss DNA to forge a hybrid, a creation that Duran ominously prophesizes will change the universe forever.

Arcturus Mengsk exterminates half of his ghost operatives to ensure loyalty among the former Confederate agents who have been integrated into the Dominion ghost program. Additionally, he establishes a new Ghost Academy on Ursa, a moon orbiting Korhal IV.
(*StarCraft: Shadow Hunters*, book two of *The Dark Templar Saga* by Christie Golden)

Corbin Phash sends his son, Colin, into hiding from the Dominion, whose agents are hunting down the young boy to exploit his psionic abilities. Corbin flees to the Umojan Protectorate, a terran government independent of the Dominion.
(*StarCraft: Frontline volume 3*, "War-Torn" by Paul Benjamin, David Shramek, and Hector Sevilla)

The young Colin Phash is captured by the Dominion and sent to the Ghost Academy. Meanwhile, his father, Corbin, acts as a dissenting voice against the Dominion from the Umojan Protectorate. For his outspoken opposition, Corbin becomes the target of an assassination attempt.

(*StarCraft: Frontline volume 4*, "Orientation" by Paul Benjamin, David Shramek, and Mel Joy San Juan)

## 2501

Nova Terra, having escaped the destruction of her homeworld, Tarsonis, trains alongside other gifted terrans and hones her psionic talents at the Ghost Academy.

(*StarCraft: Ghost: Nova* by Keith R.A. DeCandido)

(*StarCraft: Ghost Academy volume 1* by Keith R.A. DeCandido and Fernando Heinz Furukawa)

Nova encounters Colin Phash, whom the academy is studying in an effort to harness his unique abilities. Meanwhile, four comrades from Nova's past desperately seek rescue from a zerg onslaught after they become stranded on the mining planet of Shi.

(*StarCraft: Ghost Academy volume 2* by David Gerrold and Fernando Heinz Furukawa)

During a training exercise in the Baker's Dozen system, Nova and her peers at the Ghost Academy discover that the planet of Shi has been overrun with zerg. Of even greater concern is the fact that several terrans—friends from Nova's youth on Tarsonis—are trapped on the planet.

(*StarCraft: Ghost Academy volume 3* by David Gerrold and Fernando Heinz Furukawa)

## 2502

Arcturus Mengsk reaches out to his son, Valerian, who had grown up in the relative absence of his father. Intending for

Valerian to continue the Mengsk dynasty, Arcturus recalls his own progression from an apathetic teenager to an emperor.
(*StarCraft: I, Mengsk* by Graham McNeill)

Reporter Kate Lockwell is embedded with Dominion troops to deliver patriotic, pro-Dominion broadcasts to the Universal News Network. During her time with the soldiers, she encounters former UNN reporter Michael Liberty and discovers some of the darker truths beneath the Dominion's surface.
(*StarCraft: Frontline volume 2*, "Newsworthy" by Grace Randolph and Nam Kim)

Tamsen Cauley plans to kill off the War Pigs—who are now disbanded—in order to cover up his previous attempt to assassinate Arcturus Mengsk. Before enacting his plan, Cauley gathers the War Pigs for a mission to kill Jim Raynor, an action that Cauley believes will win Mengsk's favor. One of the War Pigs sent on this mission, Cole Hickson, is the former Confederate soldier who helped Raynor survive the brutal Kel-Morian prison camp.
(*StarCraft* monthly comic #1 by Simon Furman and Federico Dallocchio)

Fighters from all three of the Koprulu sector's factions—terran, protoss, and zerg—vie for control over an ancient xel'naga temple on the planet Artika. Amid the violence, the combatants come to realize the individual motivations that have brought them to this chaotic battlefield.
(*StarCraft: Frontline volume 1*, "Why We Fight" by Josh Elder and Ramanda Kamarga)

The Kel-Morian crew of the *Generous Profit* arrives on a desolate planet in hopes of finding something worth salvaging. As they sort through the ruins, the crew members discover the terrifying secret behind the planet's missing populace.
(*StarCraft: Frontline volume 2*, "A Ghost Story" by Kieron Gillen and Hector Sevilla)

A team of protoss scientists experiments on a sample of zerg creep, bio-matter that provides nourishment to zerg structures. However, the substance begins to affect the scientists strangely, eventually sending their minds spiraling downward into madness.

(*StarCraft: Frontline volume 2*, "Creep" by Simon Furman and Tomás Aira)

A psychotic viking pilot, Captain Jon Dyre, attacks the innocent colonists of Ursa during a weapon demonstration. His former pupil, Wes Carter, confronts Dyre in order to end his crazed killing spree.

(*StarCraft: Frontline volume 1*, "Heavy Armor, Part 1" by Simon Furman and Jesse Elliott)
(*StarCraft: Frontline volume 2*, "Heavy Armor, Part 2" by Simon Furman and Jesse Elliott)

Sandin Forst, a skilled Thor pilot with two loyal partners, braves the ruins of a terran installation on Mar Sara in order to infiltrate a hidden vault. After getting access to the facility, Forst realizes that the treasures he expected to find were never meant to be discovered.

(*StarCraft: Frontline volume 1*, "Thundergod" by Richard A. Knaak and Naohiro Washio)

**2503**

When Private Maren Ayers, a Dominion medic, and her platoon are attacked by zerg on the barren mining world of Sorona, they take refuge in a naturally fortified settlement called Cask. Although the area proves to be impenetrable to attackers, Ayers and her comrades soon witness the zerg's frightening adaptability when the aliens unleash an explosive new mutation to overcome Cask's defenses.

("Broken Wide" by Cameron Dayton at us.battle.net/sc2/en/game/lore/)

Dominion scientists capture the praetor Muadun and conduct experiments on him to better understand the protoss' psionic

gestalt—the Khala. Led by the twisted Dr. Stanley Burgess, these researchers violate every ethical code in their search for power.
(*StarCraft: Frontline volume 3*, "Do No Harm" by Josh Elder and Ramanda Kamarga)

Archaeologist Jake Ramsey investigates a xel'naga temple, but things quickly spiral out of control when a protoss mystic known as a preserver merges with his mind. Afterward Jake is flooded with memories spanning protoss history.
(*StarCraft: Firstborn*, book one of *The Dark Templar Saga* by Christie Golden)

Jake Ramsey's adventure continues on the planet Aiur. Under the instructions of the protoss preserver within his head, Jake explores the shadowy labyrinths beneath the planet's surface to locate a sacred crystal that might be instrumental in saving the universe.
(*StarCraft: Shadow Hunters*, book two of *The Dark Templar Saga* by Christie Golden)

Mysteriously, some of the Dominion's highly trained ghosts begin to disappear. Nova Terra, now a graduate of the Ghost Academy, investigates the fate of the missing operatives and discovers a terrible secret.
(*StarCraft: Ghost: Spectres* by Nate Kenyon)

Jake Ramsey is separated from his bodyguard, Rosemary Dahl, after they flee Aiur through a xel'naga warp gate. Rosemary ends up alongside refugee protoss on Shakuras, but Jake is nowhere to be found. Alone and running out of time, Jake searches for a way to extricate the protoss preserver from his mind before they both die.
(*StarCraft: Twilight*, book three of *The Dark Templar Saga* by Christie Golden)

A mixed team of dark templar and Aiur protoss journeys to a remote asteroid in order to activate a dormant colossus—a towering robotic war machine created long ago by the protoss. En route to the asteroid, however, their ship comes under assault by the zerg, imperiling the entire mission.
("Colossus" by Valerie Watrous at us.battle.net/sc2/en/game/lore/)

In the closely guarded Simonson munitions facility on Korhal IV, the Dominion performs testing on its newest terror weapon: the Odin. Unbeknownst to the Dominion, one of the Umojan Protectorate's elite psionic spies—a shadowguard—has resolved to uncover the military's secret project at any cost.
("Collateral Damage" by Matt Burns at us.battle.net/sc2/en/game/lore/)

A team from the Moebius Foundation—a mysterious terran organization interested in alien artifacts—investigates a xel'naga structure in the far reaches of the Koprulu sector. During their research the scientists uncover a dark force lurking in the ancient ruins.
(*StarCraft: Frontline volume 4*, "Voice in the Darkness" by Josh Elder and Ramanda Kamarga)

Kern tries to start his life anew after a career as a Dominion reaper, a highly mobile shock trooper who had been chemically altered to be more aggressive. But his troubled past proves harder to escape than he thought when a former comrade unexpectedly arrives at Kern's home.
(*StarCraft: Frontline volume 4*, "Fear the Reaper" by David Gerrold and Ruben de Vela)

A nightclub singer named Starry Lace finds herself at the center of diplomatic intrigue among Dominion and Kel-Morian officials.
(*StarCraft: Frontline volume 3*, "Last Call" by Grace Randolph and Seung-hui Kye)

When a ragtag group of Dominion marines known as Zeta Squad patrols a mining outpost for signs of Kel-Morian terrorist activity, it comes under attack by an insidious zerg mutation that can take on the guise of terrans, blurring the line between friend and foe.

("Changeling" by James Waugh at us.battle.net/sc2/en/game/lore/)

**2504**

A world-weary Jim Raynor returns to Mar Sara and grapples with his own disillusionment.

(*StarCraft: Frontline volume 4*, "Homecoming" by Chris Metzen and Hector Sevilla)

Isaac White, one of the Dominion's heavily armored marauders, is ordered to save a group of Kel-Morian miners under attack from pirates. Yet White's task proves to be more than just a rescue mission: it becomes an opportunity for him to put to rest a terrible memory that has haunted him since his bomb technician years during the Guild Wars.

("Stealing Thunder" by Micky Neilson at us.battle.net/sc2/en/game/lore/)

After four years of relative silence, the Queen of Blades and her zerg Swarm unleash attacks throughout the Koprulu sector. Amid the onslaught, Jim Raynor continues his struggle against the oppressive Terran Dominion . . . and the restless ghosts of his past.